I0460355

Chasing Faith

by

Mark Miller

Published and printed in the United States of America

Chasing Faith

copyright © 2006 by Mark Miller
All rights reserved.

Published December, 2009

ISBN: 978-0692006863

Dedicated to the child victims of abuse, neglect and abandonment.

Mark Miller

Chasing Faith

I hate my life. It's like I don't know who I am anymore. Since Mom died it's been hard to know or feel anything. It was always just us, but everything's different now. Jim used to come around every now and then but never to count on for anything. He's pretty much worthless. Now I have to live with him. I don't know what to say to him. I don't really know him. He just came around whenever he was in town, like it was just another stop on his route. Like we were just something else he had to cross off his list of things to do. Make sure you stop by and pretend you have a family for an hour or so every few months. Please. Mom and I were doing just fine without him. She was smart to divorce him. Sometimes I think he came around just to bug her and because the court said he had the right to.

I cringe every time I hear the squeak of those massive brakes pull up in front of the house. I've always been impressed by the way he could park that huge truck on our little street. I sincerely think it's his only talent. But my respect for him disappears when he comes through the door with that crooked grin calling out, "Where's my girl?" My girl? I no more belong to him than a caged bird belongs to its owner. Just because someone plants a seed shouldn't give him the right to claim you as his child.

Nothing about this house is the same. I remember waking up to the calm sound of Mom humming a soft song to herself. No matter her hectic work schedule, Mom was always home to wake me up for breakfast. I always wondered how she managed to be so happy in the morning. It never occurred to me that she was doing drugs.

Now I wake to the sound of Jim's annoying coughing. It's a nasty, hacking noise usually brought on by a night of drinking and smoking endless cigarettes. The whole house smells of smoke now. God, why doesn't he just cough up a lung? He just lies in his room while I pour myself a bowl of cereal for breakfast and pretend Mom is still sitting across the table from me. She gave the best advice at our morning breakfasts. The funny thing is she was always right. She was smart like that, like she had a sixth sense about people. God, I miss those mornings.

None of that matters now. A walking zombie, I stagger through the days like I'm having some kinda out of body experience. I can hear my teachers talking, but I can't hear what they're saying. All I think about is Mom and how much I hate Jim. Why should he have the right to make decisions for me when he doesn't even know me? Now he thinks he can just stride on in like he's been here all the time. He was never here for Mom, past sending some money, but I guess he was court ordered to do that. If it were up to him, I truly believe he would've let us starve before he sent us a dime. I just avoid him when I can.

School was important to Mom so it was important to me. She was proud that I could memorize the amendments to the Constitution or explain why the sky is blue. No wonder I never had a boyfriend. I was really into all that crap. Anyway, I knew it cost a lot to send me to private school so working hard was the least I could do. I loved the look on her face when I brought home an A or B on my report card. I'm just starting my junior year, but Mom thought it was time to start visiting some nearby colleges. We were planning a trip to Lehigh when she went into the hospital.

At least I still have Crystal and Jennifer. What else are best friends for? They're sweet to try to keep my spirits up, but I can see the sadness in their eyes. Sad because they don't know how to help me besides cracking silly jokes. How can they know? I don't even know myself. I really want to laugh with them, like before, but I can't. I do my best to hide the sadness, but how can I hide my feelings when I only feel one thing?

It's been two months since Mom passed, but it feels like it was just yesterday. I want to believe that she's up in heaven looking down on me. One day I'll see her again and we'll live through eternity together. At least that's what I was always taught. That's what everybody keeps telling me. "Your mother is in a better place looking down on us." I had always believed that and I want to believe it now, but I don't I feel it anymore.

I prayed and prayed and prayed when Mom was in that coma. I promised God that I'd make sure Mom didn't take any more drugs. I pleaded, she was sick and she needed his help and mercy. I reminded him that Mom was a nurse and she devoted her life to helping people. I begged and prayed every night and all through the day. I never gave up, even after a month in a coma when all the doctors said she was brain dead and there was no hope for her. I believed in the power of God. We had huge prayer circles at church all summer long. It seemed like the whole world was praying. I just knew my powerful faith and our concentrated prayers would pull Mom through. There was no way God could ignore all that praise and faith in his name. After all, I never asked him for anything before. I just worshiped him and did everything that was expected of a good girl. I never questioned going to church every Sunday or studying the bible until I could quote passages. I was devoted to him. Surely he would be devoted to me in my time of need. But he wasn't.

What I did do wrong? There must've been something I could've done or didn't do. How could it be God's will to take away someone so good? I know you're not supposed to do drugs, but she did a lot more good for people than bad. She was only hurting herself with the drugs. She was an angel to every one around her. She was sick and she needed God's help, not his damnation. It just doesn't make sense. Are people expected to be perfect? Is that what he wants? Is that what he needs?

Teachers and kids I haven't seen over the summer tell me how sorry they are over and over again. I know people don't know what to say and they think they're helping, but it's better not to say anything at all. It doesn't help that they're sorry. It just makes me think of her. Most of them didn't even know Mom. They never asked about her when she was alive. Why should they give a crap now? I wish they would all just leave me alone.

With Crystal and Jennifer by my side, I survive the school day enduring the condolences and acting grateful for all the concern. Crystal and Jennifer sit helpless. Knowing that I really don't want to talk about Mom, all they can do is look at me with pity. Like when you see a car heading straight at a helpless deer and you know it doesn't have enough time to avoid the fatal collision.

We go to the mall almost every day after school. It feels liberating to be free of the confining walls, but I still can't escape the heaviness I feel inside. It's an uneasy feeling floating right beneath my surface making me feel like I'll never feel right again. The mall is home to me now that Jim's a permanent fixture at the house.

I totally love the food court. I can have pizza one night, tacos the next, then Chinese, and on and on. Imagine fifteen different restaurants to choose from and thirty one flavors to top it all off with. Who cares if I gain weight? It's not like I have a boyfriend. Eating is the only thing that makes me feel okay. I don't think so much when I'm eating. I just concentrate on the food.

I decide to skip a real meal tonight and go straight for the ice cream, three scoops of pralines and cream topped off with whipped cream, chocolate sauce, and of course a cherry on top. Something about caramel drives me crazy. I never order sprinkles. They just get in the way of the natural, creamy goodness. For some reason the feeling of all that cool ice cream swirling around in my mouth and slowly slipping down my throat calms me. It's the perfect spoonful when it ends up in a good, strong brain freeze. Like the world stops for a few seconds and the only thing you can do is concentrate on the bitter, sweet pain.

"You know you're gonna die of a heart attack if you eat that," Crystal giggles at me as she scarfs down a piece of pizza. She has the annoying habit of talking with a mouth full of food.

"I don't care, it's good," I snip back.

Crystal's always pretending to watch what she eats. Her mom says she was born a big girl. She's not fat, at least I don't think so, but she is kind of chunky. I guess people say big boned. She's the tallest girl I know. It's one thing to be big, but big and tall is a double whammy for a girl.

"You're one to talk. Look at you chomping on that pizza like it's the last food on earth," Jennifer defends me.

With her slender build, round eyes, and perfect, little mouth and nose, she's the prettiest of us three, but she never rubs it in. She doesn't even think she's pretty. All she notices are her freckles which, in reality, aren't that bad. They're not the big, dark ones that cover your whole face, but the small, cute kind sprinkled nicely across her nose. Just enough to make her unique.

But don't we all hate ourselves? My list starts with my beach ball butt. Followed by my pumpkin head. My nose is way too big for my face. My duck feet point outwards when I walk. And even though everyone says I'm not, I know I'm getting fat. Oh well, I'm not about to give up my triple scoop sundaes.

We sit in silence for a minute which is rare for these two. I can tell they're thinking about something. Anytime they're quiet for more than a few moments I know something's up.

"I just want to thank you guys for being there for me. You know I couldn't have gotten through all this without you." I feel like I have to break the silence.

"I think we've been helping each other through it. I really loved your mom. She was so cool and she always took the time to listen to my problems," Jennifer reveals, like she's been anxiously waiting to tell me how she felt.

"I loved her, too. I really miss her," Crystal adds.

"You know she loved you guys too. She always told me how lucky I was to have you as friends. You don't know how lucky you both are. Jim's such a loser. I guess I have Grandma and Grandpa, but they live thousands of miles away in California. It might as well be the other side of the world. It's like I go home to an empty house every day."

"Why don't we have a sleep over at my house tonight?" Crystal offers. "My parents love having you around. I think Mom's making lasagna for dinner. It's so good."

"That'll be great. I just have to call my mom." Jennifer lights up.

I never really thought about why I like our sleepovers so much. Even when Mom was alive I really looked forward to hanging out with Crystal's and Jennifer's families. Crystal's little sister, Brittany, is the cutest thing I've ever seen. She's only ten, but she knows how to use a computer better than I do. She follows us around all the time and gets on our nerves, but when I think about how weird it would be if she wasn't there to annoy us, I become sad. Jennifer's the oldest in her family. She has two younger brothers, six and eight. They're classic yard apes, running around the house all day making so much noise you think you're gonna jump out of your skin. Jennifer's more like a mother than a sister to them. She's always bossing them around trying to get them to act right. I admire how she cares for them.

There's something about being in a home with a mother, father, brothers and sisters all there together. It makes you feel safe, like nothing can get to you. Even if you have a huge problem, you have a team right there by your side to help you. I had that with Mom. We were a small team, but we were a team. I appreciated Mom, but it would've been nice to have a bigger team. Now that Mom's gone I find myself at Crystal's or Jennifer's all the time.

The mall is only a few blocks from school so our parents allow us to walk there as long as we promise we'll stay together. When we're ready to come home we just call one of them to pick us up. It's always Crystal's mom. I've been jealous ever since we were kids. Crystal's mom is always there, helping us with projects or fund raising activities we have at school. Crystal always brings the best packed lunches to school and her hair and clothes are always perfect. You can tell she's well taken care of.

It must be nice to be a stay at home mom. Maybe I should just

10

forget about working and marry a rich guy. I could just hang out with the kids all day and spend my husband's money. Crystal's father's a doctor. He must be good 'cause they have plenty of money. Neither of Crystal's parents would be classified by most people as good looking. They're just your average overweight, upper class city dwellers. If Crystal's mom could hook a doctor with her average looks, maybe I could too.

I get dropped off at my house. Crystal and I live on the same block and Jennifer lives one block over. We've been running in and out of each other's houses since the third grade. I was just gonna grab my overnight bag and head over to Crystal's, but Jim's here.

"Hey darlin', where you been?" He greets me cheerfully.

"Don't call me darling." I really hate any attempt he makes at pretending we have a close relationship.

"What are you doing here anyway? Shouldn't you be out helping some bar owner into early retirement?" I smile when I see his face drop.

"I'm sure I deserve that, but I think you're gonna change your mind when you see what I cooked for dinner."

Great, another night in front of the TV with the microwaveable treat of the day. If there's anything worse than breakfast alone it's dinner with Jim.

"Oh, I already ate at the mall. I couldn't eat another bite." I answer before he has a chance to tell me what he made.

"You sure? It's your favorite, shrimp with cheesy potatoes and chocolate ice cream for desert."

"I got over my shrimp phase years ago, but I guess you wouldn't know that and chocolate isn't my favorite either." I actually still really love shrimp, but I wasn't gonna let him know that.

"Oh, come on, kiddo, just try a couple to see if I cooked 'em right."

"Maybe later, I'm gonna spend the night at Crystal's. I need to get my stuff together." I shout over my shoulder as I start up the stairs hoping to end the conversation quickly, but he's intent on trying to bond with me.

11

"Hey, you know, I've been tryin' real hard around here with you. The least you could do is have dinner with me one night."

"Really? Where were you last night or the night before? When did you decide to be daddy of the year?" I mean to be hurtful. He's being a hypocrite and there is nothing I hate more than a hypocrite.

"Hey, you better learn to treat me with some respect. I'm the one payin' the bills around here and keepin' you in this high rent house. You know I gave up the freedom of the road and took a local driving job to take care of you. You don't know what it's like to have to work for a livin'. You ain't earned the right to criticize me. If you think it's so easy, why don't you pitch in some of that life insurance money your mother left you?"

Just when I was starting to feel a twinge of sympathy for him, his true colors emerge. "So that's what all this dinner crap is about. You want to get your hands on my insurance money. You know Mom left me that money so I could finish high school and go to college. It's in her will." Mom always had a plan for everything.

I run upstairs to escape and find some peace behind my locked door. I can faintly hear him saying something like he didn't mean it and he was sorry over the banging on the door, but I don't care. He's pretty much always been a loser. The music in my headphones drowns out the pounding and pleading. A harsh, gripping voice calls out to me through the lyrics, "It's my way or the highway." A perfectly defiant anthem for my mood. It isn't too long before the pounding on the door stops. As soon as the coast is clear, I grab my bag and head out the door. Jim's probably at some bar drowning his regrets in beer. I don't care. I'm going to hang out with a real family.

"Cara, come in. We thought you forgot about us." Crystal's mom answers the door with an inviting look of concern.

"Your dinner's a little cold, but I'll warm it up for you. Did Crystal tell you we're having lasagna? Isn't that your favorite? Did you tell your father you're spending the night?"

"Yes, I did and I love your lasagna, thank you." I feel better the second I step through the door. It's hard to be sad around Crystal's mom. Her genuine happiness forces you to be in a good mood even

12

when you're feeling down. It seems like she's always looking out to make sure everybody's doing okay, like you're one of the family.

Crystal and Jennifer are in the family room watching *The Real World* on MTV.

"What took you so long?" Jennifer asks.

"I got in a fight with Jim."

"What happened?" Crystal asks.

"Oh, nothing special, he just wanted me to have dinner with him," I explain.

"Ugh." They both squeal.

"I know. I had to listen to him cry about how hard he's trying to be a good father now. It was pathetic."

"I'd do it with either Chris or David," Crystal blurts out referring to two of the boys on *The Real World*. She can be nasty like that sometimes.

"You're such a horny girl." I grin at her.

"Yeah and you're not. Let me give you five minutes alone with David and I bet I know what you'll do." Crystal grins back.

"Give me one minute," I confirm and we all laugh.

I'm actually laughing. That's why I love Crystal and Jennifer.

"What about it Jen?" Crystal asks, "Chris or David?"

"I don't know," Jennifer answers. "I mean I don't know about sex. I mean you could get pregnant and have a baby and then there goes college."

Leave it to Jennifer to bring it down to earth.

"You can still go to college and your parents will help you with the baby." Crystal justifies her runaway hormones.

"Yeah, but it'd be so much harder. I'd miss out on so much staying at home with a baby. Besides, I have my whole life to be a baby factory. I plan on enjoying my college years." Jennifer replies.

"That's true," Crystal agrees. "All those hot college boys. The last thing I'd wanna do is take care of a baby. But you can't tell me you wouldn't let Chris taste your cookies if he asked you."

"Who's Chris?" Crystal's mom comes into the room with my dinner tray, a generous serving of lasagna on a beautiful floral plate

13

with a huge slice of garlic bread. There's even a spinach salad and a nice glass of iced tea. It's perfect.

"Nothing, Mom," Crystal replies and we all laugh again.

We stay up until after one in the morning watching MTV and fantasizing about boys. We're all tucked away with our sleeping bags and big, soft pillows in a large, cozy family room. There's something fun about falling asleep in front of the big screen TV with images of rock videos racing past your half open eyes.

Little by little our conversation diminishes as drowsiness takes over. I can hear Crystal and Jennifer whispering under their breath as they fall asleep. I know they're praying. We're all accustomed to praying several times a day. We pray at meals, when we feel like we need a helping hand and always before we go to bed.

As far back as I can remember I always prayed to God before I fell asleep. When I was little I got on my knees, crossed my hands and said the cute little prayer I was taught by my mother. "Now I lay me down to sleep. I pray the Lord my soul to keep. If I should die before I wake. I pray the Lord my soul to take. Amen."

I must have recited that prayer the same way for years. As I grew older I started to pray more for those who I knew were in need. I prayed for starving children to find enough to eat. I prayed that people would stop killing animals just for fun. I prayed for selfish things too. I prayed for good grades on tests and for a boyfriend. Some of my prayers were answered and some of them weren't. But as far back as I can remember, I always said a prayer before I fell asleep.

For some reason, tonight's different. I had put all my trust in God and he just let Mom waste away. I think about all the prayers that fell on deaf ears while she was in that coma. I lay here paralyzed, not knowing what to think or feel. If God is really up there, why didn't he save Mom?

Before, when things looked down or when Mom was working a late shift and I felt alone, I would say a prayer. When there was no one else to talk to, he was there. He heard me and helped me through my problems. I knew God was by my side, as sure as the sun rose

14

every morning and Mom would be there to have breakfast with me. Now I'm not sure of anything. For the first time in my life, I don't know how to talk to God.

Chapter 2

The routine of school keeps me sane. I don't have to think as I move through the halls, just another can on the assembly line. The teachers divert my thoughts long enough to get to me to the final bell and it's off to the mall. My mind is consumed by boys, much worse than usual. Every time I see a cute boy I close my eyes and imagine his hands and lips all over me. It's pathetic to be fifteen and never been kissed. Crystal's like me. Maybe that's why she's always talking so nasty. We both have the horny bug.

Jennifer had a boyfriend last year. She met Roger at church. He seemed nice at first, but then she said all he did was talk about doing stuff and having sex. I would've dumped him too. Do boys ever think about anything else? I guess I think about it a lot too. Can't be a hypocrite. Maybe they just can't control themselves. No excuse. If Roger treated Jen more like a person than a piece of meat, they might still be together. Are boys really that stupid?

We like to hang out at a store called Hot Trends. It sells nose and belly button rings, rock band t-shirts, chain bracelets and necklaces, and just about anything anti-establishment. It's the perfect spot to rebel against the mainstream.

A deep voice sneaks into my ear while I'm looking through some t-shirts. I can't make out what he says at first, but he repeats it.

"You like Green Day?"

"Excuse me," I shyly reply. I'm pretty sure he's talking to me. Crystal and Jennifer are on the other side of the room looking at nose rings, like they'd ever get one, and there's no one else around.

"You like Green Day?" He asks again.

"They're okay," The words slip nervously through my lips. I have to think quickly. What are some Green Day songs? The first boy I've talked to in ages. Don't say anything stupid. Turn around and see what he looks like.

"I went to one of their concerts. They were tight. They got the best sound system in rock," the voice persists.

"I've never been to a concert." I finally notice I'm holding a Green Day t-shirt in my hand. He walks around the clothes rack and I muster enough courage to raise my head. He's gorgeous, at least six feet tall with brown eyes and curly, dark brown hair. He's wearing a black Tupac t-shirt with black jeans and a brand new pair of bright red Nikes. A beautiful, dangerous rebel.

"You never been to a concert. What are you some kind of nun or somethin'?"

"No, I've just never been," I'm embarrassed to admit I don't have a life.

"Relax. I'm just playin'."

He can tell I'm embarrassed, that's sweet. He really seems like a nice guy. "Beyonce's more my style."

"She puts on a crazy show, too. She had the crowd rockin'."

"How many concerts have you been to?" I feel comfortable. He's so easy to talk to.

"I don't know, a lot. I know a guy who works at Ticket Mart so I get in on all the good shows."

"That's cool." There's a pause in the conversation. It's only a few seconds, but it feels like forever. The butterflies start to flitter as I realize I'm running out of things to say. Say something. A great looking guy is talking to you!

"You must go to that all girl's school down the block?"

"The uniform gives it away, huh."

"What's that like? You like it with no boys at your school?" He

17

asks with a strange grin on his face that I can't figure out.

"I don't know. I've never been to any other kind of school. Some of the teachers aren't that bad."

"So, what do you do for fun there?"

"There's not much to do for fun, but I guess we learn a lot." I never really think about school as being fun. It's a place to prepare for college and to hang out with my friends. What do you do for fun at school?"

"You got that right. Not a whole lot of fun goin' on at school. The real fun goes on anywhere but school. Sometimes we hang out here, but the mall cops hassle you too much during school hours, so we hang out at my house."

"You mean you skip school?"

"All the time, school was never really my thing."

"What do you do at home all day?"

"Watch DVDs, play video games, but mostly we practice our music. We got a tight band called My World because it's my world. I do what I want."

"Your parents don't care?"

Pops ain't around and my mom works all the time so I do what I want."

"I know how that is, but doesn't the school send letters to your mom?"

"Yeah, but I know what time the mailman comes. She won't see nothin' that don't pass through my hands first."

The butterflies have flown away. It seems like we've been talking forever. I almost don't notice Jennifer and Crystal staring from across the room with their mouths wide open. Suddenly, it occurs to me that I don't know his name.

"I'm Cara," I blurt out.

"Tommy."

"Where do you go to school?"

"Jefferson."

"That must be nice. I wish I could go to a regular high school."

"Trust me, you ain't missin' much." His face tightens as if he's

18

recalling a bad experience.

"Hey man, we gotta bail." One of Tommy's friends calls out to him from near the entrance of the store.

"I've gotta be some place." Tommy looks over his shoulder to his friend. "You gonna be up here again soon?"

"We'll probably be here tomorrow," I answer immediately.

"Then I'll see you tomorrow, Cara."

He shakes my hand gently, but firmly. I'm surprised how soft his skin feels. A tingle moves through my hand and up my back. I close my eyes to enjoy the moment, but Jennifer and Crystal are bouncing up and down in front of me.

"Oh my God, who was that?" Crystal squeals.

"Does he go to Jefferson?" Jennifer asks.

"How old is he?" Crystal asks.

"What's his name?" Jennifer asks.

"He's so, so hot. Oh my God. He's so hot. I can't believe it. What'd he say? Tell us. Tell us every word," Crystal begs.

"His name is Tommy. He goes to Jefferson. I don't know how old he is. And he asked if I was going to be here tomorrow."

"Did you see that body? Oh my God. Oh my God." Crystal's still bouncing.

"You better stop saying God's name like that," Jennifer says looking annoyed.

"You're right," Crystal acknowledges her transgression. "But he is super hot."

"He's really cute." Jennifer has to admit. "Well, are you gonna be here tomorrow?"

"Are you kidding me? Of course, I can't wait." I start to feel nervous all over again. "What am I gonna talk to him about? What am I gonna wear?"

"You guys seemed to be talking okay right now," Jennifer says.

"Yeah, what were you talking about? Tell us everything." Crystal hangs on every word.

I repeat the entire conversation on our way to Crystal's. I don't know if it's an official date, but we treat it like one, like all three of

19

us were going on the date.

Crystal pulls out a Cosmopolitan magazine she has tucked away under her bed. She has a collection of about five of them that she has hidden in various locations around her room and guards with her life. Her parents would never let her read that kind of magazine. Any magazine that has the word sex anywhere on the front cover is off limits. Crystal opens the magazine and holds it close to her face as if she possesses the secrets of the universe in her hands.

"Let's see. You want to know five sure fire ways to increase the intensity of your man's orgasm?" Crystal giggles with a dirty, little grin on her face.

"That's so nasty," Jennifer blushes.

"How about ten ways to know if your boyfriend' is cheating?"

"Come on Crystal, get serious. He's not my boyfriend, yet."

"Hey, here we go." Crystal lights up as she throws down one magazine and picks up another issue with a picture of some super skinny model wearing a bikini that only covers the bare essentials. "How to make your first date your best date."

"That's perfect. What does it say?" I'm bursting with curiosity.

"Well, let's see. Rule number one- Try to be interested in what he's saying. Men love to talk about themselves, so indulge them. Find out what he really likes to do and seem interested in that activity, but be careful. You don't want to end up having to go bungee jumping with him next weekend."

"That makes sense," I agree.

"Oh, please," Jennifer replies in disgust. "Do you really want to come off like one of those air headed bleached blondes who hang on a man's every word and don't have an opinion of their own."

"I don't know. I just want him to like me." I'm blinded by the image of his crooked smile etched in my head, clouding any rational thought. "Go ahead, Crystal."

"Yeah, Jennifer, don't be so negative," Crystal continues. "Rule number two- Don't dress too sexy. It's okay to show a little cleavage, but you do not want to come off looking like the dessert on the after dinner menu."

20

"I wouldn't know how to dress trashy if I tried."

"Yeah, no kidding," Jennifer agrees.

"Oh, come on. You can't tell me that you never wanted to put on one of those sexy Victoria Secret outfits and rock some boy's world," Crystal says excitedly.

"Please, what do you know about rocking anybody's world?" Jennifer's quick to bring Crystal down to earth.

"I don't, but I want to find out."

"You need to stop it, Crystal. People are gonna think you're a slut," I scold her.

"So what if they do. You don't think I could be the school slut?"

"Get serious." Jennifer becomes impatient with her fantasies. "Let's get back to the list already. What's rule number three?"

"Okay, rule number three- Don't reveal too much personal information. He doesn't need to know about your crazy ex-husband or your last trip to the doctor on the first date. You'll scare him off for sure. Keep the conversation light. Give him just the most basic information about your job, hobbies, likes and dislikes, but don't go into too much detail. You always want to leave him wanting to know more about you."

"That one actually makes sense." Jennifer relaxes her cynical demeanor.

"Well, that should be easy for me. I don't have anything going on in my boring life to reveal. What am I gonna talk to him about? I don't have a job or any hobbies and we can't talk about school 'cause he doesn't go to school."

"What do you mean he doesn't go to school? I thought you said he goes to Jefferson," Jennifer asks.

"He does, but he said he never goes to school. He said it's not his thing."

"What does he do if he doesn't go to school? Does he work?" Jennifer keeps probing.

"I don't know if he has a job, but he says he has a band and he spends his time practicing music."

"Let's see. He doesn't go to school and he sits around the house

21

all day playing around. Sounds like a real winner to me." Jennifer looks disgusted.

"Who cares if he has a job? He's a hottie," Crystal declares.

"Yeah, it's not like I'm gonna marry him. I just want a boyfriend and he's really hot. Read some more Crystal. What else do they say?"

"Rule number four- Keep the conversation going. Avoid at all costs those awkward, lingering moments of silence. Nothing kills a date faster than boring conversation. When you find the idle chatter is starting to lull and he has run out of things he can brag about, you can always pick up the pace by telling a funny story about you or your friends. If you can't think of a funny story, make one up. He won't know the difference as long as you make it believable."

"I don't have any crazy stories. Nothing truly interesting has ever happened to me."

"Don't worry, we can make up something good." Crystal seems excited at the challenge. "We can make up a great story about a crazy concert we went to. I've always wanted to go to a concert."

"I already told him I've never been to a concert before." It bothers me to know my life is so boring.

"Okay then, what about a camping trip?" Jennifer suggests.

"Yeah, we can say we went on a camping trip and got chased by a bear," Crystal agrees.

"That's not bad. I can tell him how much I enjoy the outdoors. I've never been camping, but I always wanted to go."

"So it's agreed. We'll make up some wild getting chased by a bear story for you. What else do they say?" Jennifer's getting into it now.

"Okay, the last rule- Never sleep with a guy on the first date, unless you're just in the mood for a one night stand. Don't let him check under the hood until you are relatively sure he wants to buy the car. If you like him and you think he likes you, the general rule is sex on the third date. Besides, if he's really hot you may not be able to hold out any longer than that."

"I can half way agree with that one," Jennifer comments. "You definitely shouldn't have sex on the first date, but you should wait until way after the third date. If you give it up on the third date you better bet he is just gonna dump you and then tell all his friends you're a slut. I talked with my mom about this when I was dating Roger. She said you should wait until you're comfortable."

"I'm surprised she didn't tell you to wait until you're married," Crystal says.

"She did. I mean she told me that it'd be better if I did, but you know my mom. She knows a lot of kids are having sex. She'd rather I know what I was getting into."

"My mom always tells me good girls wait until they get married. You know that's the good Catholic way." Crystal's disdain for her mother's opinion is written all over her face.

I can't help thinking of Mom. Out of all the talks we had over breakfast the subject of sex never came up. I guess she could see that the boys weren't exactly banging down my door to date me so there was no need to bring up the subject, but I regret never having that mother to daughter sex talk. There's so much I don't know about boys.

"What do you think, Cara?" Jennifer's question brings me back to earth.

"Well, I don't think I'm stupid enough to sleep with a guy on the first date. I know enough to know they lose all respect for you when you do that. Three dates seems too short too. I don't know. I guess the right time to have sex is when it feels right. I think it has to be the right guy and you have to be in love."

"How do you know when you're in love?" Jennifer asks like I know the answer.

"You're asking me? I don't know. I think it's probably when you can't stop thinking about him and you want to spend all your time with him. He has to make you feel happy inside and make you laugh. And he has to care about you. I think that's what love means to me."

"I don't think you have to be in love to do it with a guy," Crystal adds looking like she is embarrassed by her thoughts. "I mean, don't you wanna know what it feels like, you know, sex? I could fall in love if I found a guy who loves me for who I am and not what I look like. And if he treats me good I think I would do it with him."

"I think you just want to do it no matter if he loves you or not," Jennifer smirks.

"I want to be in love if I'm gonna have sex with a guy, especially the first time," I interrupt before Crystal and Jennifer begin to annoy each other too much. "Of course I want to know what it's like, but it should be special. If he loves you he'll want it to be special, too. He'll wait until you feel comfortable to do it."

We spend a couple of hours working on my camping story. It's hard to make a story sound believable when you're making it all up, but I think we do a good job. I end up being chased up a tree by a black bear and I scare him away by throwing rocks.

Crystal suggests I wear my uniform to school as usual, but bring a change of clothes for when we go to the mall after school. I wish I hadn't been wearing my school uniform when we met. The dress code doesn't allow any skirt lengths above the knees. There's nothing sexy about a plain, button down white shirt with a long plaid skirt and socks that come up to my knees. I must've looked like the biggest geek in the world. I wonder what made him want to talk to me in the first place?

We leave Crystal's and run over to my house to rummage through my closet for something sexy, but not too sexy, to wear. My wardrobe is pathetic; mostly plain, white shirts and long skirts for school, some basic blue jeans, a bunch of t-shirts and sweatshirts, and a few nice dresses for church and special occasions.

"Man, you're really hurting for something good to wear. Are these all the shoes you have?" Crystal says in alarm.

"I know. What am I gonna do? These are the same clothes I've always had."

"Yeah, but you never had a date before," Crystal replies.

"I really don't think you have anything to worry about. Wasn't he wearing a t-shirt? You have plenty of t-shirts here. We just have to pick out a cool one, put it with a pair of your blue jeans, and you can kind of match his style." Jennifer smiles; proud that she's found

24

a solution to the problem.

"That sounds pretty good." I agree and dig right into my drawers, pull out all my t-shirts, and throw them all over the bed. The first one I pick up is bright pink with large white cursive letters that say "Girl Power". I remember Mom picked it out for me because she thought it had a positive message. Another one I haven't worn in a while says "Princess". I bought it when I was in one of those fantasizing about Prince Charming moods. There's one with a picture of a big, bright yellow sunflower and one with the logo of the Philadelphia Seventy Sixers, but I don't remember where I got it.

"That one's cute. You look so pretty in pink." Crystal approves of the "Girl Power" shirt.

"Yeah, if you're seven years old and your favorite TV show is the *Power Puff Girls*," Jennifer argues.

"That's true." I toss it to the side and I put on one that says "Sweet and Sassy".

"Wrong again. It sounds too much like a slogan for some kind of cat food," Jennifer says.

She's right again. I might as well wear one that says, "Wild Thing" or "Sexy" or "Gold Digger". How shallow do you have to be to need to broadcast your personality on a billboard across your chest. It must be some kinda pathetic cry for help. I put on a bright yellow one with a full size likeness of Mickey Mouse smiling and giving the thumbs up.

"I like that one," Crystal suggests. "It's the bright color. It looks great against your blue jeans and it makes you stand out in a crowd."

"I like this one." I pick up a black t-shirt with multi-colored print that says "You know what I mean, man?" in funky cursive print. "It's bright, it has cool colors, and it sends a message."

"What kind of message?" Jennifer asks.

"I don't know, but it says something, doesn't it? I mean it's not just a picture of an animal or a flower. How about this one," I ask pointing to one that says, "Too cool for school".

"Hey, that might work. He is a high school drop out, right?" Jennifer says in a critical tone.

25

"Very funny. My eyes drift to one of my favorites. It's light blue with a close up of Bugs Bunny chewing on a carrot and the caption reads, "What's up Doc?" I always liked Bugs Bunny. There's something about how he always finds a way to outsmart his enemies that I totally admire.

"Oh, I like that one," Crystal says. "You could wear that bright blue with your blue jeans and put this white belt in the middle to break up the color. That'll look really cool."

"I like it too," Jennifer agrees. "Bugs is the man."

We decide on some bracelets and earrings and stand in front of the mirror, scrutinizing my outfit like I was gonna be inspected by the President and the Joint Chiefs of Staff. They tell me I look good, not too cute, not too slutty. I'm not convinced.

Crystal and Jennifer both invite me to their houses for dinner before they go home, but I'd rather be alone with my fantasies about how great tomorrow will be. I practice my smile and how I'm gonna giggle when he's trying to be funny. I check out my look in the mirror twisting my hair between my fingers and batting my eyelashes. I don't know, they say guys like that.

I imagine how we'll look standing together as a couple. Five foot one is way too short for a six foot guy. I'm gonna look like a hobbit girl next to him. At least I have my girls. I never wanted big ones, but Mom had them so I knew I'd get them too. I hate the attention they bring. I thought it was just creepy guys at first, but they all stare. My pastor, the dad at the mall with his wife and three kids, even the sweet, old man who offers to help at the grocery store is only trying to get close enough for his weak eyes to sneak a peek. I usually try to hide them, but they're my secret weapon now. If he doesn't like anything else about me, he'll like the girls bulging through my t-shirt.

The house is quiet as I get ready for bed. It's around eleven o'clock and Jim's not here. I'm not expecting him. It's way too early for last call. The silence gives me time to think and remember what it used to be like when Mom was here. I practice my camping story as I lie in bed and fall to sleep repeating Cosmo's five rules: pretend to be interested in his conversation, don't reveal too much personal information, don't dress too sexy, keep the conversation going, and no sex on the first date.

My internal alarm clock wakes me up at six every morning. There's a strange vibe in the house brought on by the unfamiliar noise of shoes clumsily scampering across the wooden floors in the hallway. I know the sound of Jim's heavy shoes when he drags his feet down the hallway after a long night of drinking. The light tapping of these shoes sounds like high heels. I listen intently as the sound moves into the bathroom, the door slams and the water starts to run.

It seems like the water runs forever. An uneasy feeling festers as I realize there's someone in the house I don't know. I open my bedroom door ever so slowly and before I know it my legs are pushing me down the hallway. I lean my ear towards the bathroom door for clues to the identity of the stranger, but all I hear is running water.

All of a sudden, the door swings open and a pair of black high heels in fish net stockings trips through the passageway. I look up to see a disheveled woman. Even though she's made an attempt to freshen up, it's obvious she's recovering from a wild night of partying, with Jim no doubt. Her hair is tangled and her see through blouse and mini skirt looks like they were just thrown on. We stand there looking at each other for what seems like minutes. She runs her hands over her hair and adjusts her skirt in an attempt to fix her appearance.

"Oh, hi, I'm Terri." She holds a shaky hand out for me to greet.

"Cara." I reluctantly raise my hand to meet hers. I really don't want to touch her. I don't even want her in my house. Who is this person anyway, some bar slut or prostitute Jim bought home? "What are you doing here?" The question comes out before I can think about not being rude.

"Oh, I'm sorry. I didn't mean to hog the bathroom. Let me get out of your way." She quickly retreats back down the hall into Jim's room.

I listen at Jim's door, but I don't hear any voices, just the noise of things scrambling around. My instinct is to go back to my room before I get caught snooping, but I don't. Why should I hide? This is my house, not hers. I stand at the door determined not to give up my turf and unsure of what I'm gonna do when the door opens again.

"Excuse me, sweetheart," she sighs, disappointed that she has to see me again.

I step aside and watch her bolt down the stairs and out the door. How could Jim brought such a skank into my house? We'll probably have to get the place sprayed for lice.

Now that the intruder is gone all my attention turns to Jim, nasty, dirty, disgusting Jim. He lies, obviously passed out, in the bed where Mom used to sleep. My eyes wander around the room and my mind automatically slips into memories of what the room looked like when Mom was here. I remember her big, fluffy bed with its flowery comforter and matching pastel pillows, her perfectly coordinated oak dresser and mirrored vanity table, and the frilly, sheer curtains that always let in just enough sunlight to brighten the room. The memory of such a beautiful room and the realization that it had been grotesquely transformed into a dingy wasteland of scattered, dirty clothes angers me.

"Who the hell was that?" I yell at Jim.

He just grunts attempting to revive himself.

"Did you hear me? Who the hell was that?" I refuse to be ignored.

"Calm down, Cara. It was just a friend, that's all." Jim rubs the sleep out of his eyes.

"What was she doing in Mom's room?" I already know the answer, but I ask anyway.

"I'm sorry Cara, but you know it's my room now." His voice is calm, but I'm not in the mood to be calmed down.

"Just because it's your room doesn't mean you have the right to turn it into a brothel."

"Come on, Cara, don't be like that."

"Be like what? Don't I have the right to know who's coming in and out of my home?"

"And I have a right to live my life the way I want. I'm a grown man. You don't tell me what to do. I'm still your father."

"Are you really? What makes you think you have the right to make that claim? Do you do the things a father does?" I just love challenging Jim. It's like pay back for all the times I needed a father to help me through my challenges.

"What do you mean? Of course I do. Don't I keep a roof over your head and food on the table? What else do you want?"

"Never mind. What do you care anyway?" I don't have the patience to explain what he should already know. I hear him pleading for me to come back as I walk away, but I don't care. How could he not know what I'm talking about? He's so clueless.

Mark Miller

Chapter 3

It's so hard to shake the image of that slut in Mom's bed, but there's no way I'm gonna let it ruin my date with Tommy. I hate that Jim is on my mind. Practicing the camping story and running through the five Cosmo rules keeps me focused while I'm waiting for Crystal's Mom to pick me up for school.

The car door opens to Jennifer's and Crystal's full smiles.

"Did you bring your clothes?" Crystal can't hold her enthusiasm.

"What clothes?" Crystal's mom interrupts.

"Cara's got a date," Crystal blurts out and takes the opportunity to explain the whole plan to her mother.

She tells her all about how I met Tommy, the Cosmo rules, and why I brought an extra set of clothes to school with me. Her lips are moving so fast I think her head will explode.

"I see. How well do you know this boy?"

"I told you, Mom, she just met him."

"Where are you going on this date?"

"I don't know. It's really not even a date. He just asked me if I would be at the mall today and I said yes, that's all."

"Okay, but I want you to call me if you go anywhere with him. You know you don't really know him. How old is he?"

"I don't know, but he goes to Jefferson."

"You mean, he kind of goes to Jefferson," Jennifer sarcastically interrupts.

"Shut up, Jennifer."

"What do you mean *kind of*?" Crystal's mom asks.

"Nothing, Jennifer's just being stupid," I reply.

"I'm not the one who's stupid. At least I go to school."

"He doesn't go to school?" Crystal's mom begins to frown.

"He goes. He just doesn't go all the time, that's all. He doesn't like school."

"I don't like the sound of this, Cara. You know, boys that don't stay in school are up to no good. He surely can't be going anywhere in life if he doesn't have an education. You know that. You never know what a boy like that is into."

"Yeah, he could be an axe murderer," Jennifer says.

"A really cute axe murderer," Crystal adds.

Crystal's mom continues to ask questions and give advice the rest of the way to school. "Where does he live? What do his parents do for a living? Does he do drugs?" Part of me resents the inquisition; the other part feels reassured knowing that someone is here to bug me the way Mom would've if she were here.

The school day is just a blur. I have a one track mind; Tommy, Tommy, Tommy. I meet up with Jennifer and Crystal and we run to the mall as soon as school's out. A quick change of clothes in the restroom and we're over to Hot Trends. We're careful to slow down before we get to the store so we can make a cool entrance. We walk briskly up and down the aisles darting our heads left and right, but no Tommy.

"Where is he?" Crystal asks.

"I don't know. He forgot about me."

"Relax, we just got here," Jennifer says. "Anyway, you didn't meet him yesterday until about four o'clock and it's only a little after three now."

"You're right," I agree. "I should relax. Let's just hang out for a while."

"I'm sure he'll be here," Crystal adds.

We wander around the store looking through all the t-shirts and

31

gag gifts. I check my look in the reflective glass that covers the store front at least a hundred times. They quiz me on the camping story and pretend to be Tommy so I can practice my witty dialogue. We're having so much fun that I almost don't notice an hour has passed and still no Tommy.

"Where is he?" I ask.

"He better be here," Crystal says in an angry tone.

"You guys stop it," Jennifer calms us. "It's only four o'clock. Don't worry so much. You don't want to be in a bad mood when he gets here."

Jennifer's right. I feel familiar feelings of loneliness and sadness starting to surface. I tell myself to shake it off. Think of something happy. Right on time, Crystal picks up her favorite book of dirty jokes and starts to read.

"What did Bill Gates' newlywed wife say to him on their wedding night? . . . Well, I finally know why you call it Microsoft."

We laugh along with Crystal as she continues to read. There's nothing like a good laugh to help pass the time. The clock over the cash register reads four thirty. Maybe he isn't coming? My eyes glance down and he's standing right there talking to the pretty blond that runs the register. I suddenly experience the sharp, queasy feeling of a million butterflies floating around in my stomach and my mind races. Why is he talking to her? He's supposed to be here to see me.

"Hey, that's him." Crystal almost shouts out.

"Who's he talking to?" Jennifer asks.

"How should I know?" I snap at her.

"Okay, calm down. They could just be friends for all you know," Jennifer says.

"Oh my God, he's coming over, he's coming, he's coming." Crystal tries as hard as she can to contain her excitement.

"Okay, everybody play it cool." I warn them. "Just chill out and let me do the talking."

"Hey, Cara," he calls out as he approaches. The girl he was talking to doesn't seem to care that he's heading toward me. Maybe they are just friends.

I'm too nervous to muster enough wind to shout back so I just wave and smile.

"Hi," he says.

"Hi," I say back.

"You gonna introduce me to your friends?"

"Oh yeah, I'm sorry." I totally forget they were still there. "These are my friends Jennifer and Crystal. Jennifer and Crystal, this is Tommy."

"Nice to meet you," Crystal shoves her hand out and giggles when he shakes it.

"Nice to meet you," Jennifer is more reserved in her reaction, but she's also grinning from ear to ear.

"Nice to meet you too," Tommy replies.

He is so much more relaxed than we are. He barely glances at Crystal, but his eyes linger on Jennifer for a few moments longer than I like.

"So, what have you been doing today," I reach up and tap him on the shoulder to regain his attention.

"Just hangin' out."

"You didn't go to school today?" Jennifer asks.

"What for?" He answers, looking annoyed. "You wanna go get some ice cream, Cara?"

"Sure, let's go." I'm so relieved he showed up that I turn to leave without even saying goodbye to Crystal or Jennifer. I feel special as we walk through the mall. Like everyone staring at me with this great looking guy knows I got it going on.

He's talking about this rap song that he's been writing on our way to the ice cream place. We walk at a quick pace, not the leisurely cruising pace I am used to when I walk through the mall stopping and peeking, window shopping and taking my time.

"What kinda ice cream you like?" he asks.

I'm so busy trying to keep up with his stride I hardly notice we're already approaching the line.

"Anything with caramel. Do they have pralines and cream?"

"Can I help you?" The lady behind the counter asks.

"Sure, give me two double scoop cones, one rocky road and one pralines and cream. Is a cone okay or would you rather have it in a bowl?" He asks me before he gives the lady the final nod.

"A cone's okay." I'm not sure why I agree so quickly. I would really rather have it in a bowl. It just kind of slipped out. I want to correct myself and tell him I want a bowl, but I'm too embarrassed to change my order now.

He sits across from me at one of the many four chair tables that cover the food court. The table is small enough I could reach out and touch his hand, but I don't have the nerve. His face looks even more beautiful up close, no marks, zits, or even black heads. For the first few moments we're both too involved licking away at our cones to notice that we're not talking.

"How's your ice cream."

His voice startles me. Conversation time. Be interested in what he likes, be witty and funny, and don't reveal too much.

"It's really good, how about yours?" I answer, worried that my response is neither witty nor funny. "Tell me more about this song you're working on,"

It works. He goes on and on about his song. Cosmo was right. Guys really do like to talk about themselves. All I have to do is sit here and pretend to be interested in what he's saying. He must have gone on for at least half an hour about his band. They play a mix of rock, hip-hop and rap. He's amazing. I've never met anyone in a band before.

"I'd love to hear you guys play."

"We're rehearsing later on. Why don't you come and see for yourself."

I agree. Why not? It's not like I have anything better to do.

"You wanna go check out some CDs?" he asks.

"Sure."

We spend a couple of hours at the music store just checking out CDs and talking about music. He likes everything from rap, to rock, to pop and even jazz. He puts a jazz CD on the sampler that's just awesome. It's some guy named Coltrane playing the most amazing saxophone. It's so melodic and smooth I could listen to it all day. He knows so much about music. I can't wait to hear his band.

We leave about seven for rehearsal. He cranks the music up high for most of the ride, bobbing his head up and down to the beat. He tells me about all the rap and rock stars of today who stole their beats from old school musicians. He talks about the roots of rock and roll, from the blues to Chuck Berry and the origins of rap and hip-hop. I think he's in love with Run DMC. It's great he has something in his life he loves so much. Something he can get so excited about and he has so much passion for. I doubt I could ever feel so strongly about anything.

I can't believe I'm in such a great car. It's actually a Jeep with a sparkling green paint job and a great stereo system. He must be at least sixteen, of course, but he could be as old as seventeen or eighteen. There's tons of candy wrappers and empty food bags covering the floor, but it's still the coolest car I've ever been in. We go racing down the street with the music blaring and wind pressing across my face. It feels like complete freedom.

It takes about twenty minutes to get from my neighborhood in central Philadelphia to his house in the subdivisions that surround the city. We pass row by row of traditional, two story, red brick homes enclosed by perfectly manicured lawns. As we approach, I see his house is just as beautiful as all his neighbor's, set apart only by its unique sand colored brick and dark blue shutters.

The jeep jerks to a stop as Tommy pulls into the driveway. "Home sweet home."

"You have a very nice house."

"It's alright. My mom's a real estate agent so she got us a good deal. I talked her into lettin' me convert one of the garages into a rehearsal studio. I guess she figured I wouldn't get in so much trouble if I spent more time at home."

He clicks a button on his key ring and the door on one side of the two car garage opens. It's a nice size room cluttered with musical equipment, speakers, and a big, red couch jammed against the wall. There's two guys smoking cigarettes, leaning on three-foot tall speakers. The short one with blond hair has a big red guitar hanging over his shoulder. They're staring at me as we walk up the driveway and I feel those little butterflies flittering around in my stomach again.

"Hey man, we ordered some pizza," the short one says.

"Tight. This is Cara," Tommy puts his hand on my waist. "Cara this is Jessie with the bass guitar and Kurt, he plays the drums."

"Hi, nice to meet you." I raise my hand and wave, but I'm too anxious to leave Tommy's side.

"Wanna cigarette?" Kurt asks. He's not as creepy looking as the short one. Actually, he has a really cute smile and big dimples.

"No, thanks."

"You don't smoke, do you?" Jessie asks holding out his hand for a cigarette.

"No, I mean I've never tried one before."

"Never? Man, you sure you ain't a nun," Tommy says.

"No I'm not. I just never tried one before, that's all."

"No time like the present." Tommy grins at me.

"Okay, why not." I can't resist his smile.

They go about their business plugging in speakers and adjusting their guitars and drums. I'm amazed at how easily they hold their cigarettes in their mouths with all that smoke enveloping their eyes and noses. They breathe in deep drags, hold it in and exhale faint streams that resemble steam pouring from a tea pot. Tommy tilts his head back and little rings of smoke emerge from his contorted lips. We smile at each other acknowledging his effort to impress me.

I can hardly stand the smoke streaming up my arms and into my nose, but I put it up to my mouth anyway. I always hated the smell of cigarettes. Mom didn't smoke and I hate the way Jim's smoking makes the house stink, but I don't want to come off looking like a nun. I guess one little cigarette won't kill me. How bad could it be? They're all having so much fun with the smoke. Like it's a friendly part of them they have complete control over. I feel confident enough to take in a deep breath. The smoke hits the back of my throat like a brick wall and bounces right back out. I'm coughing like crazy.

"Is it actually supposed to go down my lungs?" I ask catching my breath between coughs. "God, how do you suck it in like that?"

"Yeah, but don't sweat it," Tommy answers over Kurt's and Jessie's laughter. "You don't have to smoke it if you don't want to. It takes some gettin' used to."

"You can just puff on it until you get used to it, and then, before you know it, the smoke will be your friend." Kurt holds in a breath and lets the smoke escape, slowly drifting from his nostrils over a silly grin.

Tommy reaches over and turns on a two foot tall air purifier.

"Your mom doesn't care if you smoke in here?"

"She knows we smoke, but she don't care. It's easier for her to ignore it. I just turn that thing on so we don't choke to death in here. It gets pretty smoky with the door closed. I had this place sound proofed so we can play all day and night. Close the door."

They warm up, only for a moment then ease into a melodic groove driven by the bass guitar. It sounds like the jazz music Tommy put on at the music store. I can't believe how great Tommy plays his electric guitar. He and Jessie have cigarettes hanging from their lips, the smoke floating and lingering above their heads. They look so professional swaying to the music, like they could be on MTV. Tommy steps up to the microphone and starts to rap over the slow, soothing beat.

> "It's my world
> I'm like a diamond or a pearl
> So rare and precious
> You don't wanna step to this
> You might get your feelings hurt
> Testing what your manhood's worth
> You ain't ready for this test
> You can't take the consequence"

The words slide off his tongue and bravado fills the air. I keep taking small puffs on the cigarette so I look like I belong there. I feel a little light headed or maybe I'm just too relaxed by the music. Anyway, it feels good. I puff away for the next three hours. I had six whole cigarettes before I knew it. Tommy smiles at me every so often and I can't help smiling back every time our eyes meet. They practice pretty hard, only stopping to talk about the song or joke around a little. Jessie seems to be the victim of most of the kidding.

They drink beer after beer. They offer me one several times, but my stomach's a little sore.

I catch myself babbling on about how much I like his band on the ride home. I hope he doesn't think I'm like a groupie or something.

"Are your parents home?" Tommy asks as his jeep slows down in front of my house.

"Nobody's home."

"Well, aren't you going to invite me in? We can hang out and listen to music."

"Okay."

He wants to hang out with me. He really likes me. This is perfect. It's only 10:30. Jim won't be home until at least midnight. He'll be drunk. He won't even know Tommy's here.

The house is quiet as usual. I give him the quick tour through the family room, around to the kitchen and dining room and back to the family room

"I like your place."

"It's not as big as yours, but I guess it's alright. There's not much to it. The bedrooms are upstairs and that's about all."

"Aren't you gonna show me your room?"

"You wanna see it?" I stall trying to think whether or not I left something embarrassing out that I don't want him to see.

"Why not? I think you can learn a lot about a person from their room."

"Oh, no way. You're gonna think I'm a total geek."

"I don't think so. You're too fine to be a geek?"

"Okay." He makes me smile. "But don't say I didn't warn you."

The first thing he sees when he opens the door is my collection of stuffed animals. I must have over fifty of them hanging from the ceiling in a huge net in the corner facing my bed or scattered around the floor and on the bed. I don't remember why, but Crystal, Jennifer and I decided to paint our rooms pink when we were in the sixth grade. Jennifer has changed her room color several times since then, but Crystal's and mine are still the bright, hot pink. I always liked the color up until this moment.

"This looks like my little sister's room," he says, laughing out loud.

"See, I told you. Let's go. Out right now."

"Come on, I'm just clowning. It's alright. A cute little girl should have a cute little room."

He grabs me by the waist and spins me around. I think he's gonna kiss me and I know I'm gonna let him. He pulls me closer. I feel every part of his body pressing against mine. I close my eyes and wait. The light touch of his finger pulls my chin upwards, finally, his lips are moving back and forth across mine. I try to mimic the motion. It's soft and wet and tingles my entire body like nothing I've ever felt before. I never imagined kissing would feel so nice.

"You're a really cool girl, Cara," he whispers between kisses.

I'm enjoying the kissing too much to respond with anything but a moan. We're lying on my bed, but I don't care. I never knew I could feel so close to anyone. We stare into each others eyes, just like in the movies. His fingers run lightly down the side of my face, and he tells me how pretty I am. For the first time in my life I believe I am pretty. I must be. Why else would this great looking guy be with me? He kisses me again and again, each time my insides burst. His hands, big and strong, touch my body in places that no one has ever touched before. His fingers tug at my shirt. Suddenly his hands are on my bare skin and my bra is open.

He's trying to have sex with me. Part of me wants it bad. Everything about him feels so good I don't want it to stop. But the butterflies going crazy in my stomach tell me the time isn't right.

"Please, we can't." I fasten my bra.

"Why not?"

"It's not time."

"It's always time."

"We can't. We just met. I don't know you. You're going to think I'm a slut and I'm not." The reasons come pouring out of my mouth. It's wrong on so many levels. And Cosmo said never sleep with a guy on the first date.

"I'm sorry, you're right. I can't help myself. You're so hot."

"You don't really think I'm hot. You don't have to say that."

"Of course I do. Can't you see it? You have beautiful round eyes, an awesome smile, and a sweet onion." He runs his hands down my back and taps me on my butt.

"Don't make fun of my butt. I know it's big."

"I ain't makin' fun. I like it. There's nothin' worse than a skinny girl with no hips, for real"

I don't care if he's telling the truth or not. We lay on my bed with my head on top of his chest just talking. I can hear his heart beating through his t-shirt. I'm an infant discovering a new sensation for the first time. Almost hypnotized by the synchronized rhythm of his voice, heartbeat and breathing, I barely notice the sound of Jim stumbling through the door around 12:30.

"Who's that?"

"It's just my father."

"He's comin' this way?"

"He never comes in to check on me. He's usually too drunk to care."

"Those footsteps sound like they're gettin' closer."

He's right. The sound of dragging, stumbling feet moves closer. I can't believe it. Finally, a guy who's willing to hang out with me and Jim's gonna mess it all up. He better not come stumbling in here trying to tell me what to do. Hell, if he can have some slut spend the night in his room, I have the right to have a friend in my room. The footsteps grow louder.

"Quick, hide in the closet."

I take off my shoes, jump on the bed and pick up a book. My heart is pounding as I wait, anxiously anticipating the door will open at any moment. But the footsteps stop and go into the bathroom.

"Is he comin'?" Tommy sticks his head out of the closet.

"Not yet, he's in the bathroom. Get back in there."

I'm quiet as a mouse until I hear him shuffle back down the hall and his bedroom door close. No need to worry. I should've known Jim would never care enough to check in on me.

I tip-toe to the closet and open the door. Tommy's mischievous grin lifts my mood.

"Is he gone?" he asks.

"Yep."

"That was close. I thought we were busted for sure."

"We don't have to worry about him."

"That's okay, my mother's probably just gettin' home too. She was out with one of her boyfriends. I'd better get home."

"Thanks for inviting me to your band rehearsal. You guys really rock."

"Thanks for coming. Can I call you tomorrow?"

I rush over to my desk and grab a piece of paper and a pen to write down my phone number. We stand at the doorway listening to make sure Jim's asleep. When we're sure the coast is clear, he gives me one last kiss and slowly creeps down the stairs. It occurs to me that I didn't even have to use my camping story. Now I have my own story to tell.

Chapter 4

Crystal calls me at 6:00 in the morning. "Oh my God, you better tell me what happened, every word. I saw him leave at almost one o'clock last night. Did you do it with him? Oh my God, you did it didn't you? Did you do it?"

"Get real. No, I didn't do it with him, but he is a great kisser."

"Oh my God, he kissed you? Did he use his tongue?"

"I'll tell you when we get to school. And don't call me back. I have to get ready."

I can still hear her talking as I hang up the phone. It's amazing how anyone could have so much energy so early. I don't mean to be rude, but the last thing I want is to be grilled with questions first thing in the morning. The only thought I want in my head is the memory of how it feels to have Tommy kissing me. They'll just have to wait until lunch time for me to spill the beans. There's no way I'm gonna talk about last night in front of Crystal's mom.

I could almost feel a cold breeze coming from the car when they opened the door.

"I can't believe you hung up on me," Crystal grumbles.

"Yeah, you know, that wasn't very nice," Jennifer adds and I know they've been talking about me.

I let them sit and pout for a moment in silence. I know they're excited, but don't I have a right to some privacy? My experience was a special moment between me and Tommy.

"So how did your date go yesterday, Cara? Where did you go?" Crystal's mom breaks the silence.

"It was really nice. He's a great guy. I went to hear his band practice. He plays the guitar and sings. He's really talented."

"I guess you didn't get home until late? I wish you had called me like I asked."

"I'm sorry, I forgot. It wasn't too late. I got home around 10:30."

"Well, I hope you're careful with this boy. I hear he has a car. How old is he?"

"I'm sure you hear a lot." I throw my eyes at Crystal. "I'm not sure. Sixteen or seventeen, I guess, old enough to drive."

Crystal's mom can tell I'm getting annoyed by her questions, so we don't talk most of the rest of the way. She asks me to wait in the car for a moment when we get to school.

"Cara, I hope you don't think I'm trying to invade your privacy, but you know I loved your mother. She had her problems, but she was one of my best friends. When she got sick, I promised myself I would look out for you. I know I'm not your mother and I can't make you call and check in with me, but I hope you feel like you can talk to me about things."

"I know. There's nothing to worry about. He really is a great guy, a real gentleman."

"I'm glad you think so, but promise me you'll take it slow. You don't know him that well, a boy like that, who doesn't go to school. Just promise me you'll be careful."

"Okay, I will. Thanks for the advice." I only halfway mean it. Anything to stop the inquisition.

"What did she want?" Jennifer asks when I get out of the car.

"She just wanted to warn me about what a bad guy Tommy is. What did you tell her anyway?"

"I just told her he has a car, that's all."

"You didn't say anything about what time he left my house."

"No, I didn't." Her face drops as she answers.

"We're gonna be late for class. I'll tell you guys all about it at

43

lunch."

I tell them all about my date at lunch, about how good Tommy plays guitar and the kiss. They cling to every word. Crystal looks like she's gonna die when I tell them about the bra. Jennifer thinks I did the right thing. Crystal wonders how I found the restraint to stop.

We go to my house after school and wait for Tommy to call. Jennifer thinks it's silly for us to sit and wait by the phone for a call, but I can't help it. Tommy's all I think about. And Crystal, she'll go along with anything having to do with boys. The phone rings about 5:00.

"Hello."

"Hi, Cara, it's Tommy." I could barely hear his response over Crystal's squealing and Jennifer's shushing.

"Hi, Tommy, how's it going?"

"It's all good. Had a great time with you yesterday."

"Yeah, me too."

"You know you're a great kisser"

"Yeah, right, shut up."

"I'm serious. Can't wait to see you again."

"Yeah."

"Some of my friends are having a party this weekend. You wanna come?"

"Sure."

"Bring some of your girlfriends?"

"Okay, but we're gonna need a ride. None of our parents would ever take us to a party."

"Don't sweat it. I'll come and pick you guys up. Saturday night, okay."

"Okay."

"Okay, well, I gotta go. We're starting practice. I would invite you to come, but the guys don't like it when we bring our dates to rehearsal all the time.

"That's okay, I understand."

"Can I call you later tonight?"

"Sure."

44

"Okay, bye."

"Bye."

"What party?" Crystal grabs me the second I hang up the phone.

"What?"

"You said something about needing a ride to a party. What party?" Jennifer jumps in.

"He invited me to a party Saturday night."

"Really. Oh my God," Crystal squeals again.

"What kind of party?" Jennifer asks.

"I don't know, but he wants me to bring some friends so you guys are invited, too."

"Unbelievable." Crystal jumps up like she just won the lottery. "We're actually going to a Jefferson party. Unbelievable."

Tommy calls me every night for the rest of the week. Sometimes we talk for only a few minutes, but a couple of times we talk for at least two hours. Crystal and Jennifer leech off the details of every conversation. I think they're more excited about the party than I am, at least Crystal is. They wonder what they're gonna tell their parents. I don't have to worry about with Jim, the only pro to having a dead beat dad. I can get away with murder. We decide to tell them we're going to a late movie with an older girl from school who has a car. I was disappointed, but not surprised when they both called me later in the week to tell me they couldn't talk their parents into letting them go. Crystal's mom knows I'm seeing a new boy and immediately smelled a rat. Jennifer's parents are just hard to fool. She says they always know when she's lying. Jennifer thinks it's because they're lawyers. I guess they tell so many lies at work they can recognize one when they see one.

Tommy picks me up around 8:00 on Saturday night. Crystal and Jennifer help me with my outfit again. Since it's a night party, we decide to pick the black "You know what I mean, man?" t-shirt to go with my blue jeans. I pretend to be crushed they can't go with me, but, in reality, I don't care. As long as Tommy's with me, that's all I need.

The party's in a big, beautiful house close to where Tommy

lives. He introduces me to another tall, great looking guy named Brick. He's a D.J. It's Brick's house and, of course, his parents are out of town.

I imagine Tommy's holding my hand as he leads me in and out of these huge rooms, each perfectly furnished like something out of *Home and Garden* magazine, but his hands are too busy slapping high fives. He knows everyone and everyone knows him. The jocks in letter jackets talk too loud, obviously trying to impress the girls with perfect bodies, long, thick hair and too much make up. They must be the cheerleaders. All the kids are dressed in jeans and t-shirts. Thank God I fit in. Not only am I with a great looking guy, but I'm in with the popular party crowd. Unbelievable!

Someone hands me a cigarette and I take it. Everyone's smoking and I am part of the popular crowd now. Tommy's standing next to me puffing away and talking excitedly about one of his favorite bands with a tall, skinny, grungy looking boy. Another greasy looking boy comes up with two beers in big, red, plastic cups. He hands one to me and one to Tommy. It's automatically assumed that I want it. Why not? I always wondered what the big deal is about beer anyway. My first cautious sip is cold and bubbly with a weird, nutty, bitter taste. It's not good, but it's not awful either.

"How's your beer," Tommy asks.

"It's okay."

"I was afraid you was gonna be a milk and cookies girl."

"Hey, I know how to have fun."

"Straight."

We stand there for a moment sipping and smoking. I scan the room looking for something interesting to comment on, but my mind is blank.

"I see someone I need to talk to. You gonna be okay by yourself for a minute?"

"Sure. Go ahead," I answer relieved by the time to think of something to talk about.

"I'll bring you back another beer."

"Okay," I can't refuse. After all, I'm no longer a milk and

cookies girl.

He takes one last big sip, lets off a loud "ahhhh", throws the plastic cup over his shoulder and disappears into the crowd. I take bigger sips trying to finish my beer before he comes back. Besides, I have nothing else to do but stand here and feel uncomfortable.

A group of boys and girls are stretched out across a U shaped sectional sofa that surrounds a big screen TV. The room is dark except for the dim glow of the TV and some light that creeps in from the adjoining kitchen. They're passing around a cigarette, but they're smoking it weird. Each one takes a couple of puffs and passes it on. I've never seen it before, but I can tell from the pungent, unfamiliar scent and the way they're passing it around that it's marijuana. I watch them intently to see how they react to it, but there's no reaction. Everyone's just sitting there, quietly puffing.

Finally, Tommy comes back. "You still nursing that beer?" He takes my cup, quickly chugs the last few sips I have remaining and throws it over his shoulder. That must be some kind of strange ritual for him. "Here you go, a fresh one."

"Is that what I think it is?" I ask pointing to the kids on the sofa.

"You mean the weed? Let me guess. You never tried that before either. What am I gonna do with you?"

"You mean you do that, too?"

"Please, everybody does it. It ain't no big deal. It's a great buzz, but I guess they don't teach you about having a good time in Catholic school. You wanna try it?"

"I don't know. I mean it's illegal, isn't it?"

"Yeah, but that's only because the religious freaks pass the laws in this country. They're such hypocrites. They condemn smoking weed, but they'll sit up all night at their parties sucking down wine and gin and tonics. I only follow the rules if they make sense. Hell, most of them have never even tried it. Believe me, drinking is much worse than smoking pot. At least it doesn't shrink up your liver and you don't wake up with a hang over."

"You know a lot about drugs, don't you?"

"I guess. I know how to have a good time." He pauses and I can

47

tell he's thinking. "Maybe I shouldn't have bought you here. For some reason I thought you was gonna be fun."

"I am fun."

"No really, it's okay. I don't want you to do nothin' you don't want to. Come on, I'll take you home."

"I don't wanna go home. I'm having fun, really."

As if on cue, some guy approaches us with one of those funny little cigarettes. His eyes are half shut and he's slurring his words "Hey man, you gotta try this. It's the best."

Tommy takes a puff and hands it to me with that "try it you'll like it" look on his face. Time to put up or shut up. I take it and inhale little puffs like I learned to do with the cigarette.

"Hey man, what you doin'? Puff, puff, pass," the boy with the squinty eyes exclaims.

"What?" I ask.

"Man, ain't you a greedy little one. Puff, puff, pass. You gotta take two puffs and pass it on. You can't be hoggin' the blunt."

"Relax man, she don't know no better." Tommy defends me. "Here, let me show you. You take in a deep, slow drag and hold it in as long as you can, then exhale. Like this."

I watch him, amazed at how much smoke he slowly inhales. He must have a room full of smoke in his mouth. The funny thing is when he exhales only a small stream floats from between his lips.

"Oh my God, did you hold all that smoke inside?" I ask.

"Yeah man, that's the way you do it. Pass it, man." Droopy Eyes is getting impatient.

"Hold on, man. Let's give virgin lungs another shot," Tommy says.

"Go ahead. You guys finish that off. I'm gonna roll another one." Droopy Eyes slaps Tommy's hand and disappears into the dimly lit, smoky haze.

"Okay, you ready?" Tommy asks.

"Sure." I'm really not, but I have to show him I'm cool enough to hang with the party crowd.

I slowly inhale as much smoke as I can, but, just like with the cigarette, I can't keep it in and the smoke comes rushing out leaving me coughing uncontrollably. I'm so embarrassed. I would apologize if I could catch my breath.

"Don't sweat that, baby. It takes some gettin' used to. I remember the first time I tried it. I thought I was gonna cough up a lung."

He hugs me and kisses me sweetly on the forehead. He called me his baby!

We find a seat on the sofa in front on the TV. I don't really know if I'm high or not, but I feel good there with Tommy, nestled against his chest with his arms around me. I feel warm, safe and comfortably sleepy. I gingerly sip on my beer and take an occasional tiny puffs off the funny little cigarette. Tommy keeps telling me how pretty he thinks I am. I believe him more with every sip of beer.

"Come with me." He suddenly grabs my hand and leads me, staggering, through the crowd, down the hallway and into a small room in the back of the house. "Yo man, we need the room."

The two boys sitting on the couch playing video games nod and slap Tommy's hand as they quietly leave the room. I'm impressed with how popular Tommy is. He snaps his finger and they jump.

He eases me on to the thick couch cushions and kisses me. I'm so relaxed with him and my body feels like it wants to be touched all over. His hands are everywhere, each touch brings a new sensation. All of a sudden my pants are open and his hands are touching my thing. I push them away, but they rise right back up again.

"No, we can't."

"Why not?"

"I don't know, we just can't."

"Don't you like me?"

"Of course I do. I'm just not ready, that's all."

He keeps kissing me gently on my neck and lips. I feel like I'm on fire. I pull him closer to me. God, I love the kissing. I don't want him to stop. He puts his hand down there again, rubbing and poking.

I never really like touching myself down there. It just looks and feels too weird. This feels weird, too.

49

Mark Miller

He's on top of me now unbuckling his pants.

"No. Stop. I'm sorry. We can't."

"Come on, Cara. It's okay."

"No, please. I need more time. I'm sorry."

"You tryin' to be a tease?" He sounds angry.

"No, please don't be mad. We just can't yet, that's all. Not yet. It's too soon."

"You know, Cara, I really like you. I just wanna be closer to you. I feel like we have this connection and I wanna see it grow. You know if we do it, it'll bring us closer together. Don't you want us to get closer?" His tone is now more relaxed, almost calming.

"I do. I really do. I'm just not ready to get that close yet. Please, try to understand."

I can tell by the look on his face that he doesn't understand. I don't really know if I understand it. My body is screaming out, do it! But my mind, still dizzy from the beer and funny cigarettes, is saying slow down. I guess it just doesn't feel right.

We get back to my house around two in the morning after a long, silent car ride.

"Thanks for inviting me to the party. It was really great."

"I hope you had a good time."

"I did. I hope you're not still mad at me. You've been so quiet."

"Not mad, maybe disappointed. I really like you, Cara." He cups my face in his hands and kisses me. "Call you later."

"Okay."

My head's so hazy. I can't wait to throw off my clothes and fall into bed. The bed is spinning so fast I think I'm gonna be sick.

Chapter 5

The phone wakes me up with a loud ring. My head feels like someone squeezed all the juice out of my brain. My first hang over. It's Crystal calling to remind me that her family will be by at nine to pick me up for church. She really wants to know how the party was, of course, but I'm way too groggy for conversation.

I give them all the details after church, everything from the cigarettes to the beer to the kissing on the couch. I leave out the part about the weed and the rubbing and poking for fear of criticism.

"You got drunk?" Jennifer disapproves.

"I bet he's a great kisser," Crystal daydreams.

"You got drunk didn't you?" Jennifer persists.

"Maybe a little. Lighten up. It's no big deal." She's really starting to get on my nerves with her high and mighty attitude.

"What's it like, you know, getting drunk?" Jennifer asks.

"It's no big deal. I mean you just feel silly and kinda dizzy. You pretty much laugh at anything. Then, after a while, it makes you sleepy and you wake up with a big headache. Now I know why Jim always sleeps 'til noon when he's been out. My head still hurts. But it does make the kissing feel really nice."

"I've never been drunk before, but I used to sneak sips of wine out of my parent's friends glasses at their parties just to see what it was like. It made me feel a little dizzy, but I couldn't stand the taste

51

of it." Crystal shudders.

"It was so great. There were so many popular kids there and they liked me too. Tommy's the best. He calls me every night and sometimes we talk for hours."

"No wonder I can't get you on the phone lately," Crystal sighs. "So, what are we gonna do today?"

"Tommy's picking me up later. We're going to the movies."

"I think he really likes you," Crystal says excitedly.

"Yeah, me too," I agree.

"God, you're so lucky," Crystal says.

"Has he tried to, you know, yet?" Jennifer asks.

"He wants to."

"They all want to," Jennifer replies.

"For real, but he's been good about it."

"Hey, if you go to the movies it will be your third date and you know what Cosmo says about the third date. Time to give it up," Crystal says.

"Just because Cosmo says so doesn't mean that's the way it is," Jennifer argues.

"Sure it does. The women that write those articles have a lot more experience with boys than we do. That's for sure. Sex on the third date, that's what you're supposed to do." Crystal stands her ground.

"It doesn't seem right to me," Jennifer looks upset.

"Me either. I mean, I know I want to do it. When we're kissing it's so hard to stop. But we've only been dating for a couple of weeks. How much respect is he gonna have for me if we do it so soon?"

Tommy takes me to see a scary movie about ghosts. I've always been especially afraid of ghost movies. I find it easy to believe there are lost, wandering souls stuck somewhere between heaven and hell. I spend half the movie with my eyes closed and my head buried in his chest. It's a safe, warm place. Exactly where I want to be.

For the next two months we spend almost every night on the phone or in each others arms. We talk about sex a lot. It's so hard not to give in, but I just don't want to do it yet. It's creepy the way he talks about it, like it's always on his mind. No matter how many times he says it, I'll never believe I'm as pretty as he says. A super model, right. I want to believe it, but I can see myself in the mirror.

I can't help thinking about family one night while we're leisurely puffing on a funny cigarette, watching *Little House on the Prairie* on the old re-run channel. We start joking about how ridiculous the idea of a whole family is. His parents divorced when he was only four and his father lives in Arizona with a new family. He hardly ever hears from him. He seems broken up about it, but he's good at not showing it. He doesn't have to. The expression on his face reminds me of how much I miss Mom. I haven't mentioned her yet. It never seems like a good time to bring up the subject. I can't exactly blurt out, "My mom died this summer," between kisses.

All he can say when I tell him is, "That's a tough break, I'm sorry." Then fall into silence and turn the channel. I don't know what kind of reaction I was looking for, but he didn't even seem to care. Couldn't he even talk to me about it, just a little? They say guys don't like to talk about stuff like that, emotions and all. I don't know, but a minute later we're kissing. It seems like every time I want to talk we end up kissing.

I love the kissing. The tingle it brings and the feel of his body pressing against mine leaves no room for conversation. It helps me forget about everything and escape to another planet, a parallel universe where I am a supermodel and I date the hottest boy in town.

I know he's mad about the sex. Our time together is different now than it was in the beginning. The kissing starts out nice, but then it turns into an awkward game of tug of war, him pushing his hands up my shirt or down my pants and me pulling them away. I've instinctively learned enough hand blocking, wrist turning moves to earn a black belt in karate by now.

Why am I even holding out? He's all I ever think about. Is this love? It must be. He calls me almost every night to ask me how my day went and he's always so nice when we go out, like I'm the only girl in the room. He makes me feel beautiful. What the hell is wrong

53

with me? Am I crazy for making him wait so long? We've had way more than three dates. Maybe I am a tease.

I give him a deep, wet kiss when he picks me up to go to a party Friday night. Someone's always having a party on the weekends. The jock parties supply an unlimited supply of beer. By the end of the night you can count on a sea of twisted or crushed beer cans blanketing the floor and the familiar sound of some cheerleader of football player praying to the porcelain god. I like watching the helmet heads running, screaming and wrestling around like they're auditioning for a career in professional wrestling. I even won a bet one night on who would loose their cookies first. For my prize I got to chug a beer and barely escaped a visit to the porcelain god myself.

Anyone who hangs out behind the cafeteria smoking cigarettes at lunch time and weed on the weekends is labeled a freak by the jocks. That's the funny thing about the jocks. They look down on the freaks for smoking weed, but they have no problem drinking so much beer and shots of tequila they end up puking their guts out.

The freak parties are a totally different vibe. The jocks would be shocked if they knew how much drugs the freaks really do. Someone's always passing around an assortment of pills at every party. There're the purple ones that mellow you out, the pink ones that make you hyper and the yellow and black ones that send you into a dancing frenzy all night long. I don't have the nerve to try any yet.

I like the freak parties better. There's always such a positive energy driven by loud music saturating every room. Sometimes it's a crazy techno beat. Sometimes they slow it down, but the thunderous beat is ever present. I'm sure it's the drugs, but everybody's always in a good mood, either hyper and happy like a lap dog or mellow and content, cool like a cat. The jocks just want to fight all the time and their cheerleader girlfriends are such snobs I'd rather ignore them than try pry into their top secret conversations.

Would I be a freak or a jock if I went to public school? No way I'd be a cheerleader, too phony. Am I too much of a good, Catholic girl to be a freak? Maybe I'd be a drama or band geek.

Tommy seems to fit in freak or jock, but he's definitely more of a freak by the way he acts and dresses. His band plays at some of the parties. Everyone loves him. They all know him everywhere we go. Tonight's a jock party with football season in full gear. The jocks are always happy to see Tommy. I'm not really sure why. He's into music, not sports.

He's pulled into the back room by two buffed football players only a few minutes after we arrive. He's always disappearing into back rooms, leaving me alone to mingle with the freaks and the jocks. I've learned the art of excusing myself during boring conversations and find a quiet place outside to smoke. It took a while, but I can actually inhale the smoke now. There's something relaxing about a cigarette, the way the smoke eases in and out at your own rhythm and pace. I think about Crystal and Jennifer and wish they were with me, only I know they wouldn't go for the cigarettes. Crystal, maybe.

It isn't long before Tommy finds me outside. I approach him like a lonely puppy when his owner comes home at the end of the day. It's like I can't help myself.

"Hey Tommy," a beautiful, tall, slender girl with small, tight braids intricately woven into her hair runs up and gives Tommy a hug. "Hey babe, what's going on? Long time no see," she says.

"Hey, you lookin' sweet as ever." Tommy beams at her.

"Yeah, you know I gotta keep it together," she says as she runs her hands down the sides of her perfectly slender hips.

"Lasenna, this is Cara. Cara, Lasenna. She graduated last year and goes to Temple."

"Hey girl, what's up?"

"Hi."

"Me and Tommy go way back. This fool is crazy. I can see the jocks are acting stupid as ever." She looks over at two guys crushing beer cans on their foreheads.

"Where's T. J.?" Tommy asks.

"He's right over there." She points to a stocky, well built boy in a letter jacket. "He's gonna to take 'em to state this year. Watch and see."

"I don't doubt that. That's one serious runner right there. Cara, T. J's our best running back."

"You know my baby's your only running back."

"He's your boyfriend, Lasenna?" I ask anxiously.

"Yeah, that's my baby. So, are you guys, you know?"

"Yeah, Cara's my girl." He pulls me toward him.

"Really, I didn't know you had it in you, Tommy. How long you been together?"

"We've been kickin' it for a minute," Tommy says.

"It's been two months," I correct him.

"How old are you?" she asks.

"I'll be sixteen in a couple of months."

"You better watch yourself girl, this one's a player." Lasenna grins at him as she walks off.

"What did she mean?" I ask.

"Nothing, she's just trippin'."

"You've had a lot of girlfriends, huh?"

"That don't matter. I'm with you now. You know you're my girl, don't you?"

He pulls me into a close, tight hug. Our arms are wrapped around each other like we're never gonna let go. My face pressed against his chest, we rock slowly back and forth. I can hear his heart beat and I know he's telling me the truth.

I'm gonna do it with him tonight. Why not? Everyone knows I'm his girl. They all call me "Tommy's girl" more than they use my own name. Everyone else is doing it. I'm tired of wondering about it. I wanna find out for myself.

I give him little kisses all night hoping he gets the hint I'm in the mood. I know it works when he turns to me before the party really kicks into high gear and asks if I want to leave early. He says his mom will be out late and he'd rather be alone with me tonight. It's like he can read my mind. We are meant to be together. Tonight's the night Everything's gonna be perfect.

I recline back into our make out couch in his TV room. He turns the big screen on to music videos, gently rests his body on top of mine and we start kissing.

"I wanna do it." I whisper into his ear.

"You sure?"

"Yeah."

I keep my eyes closed as he takes off my clothes, afraid to see his reaction to my big butt next to his perfectly thin, athletic body. Suddenly, I feel his bare skin all over mine. It's amazing, like nothing I've ever felt before. I feel closer to him, like it is bringing us together as one. I hold on to him, squeeze my arms around his back and cling to him. It's tight and it stings, but I hold on.

"I love you," slips out. I can't help it. I feel so close to him now.

"I love you too. You're so beautiful," he pants and whispers in my ear until he's finished.

He tries to get up, but I can't let him go and pull him back to me. He lies down so I can lay my head on his chest. He knows my favorite spot, cuddled up next to his heartbeat. I am connected to him, safe and happy. In a place where nothing bad can get to me.

Chapter 6

Crystal and Jennifer almost flip when I tell them. Jennifer scolds me for not using a condom, but Crystal wants to hear every detail. I describe the connection it formed between me and Tommy and how much it stings. I want to tell them about how much I love him, but I don't think they'd understand. They haven't felt the closeness.

Crystal keeps asking me to set her up with one of his friends, but she can never make it to any of the parties. I don't think any of Tommy's friends would go for her anyway. Brick, Kurt, no way. I see the kind of girls they go for and Crystal just isn't it. Maybe Jessie, but he's so short and creepy. I don't know. I feel sorry for Crystal. At least I'm cute. Tommy says so.

We have sex almost every time we're together, on the couch in the TV room, in his bed, in my bed, in the back seat of his jeep, and under the tree at the park. The more we do it, the more I like it. He even has a pet name for my fat, ice cream filled butt. It's his "bucket" and he loves the "junk in my trunk". I feel so close to him each time we do it and it doesn't hurt so much anymore. I don't know why sometimes it feels really good and sometimes it's just okay. It doesn't matter, each time I get to lay my head on his chest when we're done. He listens to me lament over Mom and complain about Jim, anything I need to talk about. He tells me about what a loser his father is too. We have so much in common. What is it with fathers anyway? Are they all pre-programmed to be idiots?

I hardly see Crystal and Jennifer anymore outside of school, but I don't even think about them when I'm with Tommy. Jennifer's really getting on my nerves lately anyway, always complaining that I smell like smoke and criticizing me for skipping school to be with Tommy. She's so jealous. She has no idea what it feels like to be in love. Tommy's totally right. School's for suckers. So what if my grades are slipping as long as they're good enough to get into college what do I care.

We go to the mall and hang out at music stores or at his or my house. Our favorite spot is the park. There's this one tall oak tree hidden behind a row of tall bushes that's the perfect place to hide and fool around. Something about the danger of fooling around in public really makes me hot. It's more exciting when I know I might get caught at any moment.

I've embraced my new wild side. I'm actually doing all the things I used to sit around dreaming about with Crystal and Jennifer, except for the drugs. I never thought I'd try that, but I like getting high. It relaxes me and I can forget about everything. Plus it makes my body feel really good when I'm fooling around, like every sensation is magnified. I haven't told Jennifer and Crystal about getting high. I don't think I'm going to. They wouldn't understand.

Sister Jane is the only one of my teachers who notices my grades are slipping. I know she has a last name, but none of us ever use it. She's nothing like the other grouchy, old nuns and priests you couldn't pay to crack a smile.

I wonder why they're so bitter, but I guess it's easy to be sad when you spend a lifetime alone. Now that I have Tommy, I can't imagine how anyone can spend their entire life by themselves. Now I understand why so much time and energy is spent on attracting the opposite sex. Choosing God as a life long companion definitely has its drawbacks. They say God is always at their side, but you can't cuddle up with God or feel his heartbeat through his chest. You can't raise a family with God. Now I know what it's like to be close and how much they're missing. It's not natural for people to live alone.

59

I wonder why the church demands celibacy anyway? Isn't it God's plan for men and women to be together? Why would he condemn the people who worship and serve him the most to a life of loneliness? It's just not right.

Sister Jane's different, so pretty she could have any man she wants. She has luxurious, sandy blond hair that goes all the way down to her waist. She keeps it in a bun, but I saw her let it down one day after school. A natural beauty with that perfect girl next door look, the kind you hate because she never has to wear make up. I could never figure out why it's so important to her to look so plain. If she really knew what it is to be plain, she wouldn't be so quick to join the party. If I had her face and body, the last thing I'd do is cover it up. Everyone would know how beautiful I was.

She asks me to stay after class one day.

"Cara, I know things have been really hard for you. I want you to know you have a lot of people in this world that care about you. You're missing so much school I'm concerned about the way your grades are slipping. Are you okay?"

"Sure, thanks for asking. I've just been feeling a little sick lately. You know, a little run down. But I feel a lot better when I stay home and catch up on my sleep." I'm surprised at how easily the lie jumps out of my mouth.

"You need to catch up on what you've missed. Would you like me to tutor you after school? It would be a blessing for me. Please say yes."

"I don't know." I know she's trying to reach out to me. She's my favorite teacher, but I can't imagine myself in tutoring when I could be hanging out with Tommy.

"I know God is testing you now, but you have to understand he has a plan for you. He blessed you with intelligence. He wouldn't have bestowed you with such a blessing if you weren't meant to use it."

"Oh, he has a plan for me?"

"He has a plan for all of us."

"Was it his plan for my mother to die?"

"Everything happens for a reason, Cara. We can't question God's plan. His ways are much too powerful for us to understand."

"If that was his plan, I don't want anything to do with it."

"Please, Cara, what are you saying?"

"I'm sorry, Sister Jane. Don't get upset." I don't mean to hurt her feelings. "It's just that you remember how hard we all prayed when she was sick and none of it did any good. Our prayers went unanswered. Is it God's plan to ignore the people that worship him the most?"

"You're so angry, Cara. I understand that, but you can't turn your back on God. You can't let despair take your soul. Let us help you find your way. Will you be at service on Sunday?"

"I don't know. I guess. Thanks for talking to me, but I gotta go. I'm okay, really I am. Don't worry about me, okay."

After my talk with Ms. Jane, I start to think more and more about God, religion and so many things I was taught growing up Catholic. Like if you don't believe Jesus Christ is your savior who was sent to die for your sins and will come again to sit at his father's side at judgment day, you're damned to burn in hell.

But what about all the different religions of the world? The Muslims who believe in Mohammed and don't believe Jesus is our savior. Jewish people don't believe in Jesus either. What about the Buddhist, the Hindus and the other religions representing billions of people all over the world that don't believe Jesus is our savior? Are they all damned to hell? It doesn't make sense.

Wandering around the mall after school helps me think about God and everything. They have a great bookstore where I look through the picture books of far off places. Maybe I'll be a National Geographic photographer one day. As I'm browsing through the shelves, I see a book on religions of the world that catches my eye.

There's so much I don't know about other religions past what I see on TV. They never mention anything about any religion other than Catholicism in school. There was no reason to question what I was being taught about God, no need to be curious. You don't think for yourself when you're young. You just do what your parents tell you and you believe what they believe. Mom believed in Jesus, so I believed in Jesus.

I flip through the pages like a kid ripping through his presents on Christmas morning. Buddhism, Judaism, Hinduism, Taoism, so many religions, some I don't even recognize. I decide to buy the book.

Chapter 7

I'm finding it harder to go to school every day. Tommy teaches me how to screen the phone calls and letters they send home. Jim wouldn't do anything about it anyway. Concentrating on school has been depriving me of some really great life experiences. I'm open and free now, free to feel good about feeling good. When we puff, puff, pass, my mind and body soar to a place where everything is easy. I can't believe I waited so long to have sex. How could anyone deny themselves the sensation and closeness of being with someone you love? It's truly a miracle and God has nothing to do with that.

Lasenna is the coolest girl I've ever met. Even though she goes to college, she doesn't look down on me or treat me like a kid. She's teaching me how to dress, walk, talk and act around the popular clique. I just love to watch her work the crowd at a party as she glides effortlessly from one conversation to the other, always with something cool to say. I guess the college experience actually does expand your mind.

Brick and Kurt are really cool, too. Stupid, silly when they're stoned, always saying the funniest things. I hate how they have new girlfriends every week. Always joking about how no girl could ever tie them down. They give Tommy a hard time for hanging with me all the time. I hate it when they talk like that, bragging about all the girls they "bang". I'm so lucky Tommy's not like that. He says I'm all the girl he needs.

Jessie still gives me the creeps, always staring at me like he's undressing me with his eyes. No wonder I never seen him with a girl. He probably goes around giving every girl he sees the creepy eye.

Either Crystal or Jennifer calls me almost every night. I don't always call them back. We just keep having the same conversation. "Are you coming to school tomorrow?" I feel guilty 'cause we used to be so close, but whenever I'm given the choice between hanging out with Crystal and Jennifer or hanging out with Tommy and my new crew, they lose every time. And they're always bugging me about going to church. Church just ain't my thing any more. The last thing I need is some Puritan telling me how to live my life and making me feel guilty about all the fun I'm having. I'm just not buying that I'm gonna burn in hell for smoking a blunt or fooling around with Tommy.

What is it with God anyway? Everything sends you to hell: premarital sex, smoking pot, even telling a lie. Guess I'm damned, for real. Can't I even feel simple, basic human emotions like jealousy, anger, greed and lust without having to confess my soul and say a hundred Hail Mary's? The last sermon I went to the priest was condemning his congregation for lusting after money and letting greed cloud their judgment when their focus should be on the Lord. Like it's a sin to want nice things. Isn't that the American dream? And he lives in nice, big house with a big, fat Mercedes in the driveway. Hello, anyone ever hear of practicing what you preach?

Sister Jane scared me enough to go to school today because of a history test. Mom always wanted me to go to college. The Boston Tea Party, The Sons of Liberty, The Constitution, it's been the same thing since the sixth grade. I don't bother to study.

Lasenna meets me at the mall after school to go shopping. All I have is twenty five bucks from the weekly allowance Jim gives me. His way of being a good father. Lasenna stops at the window in front of Victoria Secret.

"T.J. would love me in that." She points to a red lace teddy.

"He likes that kinda stuff?"

"He eats it up. You should try it. Tommy would love it."

"No way. My butt's way too big for that."

"Please girl, you know the day of the super skinny sex symbol is over. Guys like big butts. Look at J. Lo and Beyonce and Mariah. At least all them booty shakin' rap videos did somethin' for us girls. He'd love to see that big old booty you got in this." She picks up a teddy that looks just like the red one she likes; only it's white and more lacy. "You know that boy's a sex hound."

"What do you mean?"

"Look, Cara, you're cool and all that, so I don't wanna see you get hurt. I like hangin' with you. You know, like the little sister I never had."

"Thanks. You know you're the coolest girl I know. So...what's up?"

"Girl, Tommy's a dog. I didn't wanna say nothin' at first, but I can see how much you're into him."

"What do you mean he's a dog? I mean I know he's had a lot of girlfriends, but he's with me now."

"You sure about that?"

"Why, do you know something? What's up?"

"Look, I ain't saying nothin' for sure. I mean he seems to be into you, but I've never seen him with any one girl for a long time. He's not a bad guy; he's just a horn dog. Just like all of 'em. You know all they want is that cookie."

"Tommy's not like that. He loves me. He told me he does. I can feel it when I'm with him."

"Ugh, Cara, don't you know they'll say anything just to get at your goodies. I used to go out with Tommy."

"You did?"

"It was a long time ago and it wasn't for that long, but trust me when I tell you that boy's not ready or willing for real love. He's gonna be eighteen soon, but he acts like he's still fifteen sometimes."

"Hey, just 'cause you're young doesn't mean you have to act young."

"I'm not talkin' about you, Cara. You cool as Christmas for your

65

age. Look, I wouldn't tell you if I didn't like you. Tommy, let's just say he's very independent. Just promise me one thing; you'll use protection with him. You're way to smart and young to be gettin' pregnant. You do use protection, don't you?"

"We don't have to. I mean he doesn't like to. He says he can't feel anything."

"Come on girl. Use your head. Do you wanna get pregnant?"

"Please. What do you think?"

"I don't know. Don't you get all stupid on me just 'cause you think you're in love."

"What about you? Does T.J. love you?"

"I don't know. We don't really talk about that. T.J.'s only a little more mature than Tommy. I do like him though. He's got a hot body, he's smart and he may even have a future in football. But you better bet he don't come near my goodies without his party hat on. I ain't no fool and you better not be one either."

"Okay, can we talk about something else?"

"Promise me you'll think about it."

"Alright, already."

She buys the red teddy. I leave the store empty handed.

Tommy doesn't call me that night. He doesn't call me every night, but Lasenna has me paranoid. The more I think about it the more I know she must just be jealous. Tommy hasn't even looked at another girl since we met. Maybe she just wants him back?

There is one thing she said that really made me think. I don't want to get pregnant, but I really don't think it will happen to me. Everybody's doing it and I've only heard of two girls that got pregnant. I decide to call Tommy, but he's not answering his cell phone. I sleep restlessly that night and wake up with a queasy stomach. School takes my mind off things, but I'm preoccupied with worry. I shouldn't let what Lasenna said effect me so much. She obviously doesn't have the same kind of relationship with T.J. that I have with Tommy.

Jennifer and Crystal meet me after school.

"I'm so glad to see you decided to come to school today,"

Jennifer says in her sarcastic way.

"Nice to see you too." I was determined not to let her get under my skin.

"Hi, Cara."

"Hi, Crystal."

"You really shouldn't be missing so much school. Aren't you worried you're gonna fail your classes?" Jennifer asks.

"Not really. You know I never had to study that hard anyway. As long as I'm there for the tests I'll be okay."

"Jennifer's spending the night on Friday. You wanna come?" Crystal asks.

"I can't, Crystal."

"Yeah, I know. Tommy," she sighs.

"You know, Crystal's mom was right. This guy is no good for you. You shouldn't be missing so much school, you're smoking and I pray to God you're using protection because I know you're having sex," Jennifer snaps at me.

"Well, duh, I told you I was, didn't I. What the hell makes you think you can tell me what to do? You're not my mother."

"Cara, please, she's just worried about you. So am I," Crystal jumps in.

"So don't worry about it. What I do is none of your business anyway."

"Of course it is, Cara, we're still best friends. Just because you have a boyfriend now doesn't mean you can just forget about us. We are still best friends, aren't we?" Crystal pleads.

"I don't know. I mean things change, don't they? I know I've changed. I've grown and I like to do different things now. I still like you guys, but I don't know. Things are just different now."

"I understand," Jennifer says with a sad look on her face. "We still love you and we'll pray for you."

"Give me a break. Pray for what?"

I hear a familiar car horn beeping in the background. It's Tommy waving to me from his jeep, right on time. I'm not in the mood for the "we can save your soul" lecture.

"Anyway, that's my ride. Gotta go." I run to Tommy.

"You're timing is perfect." I give him a welcome kiss. "You just saved me from the moral majority."

"What's up?"

"Nothin', just some drama with the old friends."

"What'd you expect from the geek squad?"

"I can't believe we used to be friends. So, where we goin'."

"Everybody's over at Brick's right now. We're just hangin' out, but tonight we goin' buck wild. The mother of all rave parties. Brick's crew rented out this underground club downtown. Man, the music's gonna be off the chain."

He hands me a small square piece of pitch black paper with nothing on it but an address and a symbol of an old school record with a silver lightning bolt striking it. That sounds more like it, a great party with great music and my boyfriend by my side. Like I'd rather be hanging out in my jammys with Crystal and Jennifer eating popcorn and dreaming about boys. No contest.

"Hey girl, come here," Lasenna greets me. "Good to see you, 'lil sis." I can tell she's already started to party without me. "We gonna party tonight, girl," she says handing me a drink.

Now that's the way to greet a friend, happy, smiling and non-judgmental.

"You got that right, baby girl," T.J. hugs her around the waist from the back. "What's up, Cara?"

"Hey T.J., so tell me about this party tonight."

"It's gonna be off the chain," Tommy finally catches up to me. "I told you about it babe, crazy music, drinks, whatever you want."

"Yeah, the head's gonna be buzzin' tonight," Kurt jumps in. "Man, we gonna handle some business tonight."

"Shhh," Tommy gestures for Kurt to keep quiet.

"What?" I ask.

"Nothin', he don't mean nothin'." Tommy turns to Bick. "Hey Brick, you havin' a laser show this time. Man, you gonna bring the house down."

"You know how we do it, dog," Brick answers.

68

"Sweet, Cara you're gonna freak when you see the lasers. It'll blow your mind," Tommy says.

"Sounds pretty wild. I can't wait."

Tommy picks up a blunt from the ash tray, takes a couple of puffs and picks up his guitar. He looks right at me and starts to rap.

"Just a strummin' and a rollin', rockin' and a flowin'
With my girl to my right, you know I ain't posin'
Cause she lookin' quite fine to me
Bust a cap in your ass if you don't agree
Cause when it comes to her you better step with respect
Or I'll crush you like a grape, man you better come correct
I like her smile and the way she holds my hand and
You know I'll do whatever I can to
Make her happy and treat her right
Play it tight, rock it all night"

Everybody's used to Tommy's spontaneous raps. He's so talented. I've seen him go on for over thirty minutes bouncing from person to person rapping about their clothes, hair, shoes, anything he can find to comment on. He can break you down with insults or build you up with compliments. I just sway back and forth as he builds me up.

"Would you really bust a cap on someone for me?" I whisper in his ear.

"All day long," he says.

We hang out at Brick's for hours, partying, napping and partying again. It's almost twelve by the time we get to the club. I've never seen the city like this before, a ghost town speckled with bums who roam the streets like lost souls. We park in a dark alley and walk to a door with a purple light and the address, 1215, barely visible above the frame.

"How does anybody ever find this place?" I ask.

"People find a way to find out. Brick's parties are legendary," Tommy says.

The building looks like an abandoned factory of some kind. The guy at the door lets us in immediately. He knows Tommy. The inside is a reflection of the drab brick covering on the outside. There's paint peeling from the walls and you can see the pipes exposed in some parts of the ceiling. It's dark but I can tell there's really not much to it, just a big room with Brick's DJ stuff in the corner and a large, slightly raised section of floor I assume is for dancing. Lasers dart in every color of the rainbow through a fog that covers the room. Everyone's wearing glowing bracelets or necklaces and glow sticks lay all over the waist high tables. Multi-colored balloons float throughout the room and stick to the walls.

"What's with the balloons," I ask Tommy after seeing a couple of kids pick them off the wall and suck out the air.

"Some are filled with helium that makes you talk funny, you know, like those squeaky chipmunks. The other kind has laughing gas in it. It cracks you up, but the buzz only lasts for a few seconds."

"Let me try one." All the balloons and different colors emerging through the fog and darkness make me feel like a kid in a carnival. I wanna try every ride. Tommy hands me a balloon. It works. I'm laughing like crazy. Tommy's taking hits off a helium balloon. He sounds like Mickey Mouse on speed.

Everyone brings their own drinks and whatever. Tommy hands me my favorite wine cooler. I like that he knows what I like. They're sweeter than beer, the perfect little buzz in a bottle. Brick's in his corner pumping out a beat that moves right through me. Without saying a word Tommy and I instinctively gravitate to the crowded dance floor. I get as close to the speakers as I can, unable to resist the beat pulsing, rushing through my body so strong I can no longer feel my own heartbeat or hear the sound of my voice. My body surrenders to the beat. It takes the place of my own heartbeat, driving my body into sporadic movements, twists and contortions I would never attempt if I were in control of my senses. What a rush.

After a few songs, we have to take a break. Tommy leans against the wall. I gently back into him and he puts his arms around me. We're exhausted. Kurt and his date take a spot on the wall next to us and he hands Tommy a blunt. I can't believe we're just smoking like it's legal. I keep looking for the cops to bust in and arrest us all, but Tommy says I'm just being paranoid. It's an underground party. We're free to do whatever we want. The more I smoke, the more I trip on all the crazy lasers, fog and glow lights. It's so psychedelic. Lasenna's still on the dance floor, shaking it with her man. I love to watch her dance. Her hips, feet and limbs move in perfect rhythm to the beat. I must look like a spastic kid with a nervous twitch out there.

I'm swaying with my eyes closed enjoying the music, the wine, and Tommy's arms around me when I feel a tug on my arm.

"Come on, girl."

I open my eyes to see Lasenna smoothly gyrating in front of me. She grabs my hand and pulls me on to the dance floor. I try to match her moves, but she's moving in ways I can't follow. It doesn't matter. It's wild, everybody watching us. I'm the queen of the party.

"Here, try this." Tommy cuts in and places something in my mouth. At first, it feels like a breath mint, but it has no taste.

"What is it?"

"It's X."

"Okay." I don't question it. I'm *Alice in Wonderland* ready to follow Tommy down the mysterious path. He's made me feel so good in so many ways I trust him to keep the party going. It's probably some kinda upper so I can dance all night. Anyway, he gave one to Lasenna and T.J. and Kurt and his girl too. We continue to dance letting the music take us away, but I don't feel anything past the buzz I already have. Then all of a sudden I get a rush of energy and I'm ready to party like never before.

"Hey," I grab Lasenna by the arm and yell over the music in her ear. "What's X?"

"You feelin' it, ain't you girl." She smiles back and I know she's feeling it too.

"Yeah, it's great. What is it?"

"It's ecstasy."

"What?"

"Ecstasy. Get it? X. Ecstasy."

"Yeah, it feels like ecstasy. What's in it? Is it cocaine?" It feels like what I heard cocaine was like. Like I could run a marathon.

"No, it's something different."

"Then what is it?"

"I don't know. It's ecstasy, that's all. What, you don't like it?"

"No, it's awesome."

"So, don't sweat it, 'lil sis. It's all good."

It is all good. I'm flying on a cloud, swaying to the music, dancing dirty with my man.

I'm not sure what time we leave, but we end up at Brick's house again. I've come down from the X a little, but there's plenty around to drink or smoke to keep my buzz going. There're a lot of people I don't know. They must be Brick's friends. He's almost as popular as Tommy.

I don't know how, but I lost track of Tommy and Lasenna. Brick and Kurt are with their dates and Jessie's alone as usual. There must be something wrong with him. This kid keeps passing around shots of this stuff called Jaeger. It tastes kind of bitter sweet like licorice. Not good, but not bad like those nasty whiskey and tequila shots the football players like to do. I don't count how many I do, but before I know it I'm so dizzy I can't see straight. I catch myself bumping into people and walls, wandering around looking for Tommy. Luckily, I find an empty room and lie down on the sofa.

"Wake up, Cara." Tommy's shaking me gently.

"Oh my God, what time is it? The sunlight's creeping through the shades.

"It's almost six."

"In the morning!"

"What's up, boo, you never stayed out all night before?"

"I've spent the night at my friend's house plenty of times."

"You mean those two geek girls? That'll work. Tell the old man you spent the night at their house. They'll cover for you, won't they?"

"Crystal would. I'm not too sure about Jennifer."

"There you go. Problem solved. Let's get you home."

I don't notice until I stand up, but I feel sore down there, like I've been having sex. "Did we do it last night?"

"You don't remember? Man, you was a wasted, wild woman. How'd you like that X? I think it agrees with you."

"It was pretty wild. I was flying. I could dance all night on that stuff. God, I feel like hell."

"Yeah, the hang over sucks, but you'll be okay. You just need to sleep it off."

Chapter 8

Jim's asleep when I get home. I wonder if he even knows I live here. He pretty much stays to himself in the morning; just fills his coffee mug and he's out the door. Most days I don't even get a good morning. Then he doesn't come home until late at night, 'cause of the drinking. When he's home he zones out in front of the TV, "catching up on his sleep". No need for conversation. I don't care. I have Tommy to talk to and great friends to keep me company.

My head's thumping and spinning at the same time. Every time I manage to fall asleep, this crazy dream wakes me up, my t-shirt covered in sweat. I'm back at the party, on the couch. But instead of having sex with Tommy, I'm doing it with Jessie. Creepy, little Jessie. It's so disturbing. I'm just lying there and he's on top of me, doing it. It's like some kinda out of body experience, but I guess that's what a dream is.

Two days go by without a call from Tommy. He finally calls on the third day.

"Why haven't you been returning my calls?"

"I'm sorry, I've been busy."

"Too busy to return a phone call."

"Yeah, we been practicin' overtime for this gig we got at Temple. Lasenna booked it for us. If we do good, we could get a lot of work playin' frat parties."

"And where were you the other night at Brick's house. You left me alone almost all night."

"I had business to take care of."

"What kinda business. I didn't know you had a job."

"Business for the band. What's with all the questions?"

"I don't know. I mean you abandon me at the party and I end up passed out on some couch until six in the morning. Why did you just leave me there like that? Where were you? And then you don't call me back. What would you think?"

"Like I said, I was takin' care of some business. I wasn't gone that long anyway. It's not my fault you was so wasted you don't remember. Look, I can see you're upset so I'm gonna call you back later when you're not so mad, okay. I didn't call to fight with you."

"Wait, you can't hang up."

"Look, I've gotta go. I'll call you later."

He hangs up leaving me stranded with my questions and insecurities.

Everything seems to be changing as the days pass by. Maybe it's the fall turning into the winter, the way the leaves waste away from the trees or the annoying chill of the cool autumn breeze, but I feel like things are different. Tommy only calls me every three days or so and when I call him I usually have to leave a couple of messages before he calls back. We used to linger on the phone talking about nothing for hours, now we fight more than anything else. I think he has another girlfriend. Everything just feels different between us. It's hard not knowing for sure. Every time he's not with me I think he's with someone else. Not knowing is killing me, so I call Lasenna to see if she knows anything. She tells me she's been wanting to talk to me so we meet at the mall.

"Hey Cara, how's it goin'," she says with a concerned look on her face.

"Hi, Lasenna."

"You okay?" she asks.

"I guess. I don't know. Let's go get some ice cream and talk."

She doesn't say much talk as we walk to the ice cream stand. I don't mind. I'm zoned out thinking about how I'm gonna ask her about Tommy. They're really good friends. She's known Tommy way longer than she's known me. How could I trust her to tell me the truth? She'll probably try to cover for him, but I don't know what else to do. It's not like I could ask Kurt or Brick.

We sit at a table away from the other customers. She must be into her ice cream 'cause she's really quiet.

"I think Tommy has another girlfriend," I blurt out. "I don't know how. I just feel it. He doesn't return my phone calls sometimes and he acts different. He left me alone at the party the other night. Do you think he was with another girl? Have you seen him with anyone?"

"No, not really. I saw him talkin' to some girls. You know he's always flirtin', but I ain't seen him with no one else."

"Would you tell me if you did? I mean, I know you and Tommy are real tight."

"I'm tight with you too."

"Just tell me. I know what you're gonna say anyway. I know he's cheating on me."

"It's more than that. I'm sorry, Cara. I wish I could've stopped it. I should've looked out for you more. Boys are animals."

"What do you mean?"

"I tried to warn you about Tommy. I know he's a pig, but I never thought he could go so low."

"So who is she? Do I know her?"

"It's not another girl. Cara, I know what happened to you at the party. I can understand if you want to pretend it didn't happen. I can only imagine what you're goin' through, but I want you to know you can talk to me about it."

"About what?"

"You don't remember, do you? Never mind. Forget I said anything."

"No way. What are you talking about? If something happened to me I have a right to know."

"Yeah, you do," she pauses. "You don't remember nothin'

strange happenin' to you at the party?"

"No, but I don't really remember much of anything. I was pretty wasted."

"I over heard Tommy, Brick and Jessie talkin' yesterday. They were talkin' about you."

She talks in a low voice with her head down, stammering and hesitating. I'm afraid of what she's gonna tell me, but I have to know.

"Just tell me, Lasenna."

"Tommy was askin' Jessie if he liked your stuff."

"What do you mean my stuff? What are you talking about?"

"And Jessie was thankin' him and tellin' him he was right and he didn't think you woke up."

"What are you saying?"

"Cara, I think Jessie raped you while you were passed out at the party and I think Tommy told him to do it."

"What? Are you crazy? Tommy wouldn't do that."

"I'm sorry, Cara. I didn't wanna believe it, but I heard 'em laughin' and talkin' smack about how you like to moan when you do it. He probably put somethin' in your drink. You know Tommy sells all kinds of pills, even roofies."

"What?"

"You didn't know he's a dealer? Why you think Tommy's so popular? I'm so sorry. I wish it wasn't true, but I know what I heard. They were giving each other high fives and Jessie was boastin' about how he smashed it."

"And what'd Tommy say?"

"He congratulated Jessie." Lasenna's eyes became narrow. "He said, 'I told you she had good stuff'. I'm so sorry, Cara. I knew Tommy was a pig. He was always hittin' on other girls when we were together. That's why I broke up with him. But I didn't think he'd ever do anything like this. Man, what a punk."

It fells like someone's ripping my guts out. My eyes start to water and my head feels like it's over heating. She's telling me the truth. I can feel it. That's why I keep dreaming about Jessie. It was

77

real.

"It's gonna be okay," Lasenna hands me a napkin, moves to the seat next to me and puts her arm around me. "Its okay, let it out. You're gonna be okay."

"I thought it was a dream, but it really happened. Oh God, why me? Why would he do that to me?"

"I don't know, but he's not gonna get away with it. We'll have him arrested. Both of them fools can feel what it's like to get punked in jail."

"No, no, please. Promise me you won't tell anyone. Please."

"We can't let 'em get away with that. Not that. No way."

"I don't want anyone to know. Please, Lasenna, promise me. The last thing I want is for everyone to know what a drunk slut I am. Everyone'll be talking about me and laughing, pointing and blaming me for being so stupid. I just want to forget about it."

"I can understand why you feel that way, for real, but they're gonna pay for what they did to you. My cousin's a Crip. All I gotta do is call him and his boys'll hook 'em up straight. They don't even need a reason to go beat down some fool. When I tell 'em what happened to you, my home girl. Man, it's on like donkey kong."

"They can kill Jessie for all I care, but I have to talk to Tommy first. Why would he do that to me? All I ever did was love him."

"I wouldn't lie to you, Cara."

"I know you wouldn't. I just want to hear it from him first, that's all."

Chapter 9

I bury my face in the pillow and cry for hours when I get home. I'm used, like a piece of trash or the dirt off someone's worn out shoes. He just gave me away. It's like my own body doesn't belong to me anymore.

I dread having to confront Tommy, but it has to be done. I call him and tell him we have to talk. Maybe it was the serious tone of my voice, but he calls me right back and agrees to come by. The awful sinking in my stomach is constant. Maybe seeing the look in his eyes and hearing it straight from his mouth will make the knots go away.

I almost jump out of my skin when the door bell rings. My palms are sweating. It's gonna be hard not to show how nervous I am.

"Hey boo. You alright? You sounded weird over the phone." He leans in to kiss me as I open the door, but I back away.

"No, I'm not alright. What happened to me at the party?" I just spit it out before I lose my nerve.

"What do you mean what happened? You got wasted, that's all. You wild, wasted woman, what's up?"

"I know something happened to me at that party. Just tell me? Be man enough to tell me the truth. You at least owe me that."

"The truth about what?"

"About what Jessie did to me!"

"What'd Jessie do?" His voice drops and he looks down at his feet. Mom could always tell I was lying when I wouldn't look her in the eyes. I know I'm being lied to.

"You know what he did. How could you let him do that to me?" I don't want to, but I can't stop myself from crying. Here's the one person who's supposed to look out for me and protect me and he's standing right in front of me lying like a dog.

"Do what?"

"I thought I could trust you and you feed me to your friends like I'm some kinda cheap left over dinner."

"What?"

"You let Jessie do it to me! Did you watch? Did you like it? How many of your friends got a turn?"

"Look, I don't know what you talkin' about." His voice cracks and he begins to trip over his words. "What do you mean Jessie did it to you? What are you tryin' to tell me?"

"You already know. I remember now. I remember everything. It wasn't you, it was him. And you told me it was you. How could you do that to me? Why?"

"I didn't do nothin' to you." He looks like a deer in headlights. "I don't know what you talkin' about."

"I trusted you. You told me you loved me. Was everything a lie?"

"I never told you I loved you."

"What! You gonna deny that too? Why did you say it, if you didn't mean it?"

"Look, Cara, I don't know what you want from me. You're actin' crazy."

"I'm not crazy. I know what happened."

"Cara, I...I..."

"Get out, get out of my house."

Like the coward he is he took the opportunity to slither out the door without saying another word. What else could he say? He knows what he did and now he knows I know. I rush to the phone and call Lasenna before I lose my thirst for revenge.

"Lasenna, I just talked to Tommy. He did it. He won't admit it, but I know the truth. It was in his eyes."

"I'm sorry Cara, but I knew he'd deny it. What you want me to do?"

"I want him to pay. Him and Jessie, especially Jessie. I hate that little troll."

"Don't worry about it. They'll pay alright, both of 'em."

I heard Lasenna's cousin really messed up Jessie. He had a broken jaw and even had to stay in the hospital for a few of days. I saw Tommy a couple of weeks later at the mall, with another girl of course. He had a cast on his arm. I just smiled.

Chapter 10

I can't stand all the pink in my room, dripping from the walls, staring at me in judgment. Life isn't pink anymore, more like black or grey. I decide to paint my room black, all black. I change my clothes, too. Black is my new color. Black jeans, black shoes, black shirts, black nail polish, every thing black. It just feels more like me. Like I can disappear in the blackness and no one will know I'm really here.

At school, I blend into the walls and pass through the hallways like a ghost. Crystal and Jennifer keep trying to get me to do stuff with them, but I'm not interested.

Lasenna tries to get me to go out too, but everywhere we might go I'd see Tommy and Jessie so I just stay home. Sometimes she brings me a blunt to smoke. I kick back, inhale, listen to my music and forget about all the nasty boys in the world.

"What'd you do to your room?" Jim asks one morning before he goes to work.

"I painted it black, that's all. Is it a problem?"

"No, honey, it's your room. You should have it like you want it, but it's a strange choice of color."

"I like it. If that's okay with you."

"It's okay with me. I'm not tryin' to fight with you, Cara. Listen, I'm gonna make Thanksgiving dinner for us this week."

"What are you talking about? What kind of dinner can you make?"

I had just about forgotten Thanksgiving was coming up. It used to be a good holiday for me, not my favorite, but pretty good. Mom would cook a big turkey, well big for just us two, with macaroni and cheese, dressing, bean casserole, mashed potatoes with gravy, and corn bread. What the hell is Jim gonna do compared to that?

"I can do a little something, you'll see."

"I don't know. Crystal invited me to her house for Thanksgiving dinner."

"Come on, you're not gonna make your old man eat alone on Thanksgiving are you?"

"Why not? It's not like you never left me alone before, right?"

That stops him in his tracks. He stands with his head bowed for a few moments then speaks. "I know I have. I've been a pretty bad father to you, but you always had your mother so I figured you'd be alright. But she's not here and you and I are all the family we got. We have to stick together. You're my daughter, Cara, the only one I got."

"Why are you telling me all this? What, do you care all of a sudden?"

"I don't know. All I know is I'm you're father. I might not be able to take care of you right, but there's no reason why we can't know each other. Thanksgiving dinner's a good start."

"I already told Crystal I would eat with them, sorry."

I walk away wondering why I apologized. Why not let him know what it's like to be ignored?

I tell Crystal and Jennifer that I'm having dinner with Jim so I don't have to deal with the whole Thanksgiving thing. I wouldn't be good company, especially around a bunch of happy people sharing reasons why they're thankful. I have nothing to be thankful for. My first boyfriend was a perverted freak and the only person I can talk to about it is dead.

Most of my time is spent just walking around, thinking of all the happy families gathered around their dinning room tables, thankful for everything they have. I don't fit in. I'm really not going anywhere, just around the mall and up and down the street window shopping and leering at fancy dresses and jewelry I'll never have an occasion to wear. I hide my face behind my hair. Maybe no one will see how used up I am.

Is my body just a tool for perverts to get their rocks off? Is this God punishing me for not going to church or not praying to him anymore? Why does he have to be so vengeful? Like if you don't totally worship him he'll crap all over you.

Jim's not at home. Must be out drinking his Thanksgiving dinner. The book I bought on different religions calls out to me. There's got to be a religion out there that doesn't worship some arrogant, vengeful God. There's got to be a happier, more peaceful God.

Why do I have to believe in God anyway? He doesn't believe in me. He abandoned me that night on the couch, just like Tommy. He abandoned Mom too. Why did she have to do drugs? What she was trying to escape from? Now there's no one left but Jim. Does he really think one dinner will make up for years of not being there?

Who needs any of them? Has anyone ever seen any proof of any God anywhere? I need some proof, a sign or something 'cause he must be hiding. There must be a better reason for Mom's death other than it was just God's will. Some reason why the innocent die and the trusting get raped.

Let's see, *Religions of the World*. Christianity, Judaism, Islam, Hinduism, Buddhism and some I don't even recognize like Shinto, Jainism, Zoroastrianism, and Sikhism. It turns out 23 million people in India believe in Sikhism. Who knew? This is gonna be cool, learning about all the different religions of the world. This time I get to decide what I want to believe.

Jim keeps trying to make me dinner. I give in couple of times. It's not like he gives me enough money to eat at the mall every night. We hardly say a word to each other over the kitchen table. He asks about school and I give quick responses. He's always telling some story about work he thinks is funny, but it's not.

"Cara, come here," Jim yells from the kitchen one night after dinner.

"What?"

"Come here, please?"

"Yes." I stand at the doorway with my hands folded across my chest.

"What's goin' on with your grades? Your mother always said you was a straight "A" student."

He's holding a copy of my mid-term progress report. I forgot all about checking the mail. I'm getting a "D" in algebra II and my teacher says I might fail history if I miss any more classes. Not to worry. My genius of a teacher puts fifty percent of our grade on his final exam so who cares if I fail a couple of quizzes.

"Don't sweat it. I can make those grades up easy."

"Ain't you been goin' to school? I thought your friend's mother was takin' you. What you been doin' all day?"

"So what if I skip sometimes. Are you all of a sudden interested in my school work?"

"Look, if there's anyone who knows how much a lack of education can screw you up, it's me. You don't wanna start messin' up in school when you've been a good student all this time."

"Like I said, I can make the grades up. Don't sweat it, alright."

"Looks like I need to take you to school in the mornings from now on. Make sure you get there."

"Okay, like you're really gonna wake up early and drive me to school."

"School's important, Cara. I'll do what I gotta do. You don't wanna end up like me."

"Yeah, I don't think you have to worry about that."

I try to keep our conversations as short as possible slipping away before he has a chance to respond. Anyway, Jennifer already talked me into gong to school more. I'm not gonna fail any of my classes. Jennifer and Crystal sniff me out the next day at school. I've generally been avoiding them, but we eat lunch together sometimes.

"What's with all the black?" Jennifer asks.

"I just like it. My favorite color."

"Since when? I remember when it used to be pink," Crystal adds.

"It's black now."

"Why don't you come to church with us, Cara? I know it's been hard for you, but dressing in all black isn't gonna help anything. Let us help you find your way," Jennifer says sympathetically.

"I'm not lost. I just came to the realization that God doesn't give a damn about me. I'm tired of kissing his butt for nothing."

"Oh my God, Cara, what are you saying?" Crystal sounds the alarm.

"I don't know. It's just that God never did anything for me."

"So, now you don't believe in God?" Jennifer asks.

"I don't know what I believe."

"How could you not be a Christian? If you don't believe in God, what will you believe in?" Crystal asks.

"I don't know. What does it matter anyway?"

"Of course it matters. You don't want to end up in hell," Crystal exclaims.

"Really, what did I ever do to deserve to go to hell?" I demand an answer.

"You have to have faith, Cara. If you don't have faith your soul will perish." Jennifer's scorn turns to concern.

"Then I guess I'll have to look out for my own soul won't I."

I never thought I'd see Crystal speechless, but neither of them can handle my attitude. The perfect opportunity to slip away from the table. I'd rather burn in hell than sit through that lecture again. It's better to just avoid them. They accept the excuse I have to study during lunch to make up for missed time. Except for the constant staring of my peers and occasional comments like, "Halloween was last month", the library is the perfect place to read my book. I have a few new nick names, Freak Girl, Marilyn Manson, and Morticia. It doesn't matter. What I'm reading about is much more interesting than a bunch of silly school girls.

The school work is easy for me to make up leaving lots of time to read. Hinduism, "One of the world's oldest religions dating back to 2000 B.C." That's 2000 years before anyone even heard of Jesus. There's over 750 million Hindus in the world. And only 300 million people in the whole United States. There's 500 million Buddhists and 30 million Jews. Christians and Muslims are tied for first place with one billion a piece. So many people don't believe in Jesus. How can Christians know they're the only ones to reap a joyous afterlife? But I guess the Hindus believe they're the only ones that'll redeem eternal salvation and the Buddhists and the Muslims too. Who's right? Might as well put them all on one big roulette wheel and take a spin. Step right up for eternal salvation, but you better choose the right one.

"I have some good news, Cara," Jim says one night over a plate of limp, soggy spaghetti.

"What's that?"

"Your Grandma and Grandpa are comin' from California to visit you."

"Really, when?"

"Next week."

"The first week in December? Why not just wait 'til Christmas?"

"I don't know. Guess they can't wait to see you. They've been worried about you since they saw you at the funeral."

"Worried about what? What have you been telling them about me?"

"The truth. They have a right to know how their granddaughter's doin' and I'm not gonna to lie to them."

"Whatever. You didn't have to call in the cavalry. I told you I wouldn't miss any more school. Unlike some people, when I say I'm gonna do something, I do it."

Grandma and Grandpa are always so nice to me, especially Grandma. I can talk to her like I could talk to Mom. She has a warm, soft way about her that covers you like a favorite blanket.

They arrive on an unusually warm day for early December. Grandma throws her arms around me and squeezes tight. Just when I catch my breath Grandpa comes behind her and does the same.

They both look at me in my black jeans, black Outkast t-shirt, black nails and black hair. "Honey, what happened to you?" Grandma says in the most tactful way she can.

Grandpa just looks at me with shock, disappointment and fear in his eyes. He cups my face in his hands. "Where's the bright, little angel I used to know? All this isn't you."

"It's me now, Grandpa. I'll go put your bags in the guest room."

They're obviously talking about me as I walk up the stairs. Oh no, what are we gonna do about poor, little Cara? She used to be such a sweet girl. Give me a break. Like I don't have the right to dress like I want, the way I feel. What's the big deal anyway? It's not like I'm corrupting America's youth or setting schools on fire. I'm just doing what expresses me. I over hear a few, "lets save Cara", conversations over the next few days. They can conspire all they want, I'm still gonna do what I want.

It's good to have Grandma around. She's a great cook, really good, better than Mom. Finally, someone to have breakfast with. Grandpa is so funny at the table, always cracking really stupid jokes that only he thinks are funny. Jim doesn't join us for breakfast. Oh well, more bacon, grits, eggs, pancakes, and biscuits for me. My butt grows exponentially with every day she's here. But I don't want anyone looking at me anyway. Not like that.

Christmas break is coming up. Almost three weeks of no school, no staring or mocking. I don't have to see anyone.

"So, how long you guys staying?" I ask over an old fashion fried chicken, mashed potatoes with gravy and green bean dinner.

"We've been meaning to talk to you about that," Jim says.

"Cara, how would you like to come to live with us out in California?" Grandma asks.

"We'd love to have you," Grandpa adds.

"California. I don't know. I mean isn't your house surrounded by cow pastures?"

"The town's grown a lot since you last visited. You were just a little girl then," Grandpa says.

"Yeah, I bet. Don't tell me you guys have a bowling alley now."

They live in a small town called Harmony about five hours north of Los Angeles. It's a beautiful, harmless place surrounded by golden rolling hills and cypress trees. I remember a bunch of cows. The best thing is the beach is only a few miles away. It might be okay there. No one to bother me. I could disappear in all the nature.

It's not like there's anything to keep me around here. A rapist boyfriend and a school where they think I'm a freak. Crystal and Jennifer talk to me like I'm some kind of heathen. How can I fit in when I don't feel what they feel anymore? I don't belong with the new crowd either. Brick, Kurt, T.J., they're all a bunch of disgusting perverts. Lasenna's the only one I'll miss around here and maybe Sister Jane a little.

"Well, Cara, what do you think?" Grandma asks.

"I guess it'd be okay." I remember one more perk. No more Jim. "So when do we leave?"

"We want you there by the time school starts back after Christmas. You'll be going to public high school, the Coastal Beach Seals," Grandpa says.

"Cool, so when do we leave? I've never been on an airplane before."

"Honey, I'm gonna drive us," Jim says. "I got a job back with my old company and worked it out so I can make stops along the way. We'll be in Harmony by Christmas."

"What do you mean you're gonna drive us? And don't call me honey."

"It'll be great, Cara, the open road. You'll see the whole country in two weeks," he persuades.

"If you think I'm gonna spend my Christmas break in some raggedy truck, staying in flea ridden truck stop motels you're crazy."

"I wouldn't take you to a place like that. We'll only stay at very nice hotels. I promise. I've planned it all out and saved enough money to make it work," Jim pleads.

"So you've been planning this. Thanks for letting me in on the plans. It's only my life you're talking about."

"Maybe we should've included you in on all this, but it all

happened so quickly. When we heard you needed help, we had to think of what was best for you," Grandma says.

"I like how everyone knows what's best for me except me."

"I know this seems like a lot to take in all at once, but you'll see it's for the best. It'll be good for you to get a fresh start where you can really concentrate on your schooling. What do you think?" Grandma asks.

"It obviously doesn't matter what I think. I'm just going along for the ride."

"That's not true, Cara, please don't walk away," Jim insists as I turn my back on them.

"Just leave me alone."

My life is changing and I have nothing to say about it. They could've asked or am I just a marionette, everybody pulling my strings. It's not like I don't wanna go. Wide, open spaces where I can be alone, away from the congestion of the city. I can finally go to public school. That's a scary thought. If I couldn't fit in at an all girl's school, how will I fit in at public school? I was part of the cool crowd, but they were just users. Is there any where I can really fit in? Probably not.

"Can I talk to you, Grandma?" I catch her the next morning alone in the kitchen making coffee.

"Of course sweetheart, here, sit." She hands me a glass of orange juice.

"I wanna go to California, I really do, but why can't I just go back with you on the plane?"

"It's Jim's idea, honey. He insists on driving you out. He wants to spend the time with you. It's the only way he'll let you stay with us. You know he is your father, your legal guardian."

"Are you kidding me? What's he trying to prove anyway? All of a sudden he has to spend time with me? We've been living in this house together all these months and he wants to spend time with me now? Unbelievable."

"You may regret not having a relationship with him as the years pass on. You really should try to get to know him."

"He should get to know me."

"I think he's trying to, honey."

"If he thinks he can make up for fifteen years of parenting in two weeks he's crazy. Why can't he just leave me alone?"

"You know, Cara, your grandfather and I aren't going to live forever. One of these days your father is going to be the only family you have. At least he's trying."

"Yeah, by dumping me off on you. Don't you see? He's just gonna drop me off and hit the road, just like he's always done. This little trip is just his way of dealing with the guilt."

"You may be right. How'd you ever get to be so smart?"

"I know Jim. It's better if you don't expect much."

Chapter 11

Grandma and Grandpa left yesterday. Finally, Christmas break. I can't wait to leave that school. I stuff most of my clothes in an oversize duffle bag and my books, CDs and pictures into boxes. My phone, MP3 and computer ride with me. The stuffed animals stay here.

I want to call Crystal, Jennifer and Lasenna, but I wouldn't know what to say. Maybe I'll write them a letter when I get there. Christmas at Grandma's is bound to be better than spending it with Jim laid out on the sofa watching football, snoring his way through the holidays.

I wonder if we'll go to midnight mass on Christmas Eve, like I used to with Mom. Then it was back home for hot chocolate, with marshmallows, of course. We always opened one present before we went to bed to ease the anticipation. And we'd sleep in late on Christmas day, open the rest of the presents and eat a late breakfast. Grandma and Grandpa flew out a couple times, but not recently. Jim would always show up few days later making excuses, drop off some lame present for me and be on his way. I was only four when they divorced so I don't really remember when he was around the house all the time.

"Cara, come here," Jim bellows from downstairs.

"What?" He better not plan on shouting at me like that for the next two weeks.

"You all packed?"

"Pretty much."

"Good. Our first stop's West Virginia, Lewisburg. We'll hit the road early, 6a.m." He's all business.

Jim's truck is one of those huge big rigs that can haul anything cross country. The enormous grill is surrounded by crimson red paint with subtle yellow flames stretching out on both sides. I'm on top of the world when I climb inside and look over the dash. The big, comfortable front seat is more like a sofa than a car seat and there's a large sleeping space behind the seats. I can see why Jim likes to spend all his time on the road. This is a power machine. A get out of my way or get rolled over king of the road.

We move out at 6a.m. on the dot with a box of chocolate glazed doughnuts set on the front seat between us. Jim places my duffle bag and boxes in the storage area by the sleeping space. There's more room here than I thought there'd be. I keep my book on religion with me. Jim sips on coffee in a huge thermos with a picture of some race car driver on it as he pulls away from the curb.

"Well, kiddo, we're on our way. First to the warehouse to pick up a load of lumber, then it'll take us about five hours road time to get to Lewisburg," Jim says as the chilly morning air forms wisps of smoke off his lips.

"So what's Lewisburg like?"

"I'm sure it's no different from any other small, southern town. Not much of anything."

"Great, what kind of hick town are you taking me to?"

"Relax, we're only there overnight, then we pick up another load and we're off to Athens, Georgia"

"Hey, isn't that where the University of Georgia is?" I remember Lasenna talking about how it's such a great party school. She went there for a visit when she was applying for colleges. "How long are we gonna stay there?"

"We got a three day wait for another load to come in."

"Cool. I get to check out the college scene."

"What's so cool?"

"Nothing, I'm gonna lie down back here."

I sleep until about 10a.m. woken up off and on by the sound of men working around the truck and the constant shaking a big rig hauling lumber makes when cruising down the road. The front seat presents a panoramic view of assorted pines, evergreens and half bare trees. Small, single story, wood framed houses dot the scenery. This must be farm country. So much space between the houses, separated by row after row of some leafy, green crop. This was how I remembered Grandma's house to be like, fresh air, plenty of room and quiet.

"Welcome to West Virginia," Jim says.

I don't respond, consumed with the view, deep in thought about nothing at all. The scenery is mesmerizing to a city girl. Mile after mile of nothing but space. The higher we climb up into the mountains the more ragged the houses look. Little one or two room wooden shacks tucked away in the hills. I wonder if they even have electricity and running water. It's depressing, knowing people live like this.

Jim drops off the lumber and we have the rest of the day to bum around. He tries to take me to some truck stop diner for lunch, but I insist on a better restaurant. I remind him of his promise not to stop at any run down places. That includes hotels and restaurants. I'd prefer McDonalds. At least I know what I'm getting. He asks one of the other truckers and comes back with the name of the "best steak joint in town". According to Jim, it has to be great 'cause there's a huge statue of a cow or a bull or whatever on the roof.

I'm not really hungry, but I order some chicken wings and a salad.

"Is that all you want? Hell, that's not even a meal. Those are just appetizers."

"Yep, that's it."

"You know, Cara, I wanna thank you for comin' on this trip. It means a lot to me."

"It's not like I have a choice, do I? I'd rather be on a plane."

94

"Yeah, but you could've made a big stink about it and you didn't. So, thank you."

"Whatever. So, where are we staying anyway?"

"There's a nice little hotel down the road. Nothin' fancy, but it's very clean. Almost like a bed and breakfast."

"Yeah right, I'm not staying in some backwater dive."

"Look Cara, there are no big hotels around here. This place is nice and it's clean, that's what I promised you."

The hotel isn't so bad, like something out of *Little House on the Prairie*. There are several small, white cottages forming a horse shoe with only a few feet separating them. We have the one on the end. I'm not at all looking forward to sharing a room with Jim, but I tell myself it's only two weeks. Then he'll be back on the road and out of my hair.

It looks pretty nice inside. Flowery draperies cover the windows, the pattern matching the quilts on two nice size beds. The carpet is dark blue, soft and plush. There's even a HDTV sitting in the middle of a large dresser that extends across most of the wall. Huge mirrors on both sides of the TV make the room seem much larger than it is. The bathroom has hard, shiny wood everywhere. It even smells like wood, pine, I think. It's like we're in a log cabin in the middle of the woods.

"Nice room, huh kiddo," Jim calls out from the position I knew he'd take, in front of the TV.

"It's okay."

"Good, they got cable. Let's see if we can get a ball game on. You like football, right?"

"No. Watch whatever. I'm gonna to take a look around."

Jim's always watching some kind of game on TV. When there's not a game on, he's watching these guys talking about the game. Why do they have to spend so much time talking about a game they just saw? They all saw the same game, didn't they? Someone wins and someone loses, what else is there to talk about?

I find this nature trail near the hotel and decide to take a walk. My thick grey sweatshirt and oversize black denim jacket turn the

95

cold into a slight chill. The ground is carpeted with dead, brown leaves. Trees are lucky like that. They just die in the winter, shed all their bad leaves and fall asleep avoiding the bitter weather until awakened by the warm, soft touch of spring. A nice long sleep feels right. Fall into unconsciousness for a few months and wake up a new person with new energy, a new attitude and no memory of what happened before the harsh winter.

A scenic overlook of the valley and the city of Lewisburg provides a perfect resting place. Everything's brown with a few patches of green from a variety of pine trees, but the lack of color doesn't ruin the beauty of the overall scene.

I open my book and read about Hinduism, one of the oldest religions going back to 2000 BC. I'm curious about it because I know they believe in reincarnation. That's pretty wild, being able to die and come back as a whole new person, a second chance at life. Karma makes sense to me. If you do wrong in this life you'll be reincarnated to a lesser status in your next life and if you're a good person you'll come back to reap positive status in your next life. So you reap what you sow. If you were really bad you might come back as some kind of animal like an insect so it's harder for you to gain wisdom. I must've been a beast in my previous life. Maybe I was a rapist, a filthy perverted man who preyed on defenseless young girls.

They have three main gods, Brahma (the creator), Vishnu (the preserver of the universe), and Shiva (the destroyer). But there's also thousands of other gods and goddesses who visit the Earth in a variety of animal and human forms. It reminds me of the ancient Greek and Roman gods and goddesses. They all have gods that come down to earth to mess with people's lives. It's kind of weird that people can believe in such things, but there are 750 million who do.

Vishnu is prophesized to return to earth riding a white horse to destroy the wicked and re-establish order. Uhm, where have I heard that story before? It says that many Hindus choose a god or goddess as their favorite to worship, but all these gods are just part of one supreme unchanging reality called Brahman. If you can gain enough knowledge you will be able to see the one true reality, Brahman.

It all seems very complicated to me, but some of it looks familiar. Vishnu's pretty much like Jesus. That's easy enough to see. The whole karma thing sounds like, "Do unto others as you would have them do unto you." But I'm not sold on the reincarnation part. I just can't see people coming back as animals or insects, but it's a cool idea. It's just weird, all those gods and goddesses. So prehistoric, but I guess the religion is over four thousand years old.

I get lost in the book, distracted only by the sky changing from blue to orange to red and back to blue as the sun fades behind the mountains. I love how the sky changes color at sunset, but I've never seen anything like this. Nature is awesome. Time stops watching the stars emerge from the twilight like a dazzling, diamond studded map revealing the secrets to the universe. I know from science class and TV about the trillions of stars out there. Like a dream, always camouflaged by Philly's light pollution, they were too distant to imagine until now. So many, bright ones and clusters, it seems like I can just reach out and touch far away galaxies. There's gotta be life out there somewhere. Why would God create the entire universe and only put life on our itty bitty planet? I don't know. It's crazy to think about.

Jim's not in when I get back, probably out searching for some local dive to quench his thirst. I order a cheeseburger from room service. They actually have room service. It's good to have the room to myself. There's a bunch of channels on cable, but none of them interest me. I'm in the mood to turn up the volume and let Nirvana, sad and smooth, take me away from my present reality. There's solace in the lyrics, knowing that I'm not alone in being alone.

A weird noise, coming from outside, creeps into my ears when I take off my headphones to use the bathroom. It's music, loud and strange, like the typical battling banjo and fiddle music people think of when they think of the hills of West Virginia. It's coming from across the street. I cross a small, two lane highway to get to the curious noise. The road is dark enough to fear a hit and run, but I would be able to see the headlights of any approaching cars from far away, through the pitch black night.

The music, growing louder and louder as I get closer, guides me to a small, two room building with a big front porch. Even in the dark I can see white paint peeling from its weathered wood. There's a large cross on top of the roof. This must be a church. I creep on to the porch and sneak a peek through the window. There's a group of about 20 people congregated in a circle, dancing, hollering and singing about Jesus. The wood vibrates under my feet from all the music and foot stomping going on inside. Their attention is focused on the middle of the circle, but I can't see what's going on inside.

The music begins to play at a more rapid pace, the banjo strumming, the violin wailing, the harmonica screeching and the feet stomping out a ferocious beat. They work themselves into a frenzy. All of a sudden one of the taller men sinks down into the circle and emerges with his hand reaching straight up to the ceiling. He's holding a snake. It's black, thin, sinewy body contrasts against the man's pale arm as it squirms and bites. A quick strike to the man's hand and the snake wins his freedom. The crowd moves back and allows the man to pick up the snake and get bit over and over again.

These people must be crazy. Dancing, hollering and flailing around like some jungle tribe on the National Geographic Channel, only they're white. Instinct tells me to leave before I'm discovered snooping around so I scamper back across the street and hide behind the secure walls of the hotel room. I peek through the window and peer across the street, through the darkness, like my x-ray vision could see into the church. I try to muster the nerve to go back, but it's so dark over there. I wonder what they're doing in there and how many more times the man got bit. Why would anyone do something like that? That snake can't be poisonous.

I remember a TV documentary on life in the Appalachians. They showed a film clip of people dancing with snakes. Their beliefs come from some passage in the *Bible* where Jesus or God or someone takes up serpents. These people must be like that. Even when I believed in all that I didn't take every passage, story and scripture in the Bible word for word. Should we take all those stories literally? Did Moses really part the Red Sea? Did Noah really have an ark with two of every animal on it?

Every culture has stories about how their people interacted with some god to persevere through some hardship or discover how the world works? I just read about how the Hindus have many gods of nature, war, creation, and morality who interacted with people and helped them figure out how the world works. In Hinduism the book is the *Vedas*, a collection of verses and poems passed down over centuries. It's like their bible. Do all Hindus believe word for word the fantastic stories in the *Vedas* of gods coming down to earth to create, influence and destroy with as much conviction as Christians believe in the creation stories? Probably so. They've believed it for thousands of years. Maybe it all just depends on what you believe.

I wake up early the next morning after sleeping restlessly between Jim's snoring and the images of that snake bouncing around in my head. At the diner in front of the hotel, I sit at the counter contemplating the role God, or the gods, had in creating Earth over French toast, bacon and orange juice. There's an old man sitting one stool down from me. He was at the church last night. I know I'm not supposed to, but I have to say something. How am I ever gonna shake the image of that snake if I don't learn more about these crazy serpent worshipers?

"I saw you at that church last night," I call out to him as if I already know him.

"Excuse me, Miss." He turns his head slightly toward me, just enough to acknowledge my presence.

"I saw you at that church last night. I don't mean to bother you, but can I ask you a question?"

"Miss, we don't take kindly to people snoopin' around in these parts. What do you want?" It's hard to tell if he's angry or not, his expression is so camouflaged by the wrinkles of age.

"I was just curious. I didn't mean to snoop. And I don't mean to be rude. I just wanna know something, that's all." I know I'm annoying him, but I'm not afraid. His body is so old and weak I don't think he could hurt me if he tried. "Are you a snake worshiper?"

"I don't worship serpents. I worship the savior, Jesus Christ. The *Bible* says the true believers of God took up serpents and the Lord kept them safe"

"So you believe everything you read in the *Bible*?"

"It's the word of God. Do you know the word of God?"

"I used to. I don't know anymore. So, you play with the snakes to show God how much you worship him?"

"No, Miss, we don't play with snakes. We take up the serpent to show our faith that the Lord will keep us safe in the hands of the devil's evil. We take up the serpent to show the strength of the Holy Spirit always dominates over the evil of the devil. We take up the serpent to show our faith in God's awesome power. Now I have a question for you, Miss. Do you have faith in the Lord Jesus Christ as your savior?"

"No, not really."

"What do you believe in?"

"I don't know. I don't think I believe in anything."

"Poor thing, so lost. Look to the Lord. You'll find peace in him. Only he has the answers to all your questions."

I politely thank the man for his advice, but if he thinks playing with snakes is the answer to all my questions, he's crazy. I can't believe how quick these people are to believe everything they read in the *Bible*. And why just pick out that one passage from the *Bible* to base your whole religious philosophy? That's like limiting your diet to only fish and bread because the *Bible* said Jesus fed thousands of people with a fish and a loaf of bread. The whole thing is very bizarre. I like that word because it means more than strange and this is stranger than strange. It makes no sense at all.

Chapter 12

We head out early the next day with a new box of donuts sitting between us for breakfast. I know they're not healthy, but they rock. We're on our way to Georgia, the University of Georgia. I plan on exploring the whole campus. Jim says it'll take about seven hours to get there. My headphones save me from having to endure his feeble attempts on bonding.

We're taking the Blue Ridge Parkway through North Carolina and on into Georgia. It's a beautiful drive through the Appalachian Mountains. The landscape interrupts my reading. Staring out the window is like driving through a post card; climbing the mountain hills, overlooking the valleys, taking in the vast power of nature. Philly's nothing like this. The park was the best part of the city, an oasis in the concrete desert. This is like the park on steroids, mile after mile of untouched nature.

A small, green lizard scampers across the boxes in the storage bin behind the front seat. Jim laughs at my futile attempts to catch him. He's way too quick. What's he even doing back there? Lizards are supposed to hibernate in the dead of winter. I wonder how he's surviving. There's no sunlight and I'm not sure what lizards eat, but there can't be too much of that back there either.

"What do lizards eat?" I take off my headphones and ask Jim.

"You talkin' to me? To what do I owe this great honor?"

101

"Do you know what lizards eat or not?"

"I know, but why should I tell you with that kind of attitude."

"Whatever." I put my headphones back on.

A light tapping on my arm tells me he's not gonna leave me alone until I talk to him, so I remove the headphones.

"Lizards eat insects, any kind of bugs really. I don't guess there's a lot for him to eat back there, maybe some flies."

"Can we feed him?"

"I guess, but we'd have to find some insects. Live insects, they won't eat anything dead. Any wild animal likes to hunt and kill its own food."

"Where can I get some live insects?"

"I wouldn't be too worried about that. He'll find his own food. He wouldn't be alive if he didn't already find something to eat."

"You really think he'll be okay?"

"He'll be fine. I'm more worried about you. I know it's been hard on you. I miss her too, more than you know. Did she ever tell you about how we met?"

"She never talked about you much."

"Yeah, guess she wouldn't. Believe it or not I was the starting running back on our high school football team and your mom was on the pom-pom team. I still remember how cute she looked in that little uniform. I saw her talkin' to her friends as I was walkin' off the field after a game. I had to meet her. We started dating and as they say the rest is history."

"What was she like back then?"

"Your mom, she was beautiful, popular and smart as a whip. I never had the smarts for college, but she was a natural at the books. I see a lot of her in you. All your smarts are from her, that's for sure. She was stubborn too, just like you. Once she put it in her mind she was gonna do something, there was no stoppin' her. No wonder she outgrew me, huh. The most I'm ever gonna be is a truck driver. It wasn't enough for her."

"So you're blaming things on her."

"No, I just want you to know I didn't leave your mother. I don't know why it surprised me so much. I should've known she was gonna leave me. She always wanted more out of life than I did. She was too good for me. You know, I never stopped lovin' her."

"Sounds like you're blaming her to me. So what stopped you from coming around more?"

"I messed up, Cara, I know. I'm not gonna make excuses. I should've been there for you more. I used the road as an excuse. Told myself your mother didn't want me around. Let self pity keep me from you. I'm sorry."

His expression reveals she really did break his heart. I recognize the pain of heart ache in his eyes.

"I never was real big on responsibility. It's a good thing your mother raised you. I would've screwed you up, for sure. Your Grandma and Grandpa can do a better job raisin' you than I can."

He seems to want to pour out his soul, so I let him.

"To be honest with you, Cara, I was just hoping we could get to know each other a little bit better on this trip. I missed so much of your growin' up. I feel like I don't even know you."

"You don't."

"But I can get to know you now."

"I don't know, Jim. Do you really think you can get to know me in a two week trip? What about after that? Where are you going after you drop me off at Grandma's?"

"I have to carry a load to Seattle, Washington."

"And when will you be back?"

"It'll be a while. I have a full schedule coming up, Cara. That's my job."

"Yeah, I know. You're not gonna be there if I have a problem or need help. You never have been. You don't just leave the people you care about, Jim. Even I know that."

He has nothing to say. He's not trying to change at all. I put my headphones back on leaving him wallowing in self pity and remorse.

The rest of the drive is spent staring out the window. Jim tries to talk to me a few more times, but I just tune him out. I'm reading about the big questions religion tries to answer. The questions science can't prove like why and how the world was created, what happens to us when we die, why do people suffer so much, and do we have a soul?

These kinds of questions can't be tested in a lab. Even the scientists only have theories about how the universe was created. I guess you either have theories or you have faith. Theories make sense. You can think about them logically. There are reasons and explanations for why things happen in science. With faith you just have to trust and believe. The book says another word for religion is faith. But I don't have the faith to trust anything.

We start descending down the hills. It's sad leaving all that beautiful nature behind, but I know I'm gonna see more of it when I get to Grandma's.

"We'll be there in a couple of hours," Jim says.

"I wanna stay in a hotel near the university so I can check it out, okay."

"Sure, can I go with you? I've never seen a college campus before. It'll be as close to goin' to college as I'm ever gonna get."

"Do you have to? I'd rather check it out alone."

"If that's the way you want it, but I'm gonna check it out too."

"Whatever."

"I'll drop you off at the hotel, then I have to go drop my load. Do you wanna have dinner together later?"

"I don't know. I'll probably be out."

"Don't stay out too late. You should be home by, I don't know. What time did your mother set for you to be in?"

"You never cared about what time I came home before."

"I do now. You know you're not an adult yet and whether you like it or not I am responsible for you. That's just the way it is, so let's not fight about it."

"Whatever."

"How about nine o'clock?"

"Please, I'm not ten years old."

"Okay, you tell me. What's fair?"

"Somewhere around one sounds fair to me. Mom never really set a time. She used to let me spend the night at my friend's houses all the time."

"One, in the morning, out of the question. I'm sure your mother knew your friend's families and their parents were home, right? This is different. You don't know anybody out here and you'll be all by yourself. What on earth are you planning on doin' until one in the morning anyway?"

"Just checkin' out the campus."

"There's nothin' open at one a.m. and there's nothin' goin' on except for parties that you're way too young to go to."

"Okay then, twelve." If he only knew the kind of parties I've already been to he'd flip.

"You know you're only fifteen, right? Do you know how young that is?"

"I'll be sixteen next month."

"Right and sixteen is just a year older than fifteen. Ten o'clock and that's my best offer."

"Whatever." I don't care what he says. I'm gonna stay out as late as I want. What's he gonna do, ground me? He'll probably be out drinking at some bar anyway.

Jim drops me off at this nice, big hotel with all the amenities. I ask the lady at the front desk how far it is to campus. She says it's only a couple of miles and there's a taxi service that'll take me there for five bucks. Jim gave me a twenty. He says it's enough for food and taxis, but not enough to get in trouble. He has no idea. I don't need money to find trouble.

Chapter 13

The campus is huge. All the perfectly manicured grass and towering oak trees remind me of a massive park only with houses and buildings. The old, wooden houses with the huge columns in front look like they're left over from the Civil War, except for the fresh, white paint. The brick ones look more modern, but they're no less intimidating. I ask the cab driver to drop me off at the visitor center where the way to bubbly, bleached blond at the counter tells me how to take the bus all around campus. She can't really be that happy.

My face presses against the oversized windows on the bus as my eyes soak in everything from the dormitories to the huge halls where they hold classes. Lasenna said some classes have over two hundred students. That'd be crazy. I get lost in the library, climbing floor after floor, looking through the stacks of books at students huddled in study areas. The whole campus is like a city all to itself. There's even a cemetery.

A weird feeling sinks in walking across campus, like I'm the only person on Earth. Completely surrounded by people, but nobody knows I'm here. Total disconnect. All dressed in sweaters and scarves, the latest winter wear from The Gap, nobody looks like me. A freak in black, I could never fit in here. Haunted by hundreds of conversations I'm not a part of, I feel too much like a party crasher to sit in the cafeteria, so I order a cheeseburger, fries and a coke to take back to the hotel.

Zoning out in front of the TV is my new favorite hobby. I fall asleep channel surfing through the usual barrage of infomercials and sit-coms, but wake up in a sweat from a terrible nightmare. Someone was on top of me, smothering me. I couldn't move or breathe, totally paralyzed. He had blond hair and no face, but I knew it was Jessie.

My skin crawls from head to toe. My body's wasted, a piece of trash, used up inside. Like an empty wrapper thrown down the sewer to be washed out with the rest of the trash. I can feel him on me all over again. A wave of sadness rushes over me like I've never felt before. It's like my head is overheating, so much pressure. I don't know how to let it go. I scratch my nails against my arms, lightly at first, but the deeper I scratch the more it helps to ease the pain. Like the pain transfers from the inside to the outside. I don't know what's happening to me, but it feels good.

Fear of another nightmare leaves me channel surfing through the sit-coms and infomercials and allows my mind to go blank. My fingers caress the raised skin on my arms, a testament to my pain. Oh well, better on the outside than the inside.

Jim comes in around three, but I pretend to be asleep. He's stumbling a little, trying hard not to make any noise.

He's still in bed when I get up around ten. He said we're gonna stay three days in Athens waiting on another load, so two more days to go. I might as well go back on campus and see what's up. I don't know why I didn't see it yesterday, but there's a huge bulletin board in the cafeteria covered with announcements for upcoming events. It's plastered with flyers announcing fraternity and sorority parties all over campus. I know where I'm going tonight. Lasenna said college parties are crazy wild.

"You ever been to a Delta party?" A cute guy in a long, smooth leather jacket and tan Timberlands pokes his finger at the Delta party flyer.

"No, I'm new in town. I mean, I'm just visiting."

"Deltas, that's what's up. You gonna be hangin' out tonight?"

107

"I guess."

"Alright then. Let me show you where the house is." He points to a campus map in the corner of the bulletin board. "I'm Jason."

"Cara."

"Well, Cara, you've been personally invited by one of Delta's best."

"Yeah, best con artist."

"Damn, girl, that's cold."

"Like you don't personally invite every girl you see."

"Just the hotties. There's somethin' about a girl in black."

He makes me smile. "You might see me there."

"That's what's up. Bye Cara."

As he walks away I realize that's the first boy I've talked to since Tommy and he was hot. I don't know why I like tall guys, it shouldn't matter as short as I am, but he was tall and I like that.

I sleep away the rest of the day at the hotel, waiting for night to come. Thank God I don't have the dream again. Jim comes in and out of the room to offer me something to eat and to try to spark a conversation. He wants to go to the diner for dinner, but I brush him off and ask him to bring me back a cheeseburger. He decides to be clever and bring his dinner back to the room, too. I put up with him explaining the rules of some football game on TV for as long as I can before telling him I'm going to a movie on campus. He warns that I should be back by ten and I'm out the door.

The closer I get to campus, the more I feel like partying, craving the numb buzz a beer, a blunt or some wine can bring. That ecstasy buzz was unreal, but I'm afraid of what might happen. Maybe it wasn't the X? Maybe Tommy did give me a roofie? I don't know. Anyway, I don't really want to meet some new guy. They're all pigs. But that guy at the cafeteria was pretty cute.

I have a few hours to kill before any parties start so I decide to go to the movies after all. It's a small two screen theater so I don't have much of a choice, one of those silly romantic comedies or a cartoon kiddie movie about talking animals on a farm. I go for the romantic comedy and regret it about fifteen minutes in. It's gonna be one of those cookie cutter plots where everybody finds love and lives happily ever after. I allow myself to be caught up in the fantasy for a while before I realize those are just people on a screen and the live happily ever after thing only happens in the movies. Now I really need to get numb.

I get to the Delta house about ten. Guess Jim's expecting me back at the hotel by now, oh well. The frat house is one of those old southern homes with the tall columns in front. It feels like I'm approaching some kind of regal mansion at first, like where the governor should live or something. But as I get closer it becomes obvious that no one important lives here. The paint is peeling off the wood in some places, there are beer cans spread across the grass and two horrible looking bold flower print couches sit on the lawn, right in front of the house. The living room is huge with wood everywhere, but it's faded and stained from spilled beer no doubt. The room is actually pretty empty. There's a pool table, a card table in the corner and a bar in another corner. Several big, leather couches are placed randomly around the room. Everything is functional, but nothing is pretty.

There's not many people here yet, just a few boys gathered around the bar and some couples scattered around the room. I lack the nerve to go to the bar with all those boys around so I just walk around the room pretending to be interested in the pictures of the past Delta classes on the wall.

"Hey." A boy with a heavy southern accent pops up in front of me. "What you doin' over here all by yourself?"

"Just checkin' things out."

"You don't go to school here, do you?"

"No, I don't. How do you know?"

"I'd a noticed you before. You wanna beer?"

"Sure."

"Here you go." He comes back after a minute and hands me a big plastic cup.

"Thanks."

"Ever been to a Delta party before?"

"No."

"I'm Dave."

"Cara."

"Well, you come on the right night. This party's gonna be epic. We got three kegs and two tall cans of fruit punch."

"Fruit punch?"

"Yeah, it's grain mixed in with fruit juice. You never had it?"

"No. What's grain?"

"Grain alcohol, you know, 100% alcohol Most liquor's only 40% alcohol like vodka, whiskey and gin. This stuff is 100%. One glass and you're buzzin, two and you're bouncin' off the walls. And three, let's just say good luck remembering what happened the next day. You'll be buzzin' like bear in a bee hive."

"Shut up man, you're gonna scare our guest." It's the boy from the bulletin board. "Don't worry about him. I think he's already had too much. It's not that bad, but it'll sneak up on you if you don't look out."

I'm glad to see him. This other guy's starting to get on my nerves.

"Good to see you could make it." He turns to me and puts out his hand. "Jason."

"Yeah, I know."

"You have a good memory, Cara."

"Thank you. I see you have a good memory, too."

He maneuvers his way between me and Dave.

"That punch sounds crazy."

"It's not that bad. You just gotta watch yourself." He smiles. He's much cuter than I remembered. He has the most perfectly straight teeth I've ever seen, big, round, brown eyes and the sweetest dimples on both sides of his cheeks that emerge when he smiles.

"So, what's it like goin' to school here?"

"It's cool. Some of the classes are tough, but you know, you work hard, you play hard. And I plan on playin' hard tonight. My eyes are bleedin' from all the studyin' I've done this week."

"What's your major?"

"Business with a minor in accounting, But I don't wanna talk about school. I'd rather talk about you."

"What about me?"

"How long you gonna be in town?"

"A couple of days. I'm traveling from Philadelphia to California over the Christmas break."

"That's what's up. So, what's Philly like? One of my boys is from there and he says it's off the chain."

"Yeah, the parties are a lot better. That's for real."

"Just wait, things don't really start jumpin' off 'til after twelve. We got a band startin' up here in a minute. Reggae, you like reggae music?"

"It's cool. Are they any good?"

"They're pretty tight."

They look like the real thing, dread locks and all. More people are starting to come in. There's a line at the bar and the band is tuning up. Things are getting ready to kick into high gear. Jason's hot, funny and smart too. He's really easy to talk to.

"What's that in the garbage cans?" I ask pointing to two large plastic cans, like the kind you set out on the curb for the truck to pick up.

"That's the grain punch. We fill the cans up with ice, then add the grain and fruit punch."

"That's it?"

"That's it. Wanna try some?"

"Sure, why not." It sounds like the perfect thing to make me numb.

He brings me back a tall cup. "Here you go."

We touch cups, making a silent toast. I gulp down a big sip. "That's not so bad. It doesn't taste strong at all. I don't taste anything but punch."

"I know. There's more where that came from. You like the band?"

"Yeah, they're great. "Where're they from?" I have to stretch my neck to shout in his ear over the music.

111

"They come from Jamaica, but they play around at a lot of different schools. You wanna dance?"

I nod and he grabs my hand. The floor gets crowded quickly so we have to muscle our way through the bodies. The music is strong and rhythmic. I don't know if it's the crowd or the punch, but I'm starting to feel warm inside. I sip and sway as the music flows from song to song. His friends keep bringing us refills of punch so we don't have the leave the floor.

The strength and pulse of the music taps into something tribal, lying dormant inside me. I feel free. No shame, no pain, just free. His body moves in perfect rhythm to the beat. All the other kids are dancing close and tight, hip to hip, rubbing and grinding. I turn around and back up into him. I'm comfortable with him and I'm in charge. His body presses tight against mine. He grabs my hips and matches my swaying. This is nice, like it should feel. The band announces they're gonna take a break so we do too.

"Let me show you around the house." He holds my hand and leads me up the stairs. Everywhere I look there are couples leaning up against the walls, talking and kissing.

"Hey Jason, get in here." A voice calls from down the hall.

"What man? I'm busy."

"Come here, man. You gotta meet the band."

"Who's that?" I ask.

"That's my boy, Turner. Let's go see what he wants."

"What's up, dog?" Jason slaps his hand.

"Check it out." Turner pushes the door open.

We walk into a cloud of smoke, weed smoke.

"Close the door, man, you gonna let out the smoke," a deep voice with a heavy Jamaican accent calls out.

Just the smell of it makes me dizzy. They're playing a familiar game, puff, puff, pass, only these guys are pros. The four members of the reggae band anchor a circle of about ten kids passing around a blunt the size of a cigar, the biggest blunt I've ever seen in real life or on TV. Jason and I sit in and wait for our turn. It's amazing how much the reggae guys inhale. They've probably been smoking this stuff all their lives. I take a small puff when my turn comes, but it's more than enough. It's so strong, much stronger than anything Tommy ever had. Jason takes a bigger puff, but he coughs most of it out.

"You're from Jamaica?" I ask one of the band members sitting next to me. He's older, but his skin is so dark and smooth it's hard to tell how old. His dread locks drag half way down his back. I wonder how he can stand all that hair on his head. It could be nice in the winter, like a natural hat, but I bet it's hotter than hell in the summer.

"Ya man, Ras Tafari," he says as he rolls another fat blunt. You gotta be kidding. The first one's still circling around the room and I'm already flying.

"Rastafari, are you a Rastafarian? What's Rastafari?"

"Not what, girl, who. Our savior who leads us to Zion."

"Zion, that's your heaven, right? Is Rastafari like Jesus?"

"Zion is here on Earth."

"On Earth? Do you believe in Jesus and the Bible?"

"I know the Bible. Jah came to us as Jesus and as Ras Tafari. Jah walks the earth with man. Jah is in you and in all of us. Why you askin' me all these questions?" He takes a long, slow drag and passes the second joint to me, but I just pass it along.

"I'm sorry. I know it's none of my business. It's just that I never met a Rastafarian before. I hope you don't mind."

"I see child, you have a curious soul."

"So, what do you have to do to get to Zion?"

"Anyone can go to Zion, child. Zion is mother Africa."

"Africa is your heaven?" He nods. "And what about when you die. Where does your soul go?" I look up to see Jason chugging a beer with some guy. I hope he doesn't forget about me.

"Ashes to ashes, dust to dust. There is no life after death. We bury the body in the sacred earth, Zion, where all life come from. Do you believe in Jah?"

"You mean God. No, not really."

"Child, everybody gotta believe in somethin'. Here, smoke this. You gotta free your soul child. This is holy herb. It give you

113

wisdom, make you see everythin' clear."

The first blunt is coming back around the circle. This is crazy. I just passed on the second one. I'll pass out if I smoke anymore, but I don't wanna offend him, so I pretend to inhale more than I actually do and pass it on.

"Man, this is some crazy smoke." Jason comes back to my side and puts his arm around me. "Wanna cig?"

"Sure." I take one and offer one to my new friend.

"No thank you, child, them cigarettes no good for you."

"But you smoke weed?"

"Ganja is natural, from the Earth. Jah provide it for your health. Man make them things and put anythin' in 'em they want. No, no, thank you."

The smoke has the room and my head in a foggy haze, so I head for the door. No way I'm passing out in a room full of guys.

"Are you okay?" Jason's right behind me.

"Yeah, I just needed some air." It's better in the hallway. My head stops spinning enough to really enjoy the buzz. "That Rasta guy was really cool."

"That smoke's what's up. I'm wasted."

"Me too."

He smiles at me through half closed eyes. I can't believe he's so into me with so many hot looking girls around. We stare and giggle at each other like there's nobody else in the place. I have his full attention. A gorgeous, college boy. No, a gorgeous, college man, strong and tall.

The weed has my whole body tingling, wanting to be touched. Without thinking, I reach out and squeeze his arm right above his elbow. His muscle is a redwood trunk compared to Tommy's twigs. What the hell did I ever see in that a weak, little punk? Not when I can get this man.

Just as Jason puts his hands on my hips and pulls me closer, the sound of someone throwing up invades my ears. It's a boy running up the stairs desperately trying to make it to the bathroom. Everybody's laughing at him as his puke runs down his shirt and splatters on the hard wood floors.

"Too much punch for him." Jason laughs and wraps his arms around me. I lay me head on his broad chest. I can't hear his heartbeat, but I can feel his growing bulge.

"God, just hearing it makes me wanna puke." I feel the churning in my stomach, that lump in my throat.

"I know, me too. Let's go to my room."

He's reading my mind. He wants what I want.

His dorm room looks like I imagined; two small beds and matching desks. I shouldn't be surprised at the clothes scattered everywhere. He leads me over to an oversized, plaid, cloth sofa underneath the window sill. We push some clothes and books to the ground and sit down.

"You know, Cara, you the finest girl I've seen on this campus in a while."

"Yeah, what's so fine?" I feel dizzy again when I sit down.

"You got crazy, sexy eyes and you got them perfect lips." He moves in to kiss me. His kiss is nice at first, then I feel that lump easing up from my stomach and into my throat. I'm gonna throw up! I jump up and run to the bathroom he shares with the room next to his. I can't believe I threw up in front of him. I wash my mouth out as good as I can and go back into the room. He's waiting on the sofa smoking a cigarette.

"Are you okay," he smirks at me.

"Stop it. It's not funny. I'm so embarrassed. I must look like hell."

"Come here." He strokes my face and hands me a piece of gum. "You still the finest girl on campus."

We start kissing again. How can he still want to kiss me after what I did? He must really like me. Could I really be a hotty? My breath must smell like hell, but he doesn't seem to care. I don't care either. It feels good to be kissing. It feels better lying next to him, feeling the closeness again.

It's not long before he finishes. I'm looking forward to my favorite part when we lie coiled up in each others arms, but he jumps out of bed leaving me naked, hugging a pillow. He comes back after a few moments in the bathroom and sits on the side of the bed, putting on his pants.

"Guess I better get you home. I got a lot of studying to do for a test on Monday."

"That's it? We're done?"

"Yeah, it was great, wasn't it? You were great."

"What time is it?" I ask.

Doesn't he notice the disappointment in my face? Doesn't he care? He acts like I'm not even here. Why can't he look at me as he puts on his clothes?

"A little after three," he answers.

I scramble around the room for my clothes. His awkward silence feels like he's rushing me. He smiles a lot at his buddies as we make our way down the stairs and out the door. A couple of them give him high fives. They're all smiling at me too. It feels so weird. I have to dodge three piles of puke on my way out. Guess I wasn't the only one to fall victim to the fruit punch. We hardly talk on the car ride back to the hotel. He's speeding, like he can't wait to drop me off.

"I'm not leaving until the day after tomorrow," I say in a low voice hoping to mask my need for him to acknowledge my existence.

"Alright, maybe we can catch a movie or somethin'. I'll call you at the hotel. What's your room number?"

"302. You can just drop me off here." I point to the parking spot in front of our room. "So you'll call me tomorrow?"

"You bet."

He gives me a quick peck on the lips and speeds off as soon as I get out the car. I wonder why he speeds off so fast, but I'm more worried about facing Jim when I walk through the door. Luckily, he's asleep, snoring up a storm. I'm safe as long as I don't make any noise.

My head starts spinning again when I lay down, but my stomach feels better since I threw up.

"Wake up." Jim's standing at the foot of the bed and he's pissed.

"What time is it?" My head feels like I'm still buzzing.

"Never mind about that. Where the hell were you last night and what time did you get home?"

"I don't know. It was late."

"Where were you?"

"I made some friends and we went to a late movie, then we went to a late night restaurant where all the students hang out." I don't know where I'm coming up with this stuff, but it's good.

"Did you even think about calling? You don't answer your phone. Do you have any idea how worried I was? I called the hospital and the police. They told me you were probably at some party on campus so I spent half the night looking for you at those frat parties. You know what; from now on you don't leave the hotel. If I can't trust you to do the right thing, you're not going out at all 'til you get to your Grandma's. You could've been killed out there for all I knew."

"So you wanna keep me caged up like a prisoner?"

"I can't see where I have a choice."

"Whatever." I'm not worried. No way Jim's gonna hang out all day and night with me in some hotel room when there's a perfectly good bar somewhere in town.

I hang around the hotel the rest of the day. They have an indoor pool and a Jacuzzi that helps me get over my hangover. Plus, I can't help checking for messages. Jason might be trying to reach me to make plans for the movies. Five o'clock rolls around and I don't hear from him. Six, seven, eight o'clock, still no call. It's hard to admit he's blowing me off.

My first instinct is to sneak out behind Jim's back and go find him. Maybe he forgot my room number? Maybe he's been trying to reach me all this time? But I remember how he rushed me out of his room when he was finished with me.

How could he do this to me? Why do boys always say one thing then do another? Why do they all treat me like dirt? Lasenna was right. All they want is my thing. Is that all any of them want? Is that all I have to offer?

117

Chapter 14

I dream about Jessie again. This time Tommy's there, too. They're chasing me, but they're not on foot. All I see as I glance over my shoulder running through the woods is two huge faces the size of Thanksgiving Day parade balloons floating behind me, gaining on my every step. They laugh and taunt me through over sized jack-o-lantern grins filled with shiny, sharp, white teeth. I run and run and run, sweating and stumbling with no way out and no end in sight. At least I wake up before they catch me, my body drenched in sweat.

A surge of emptiness and shame strikes my body like raging waters crashing through a damn. I hardly notice my nails scraping against my arm at first. Each stroke brings relief from the pain.

I must've been crazy to believe any guy would want to hang out with me just for me, especially a college guy. How stupid can I get? It's obvious I'm only good for one thing.

Jim wakes me up about seven and we're on our way to Lafayette, Louisiana to pick up another load. I don't really care where we go. Louisiana's just as good as anywhere else. I look for my lizard, but he's not around. He must've taken off. Who could blame him? We have about nine hours on the road today. I'm gonna get a lot of reading done. The book takes my mind off things.

I think about the Rastafarian. The book says Rastafarians believe that the former Emperor of Ethiopia, Halie Selassie, is a living god on Earth. He is Ras Tafari, their god who previously came to Earth as Moses and Jesus. He was overtaken and killed in a military coupe in 1974, but they believe he's still alive today. Immortal, his atoms are spread throughout the world and become part of all of us. They believe we are all one with Jah. I guess that's what the Rasta guy meant when he said Jah was in me and in all of us.

It's a nice sentiment, bringing all the people on Earth together instead of implying that one group was chosen over another for eternal redemption. They don't even believe in an afterlife. There's only Zion, mother Africa. Their heaven is here on Earth. A religion where all people are connected as one and grounded to the Earth. When we die we go back to where life first emerged, Africa. So far it makes more sense than being Catholic with all the guilt and damning people to hell who don't believe what you believe. Plus you get to smoke ganja all the time. It's actually part of their religion to smoke it. They think it's a holy herb.

It sounds good, but I couldn't be a Rastafarian. I can't see believing that a regular man, an emperor or king, is a god. That just sounds like a way for the king to gain more power. Like the Egyptian pharaohs who used to declare themselves as living gods. That's arrogance, not religion.

"I never thought you'd end up being a party girl," Jim interrupts the first relaxing thoughts I've had in hours.

"What?"

"I know you were at some kind of party the other night."

"I don't know what you're talking about."

"I could smell the alcohol on you. How much did you drink?"

"I don't know, not much."

"You know, Cara, it's no secret that I like to taste the sauce a little."

"No kidding."

"Yeah, so I know what I'm talkin' about. Both me and your mother have struggled with the stuff. I just want better for you. Trust me. You don't want that monkey on your back.

"Why did Mom take drugs?"

"Your mom was a good woman, a great woman, but she wasn't perfect. The thing is she was obsessed with movin' up in the world. I wasn't good enough for her. I think she figured if she could marry a doctor, a rich doctor, things would be easier, especially for you. We started goin' to all these high brow parties. I was a fish out of water, but she loved it. That snooty crowd wasn't for me, so I stopped going with her. She had a whole new group of friends That's when we drifted apart. Them doctors got her hooked on cocaine and started writing prescriptions for her. They were all doing it, the doctors, the nurses, the girlfriends, the wives, everybody."

"You make her sound like some kind of gold digging junkie. If you knew she was doing it, why didn't you stop her? Why didn't you try to help her?"

"It's not that easy, Cara. She was just caught up in it all. And I was caught up in my own thing. I didn't see it or want to see it until it was too late. It's so easy to fall into it, but once it's got you it's hard as hell to break free. That's why I'm worried about you. I know how hard it is to break free."

"So you're saying she was doing drugs the whole time. How come I never noticed anything? I never saw her do it. She never looked high to me."

"That's the thing. When you've been doin' it that long, you get to be pretty good at hiding it. You don't even do it to get high no more. You do it just to get through the day and feel like a normal person. Nothin' good can come from doin' drugs, Cara. It's better not to start at all. Just leave it alone, please."

"I don't do drugs."

"I don't expect you to admit to it, but I know weed when I smell it and your clothes reeked of it."

"You think you know me. You don't know me."

"Hey, we're not having this conversation again. I know I don't know you. This isn't about me being a bad father. It's about you doin' drugs."

"Don't worry about it. You never cared before."

"I care now."

"Oh well." I've heard enough. I'm not going to turn into some kind of junkie. That could never happen to me. I'm not hooked on anything.

"Cara."

"Please, just leave me alone."

I put on my head phones and stare out the window, totally expecting Jim to keep bugging me, but for some reason lets me be. It's good to be alone with my thoughts, staring down the highway at nothing. Suddenly, my eyes catch something in the rear view mirror. It's my lizard, darting between the logs on the back of the truck. He must've found some bugs to eat in the wood. Animals are resourceful like that. Whatever they need they find for themselves. They don't need anybody. And if they can't make it, if they're not strong enough to survive or smart enough to find food for, they die. It's that simple. I admire him for that.

I wonder if the Hindus who live a really good life get to pick what they want to be reincarnated as. Maybe I could come back as a lizard. They're so cute. That'd be cool just hanging out, catching bugs all day, nobody bothering me. Maybe not. I'd have to eat bugs.

We pull into Lafayette around dinner time. Jim takes us to a nice restaurant in a cool part of the city. It's like an outdoor mall. All the restaurants have patios where people casually eat and enjoy each others company. The storefronts have huge windows so people can stroll by and check out their stuff. It looks like Philly, except in some small almost imperceptible way it's different. There's an easy feeling that saturates the air reinforced by soothing, melodic jazz coming from every direction. Street performers line the street; a man doing card tricks, a one man band with a banjo, harmonica, bass drum and some kind of washboard dangling from his neck, an old woman in gypsy gear telling fortunes, an old black man strumming a beat up guitar and singing the blues, and a clown faced man on a unicycle juggling torches and eating the flames. It's like a huge circus.

"Where do you wanna eat?" Jim asks.

121

"Anywhere, I guess. They all look fine to me." I'm too distracted by all the beautiful paintings the street vendors display to care. I can't believe how talented they all are. I could never do anything so beautiful.

"How 'bout this one?" Jim says pointing to a cardboard cut-out of a jazz trio. "Authentic Cajun Creole, that sounds pretty good. They say Creole is some of the best cookin' around. It's a chance to try something we don't get in Philly."

"That sounds okay to me."

I have something called seafood etouffee. Its shrimp and crab with rice in a great tasting sauce. It's awesome.

I'm expecting another lecture about doing drugs, but he spends most of his time flirting with the waitress. The crazy thing is she's actually flirting back. She's pretty, but I can tell she's lived a hard life. Maybe she smokes too much or spends too much time in the sun, but she has the kind of hard lines in her face that shouldn't show up until her forties. She's not that older than me, maybe early twenties, but she still has the lines. I hear her tell Jim she'll be getting off at ten. His eyes fall in embarrassment then he turns to her and smiles. Guess he has a date tonight. That's a free night for me. He hasn't figured out how he's gonna keep me on restriction when he's out running the streets? He really needs a lesson in basic parenting skills.

We walk up and down the street for a little while after dinner just looking around then we go back to the hotel. Jim picked another nice one. The beds are big and comfortable. I decide to change into my night shirt and get into bed with my book so Jim will think I'm content just staying in for the night. He comes out of the shower humming, singing and brushing his hair back like he was some kind of male model.

"What do you think, the red or the blue?" He holds up two plaid shirts, identical in design except for the color.

"The red, definitely," I answer quickly hoping that'll stop the conversation.

"That waitress was pretty cute, don't you think?"

"I'd rather not talk about your conquests if you don't mind."

"She's not a conquest. We're just gonna have coffee or a drink or something."

"You better not be planning on bringing her back here."

"Cara, please, do you really think I would do that? What's that?"

"What's what?"

"That." He's pointing at my arms. I usually wear long sleeves to cover the scratches, but I put on the night shirt without thinking about it.

"Oh, it's nothing." I pull my arms into my shirt to cover up the marks. "I was playing with a stray cat the other day and it scratched me. Guess I shouldn't have tried to pick it up."

"Let me see." He comes closer and puts out his hand. "Cara, let me see."

"It's nothing, I told you." I look down at my arms and for the first time I see how deep the scratches really are. My skin is scarred and raised in some places.

"You know better than to be playin' with stray animals. Man, that looks nasty. Did you put some alcohol or something on it or so it don't get infected? Maybe we should get you a rabies shot."

"I can't get rabies, Jim. He scratched me, he didn't bite me."

"Okay, smarty pants, but it could still get infected, right?"

"It's healing up fine. Aren't you going to be late for your date?"

"Oh man, I gotta go." He looks down at his watch. "Remember, you're not to leave this room, got it? I'll be callin' to check up on you and you better answer your phone."

"Right, right, I know."

"I won't be out too late," he says as he bolts out the door. Like it's some kind of promise. Like I care anyway.

I watch out the window until I see him leave the building and his image disappear into the crowd of people making their way down the street. Our hotel is in the middle of the city in the downtown area where everything's going on. It'll be easy to blend in the crowd in my black jeans, black long sleeve t-shirt and a black jean jacket. I just have to keep my eye out for Jim. I'm sure he'll be cruising the

123

bars with his new girlfriend.

I can see my destination from a block away lit up by an elaborate show of Christmas lights. I stroll along the sidewalk halfway window shopping and halfway looking out for Jim. The cold air stings my face but the music warms me, filling my head so I don't have to think about anything. It leads me to a trio, drums, bass and piano. They're playing the old Christmas standards, but with a real nice jazzy twist, especially the piano player. He makes the song come alive. I can see each note he plays dancing through my head as I lean against a light pole with my eyes half closed.

"Excuse me, Miss, can I offer you a *Bible*?" A timid voice gently interrupts my solace.

"What?"

"A *Bible*. Do you know the word of God?"

"What religion are you?"

"I'm a Jehovah's Witness. A servant of the Lord sent to spread his message and grace."

"Really."

"Will you be ready for Armageddon?"

"Armageddon. Yeah, I guess. I mean I got a flashlight and some batteries in case of emergency." I'm finding it hard to take this guy seriously.

"A flashlight won't help you unless you have the light of God in your heart. Can't you see the signs? In the *Bible* Matthew said nation will rise against nation and kingdom against kingdom, there will be food shortages, great earthquakes, pestilence, and uncontrollable disease. Can't you see? People are starving all over the world, the hurricanes and earthquakes grow worse year after year, and AIDS is just a warning of much worse to come. The *Bible* foretold it would happen and everything it says has come to pass. Can't you see the signs are clear? You must be ready for the rapture."

"So you think the world's coming to an end?" He's talking kind of crazy, but I can't resist the chance to get into his head. He looks harmless enough, just a skinny kid, not much older than me.

"Yes, we are in the End of Days. Only the saved will live to inherit the earth and be granted eternal salvation. God allowed us to live independent of his judgment for too long. We screwed it all up, but he will soon come to pass judgment. The earth will be purged of the wicked. And millions of people who are blameless shall inherit the earth for a thousand years of bliss. Millions more will be resurrected to join Jesus in God's heavenly kingdom. After 1000 years of Christ's reign the earth will be filled with perfect men and women, as God intended it to be before Satan corrupted Adam. Are you ready for the purge?"

"Do you really believe all that?"

"Of course I do. It's in the *Bible*."

"And you believe everything in the *Bible*?"

"You can't doubt the word of God."

I can't help but feel like I'm talking to a robot, some kinda automaton programmed to spit out *Bible* scriptures. "What about the 500 million Buddhists who don't believe in the *Bible*? Do you really think they're all going to hell?"

"Accepting Jesus as your savior is the only way to be saved when the rapture comes," he replies with a puzzled look on his face, unable to digest my logic.

He turns his attention away from me, knowing I'm not buying the whole rapture trip. "Can I offer you a *Bible*," he asks a young couple passing by.

There's only so many times I can walk up and down the same street before I get really bored. Its only 11:30, enough time to beat Jim back to the hotel. Might as well avoid a fight.

My book doesn't have anything about Jehovah's Witnesses, but I know what they're all about. They believe in giving testimony, a nice way of saying I'm gonna be in your face 'til I can scare you into believing what I believe. Why do they have to force their beliefs on other people anyway? Why can't they just let people believe what they want to believe?

Guess it's always been that way for Christians, going back to the crusades and inquisitions. They conveniently skipped those parts in history class at school, but I researched it on-line. They had no

125

problem slaughtering innocent men, women, and children in the name of Christianity. I know the world was a much more brutal place then and waging war was a way of life, but that's bananas. Was it really all about spreading the word of God?

Luckily, Jim's not there when I get back. I'm looking forward to vegging out in front of the TV. There's a great show about evolution on the Discovery Channel. It's hard to argue with Darwin and natural selection. From the amoeba to the dinosaurs and their extinction to the rise of mammals into apes into us, it all just seems to fit together perfectly. We even share 98% of our DNA with apes. I'm starting to find it easier to believe the logical steps of evolution than to believe there's some god that living in the sky making universes.

I'm not sure how the Earth was created. I guess the big bang theory makes sense, but I don't know. No one knows what caused the big bang, so don't you have to wonder where that first atom of hydrogen or carbon or whatever came from? How does something just appear out of complete nothingness? I remember what our pastor said in his sermon about the big bang theory and evolution. He figured the Earth is too orderly a place to have been created by the random nature of evolution. He concluded that God was the only logical explanation for the creation of such a perfect world. But if you follow that logic, don't you have to ask where God came from? Who created him? Does he have a mother and a father? Is there a race of gods out there that go around creating universes? Wouldn't that just be an alien race?

Maybe that's the answer. Aliens created earth. That would explain the pyramids. I never was convinced that man alone could have built those massive structures with the technology they had back then, but I can believe an alien race visited earth at some time in the past. So many people have seen UFOs. The pyramids actually line up with the stars. Maybe they left them as landmarks for when they return. There's literally billions of stars in the universe and each one of those could have planets around them. It's inconceivable to think that we're the only life in the whole universe.

I start channel surfing after the evolution show is over. Ironically, I come across a Christian program talking about the millions of Chinese that believe in Buddha, not God. This middle aged man and woman are making a passionate plea for people to send them money to support their mission to introduce Jesus to China and save all those poor, lost Buddhist souls. They can't understand how the people of China don't believe in God. They think that if the Chinese can just learn how to believe in our God it will bring order to their lives and all their troubles will magically disappear.

What's difference between these missionaries and the crusaders of the past? You don't see Hindus or Buddhists setting up missions in Des Moines, Iowa or walking up and down the streets of Lafayette, Louisiana trying to convert people to their way of life. Why is it that Christians are so compelled to convert others to their religion? Both Buddhism and Hinduism are older religions than Christianity. Those people have been happy and secure in their beliefs and their way of life for thousands of years. How could anybody be so arrogant to go over there and tell them that the backbone of their entire society, their traditions, beliefs, and the religion of their ancestors going back thousands and thousands of years, is wrong?

People should be left alone to believe what they want to believe. Everyone has their own perception of what God is. It's not like anyone has any proof that God really exists. The *Bible* says that God revealed himself to Abraham and Moses among others, but the *Qur'an* claims he also revealed himself to Mohammed. The *Vedas* describes many interactions between man and the Hindu gods. The ancient Greeks and Romans also wrote about how their gods revealed themselves to every day people. So who's right? I don't know. How can anybody really know?

I get up early the next morning. Jim's snoring away. I'm not sure what time he got in last night Back to my favorite street for a morning walk. The energy from the night before isn't there, but there's still a positive vibe in the air. The street vendors are just setting up, but the old gypsy fortune teller is already open for business enticing and offering a glimpse of the unknown.

I used to only drink coffee to relieve hangovers, but now I like the taste and pick me up it gives me in the morning. I order a tall caramel latte in a small coffee shop and find the perfect spot near the front window to read. Buddhists don't really believe in any kind of god. They aren't even concerned with the idea of an afterlife. All they care about is avoiding suffering in the here and now. They're always striving to reach a state of Nirvana, a condition of enlightenment and total freedom from our world. I guess you have to totally detach yourself from the world to avoid any suffering. I can relate to that.

It all started about 2500 years ago when Sidhatta Gotma, the son of the emperor of a small kingdom in India, decided to explore the part of humanity that lived outside his life of luxury. He witnessed, for the first time, the suffering of mankind; illness, old age and death. He was so disturbed he traded his royal robe in for a beggar's robe and became a wandering holy man. He gained a strong following and became known as the Buddha. He concluded that the only way to avoid suffering was by living a simple life of meditation. By seeking self awareness, one may find their own true happiness in life. Buddha believed everybody has the ability, without any divine intervention, to rise above the evils of the world into a state of Nirvana. Every man is responsible for his own salvation.

Imagine that. No God to depend on and then just say, "Oh well, that's God's will," when things don't turn out as planned. You and you alone control your destiny and how your life turns out depends on your actions. There's one thing that would be really hard to get used to. Buddhists believe that the cause for all suffering is desire and attachment to possessions. You must free yourself of the desire for things like money, cars, expensive vacations and all the other good stuff most red-blooded Americans love. No wonder Buddhism never caught on here. There's no way we're giving up all our stuff.

Jim's watching TV in his underwear when I get back to the hotel.

"Oh God, could you please put some clothes on."

"Hey, sorry, where you been?" He slides on a pair of jeans.

"The coffee shop."

"You eat already?"

"Yeah, it's almost noon."

"I'm starving. I'll be out for a while. I gotta get the truck ready. We hit the road for San Antonio tomorrow." He leaves in a groggy, quiet mood.

The hotel is nice, but there's not much to do, just a small pool and an arcade room with two outdated pin ball machines. Nothing to do but watch TV. I shouldn't be alone with my thoughts. Tommy, Jessie, Jason, Jim, they all run through my mind like members of a relay team, each one passing me on then dropping me at the finish line.

There's no room on my arms for scratching, but my legs are clean and smooth so I just keep scratching, just keep scratching, just keep scratching until I don't feel anything inside anymore.

The day moves along at a snails pace. I could be go back downtown, but I don't feel like being around a lot of people. I could fall asleep to make the time pass faster, but I'm afraid of the nightmares. It really doesn't matter. The memories follow me asleep or awake.

"Wake up, sleepy head, I've got dinner," Jim calls out.

"What? What time is it?"

"Six o'clock. Don't tell me you've been sleepin' all day."

"I guess."

"Come get some pizza."

I carefully cover my arms and legs as I get out of bed.

"So, you goin' out with your new girlfriend tonight?"

"No, I thought it'd be nice to stay in tonight. Got a lot of driving to do tomorrow. You know how to play poker?"

"No."

"Wanna learn?"

"Why not."

"Great." He jumps up and pulls a deck of cards out of his duffle bag. "Okay, there's a lot of different ways to play, but these are the basics. We both get five cards to start. Now if we're playing stud you just bet the hand you're dealt and the best hand wins. But if we're playing draw you get to trade three of your worst cards for three new ones or four cards if the one you keep is an ace. Here's a list of what beats what." He hands me a card with all the winning combinations on it. "Don't worry. It'll all make sense when we start playing. Let's see, I'll give us both a hundred dollars worth of chips."

"You have your own chips. You're not some kind of gambling addict are you?"

"No, kiddo, I just like to play sometimes."

"So, are we playing for real money?"

"Do you have any real money?"

"Just what you gave me before."

"Then I guess we can't play for real money. I don't wanna take your money. This is just for fun."

I pick up my cards. "Let's see, I've got a queen of hearts, three of clubs, seven of diamonds, eight of clubs, and an ace of spades. Is that good?"

"It's not bad. You have an ace which is good, but I can beat you if I have a pair of the same kind of card. I got you beat so far. I've got two fours, see, a four of hearts and a four of spades. A pair of anything beats an ace high. Now if we were playing draw you could trade in up to four cards for new ones since you have that ace."

"Then let's play draw."

"Okay. I would trade in your three, seven, eight, and queen and keep the ace. And I'm gonna keep my fours and trade in my other cards. Now, you know if we were playing for real we wouldn't be looking at each other's cards."

"Duh. Let's see, now I've got a ten of spades, a two of diamonds, a six of hearts and another ace. Hey, I've got a pair. Aces are good, right?"

"Aces are very good. It's the highest card in the deck. I didn't get any help from my draw."

130

"So, I win."

"You win. You catch on quick."

"Yes," I shout. I don't know why I want to beat him so bad, but I do. We play for a few hours before we go to bed. He teaches me a bunch of things about poker. He's actually pretty cool. It's been a long time since I can remember having a good time with Jim.

"Mind if I keep the TV on?" I ask him. "I like the noise while I'm trying to fall asleep."

"That's fine." He rolls over and tucks himself in tight between the sheets.

"Jim."

"Yeah."

"Do you believe in God?"

"What?"

"Do you believe in God?"

"Of course, doesn't everybody?"

"Well, not exactly, there are millions of people all around the world that don't believe in God at all."

"Really, so what do they believe?"

"That depends. Some believe in many different gods and some believe that there is no God at all and man should look inside himself to ease his suffering."

"Is that right? Well, I believe in God."

"Do you believe in the *Bible*?"

"Yes. Why you askin' all these questions about God all of a sudden?"

"I just wanna know, that's all. Do you believe everything it says in the *Bible*?"

"Yeah, sure."

"So, you believe all mankind came from Adam and Eve, and God destroyed the earth in a huge flood and asked Noah to save two of every animal in a great big boat, and he parted the Read Sea for Moses?"

"I don't know about all that."

"But if you believe in the *Bible* don't you have to believe all that? Do you believe in miracles?"

"Miracles, those are hard to believe in. I don't know, Cara. I guess some of those stories are pretty crazy. I bet people believed in a lot of stuff back then."

"Yeah, but what do you believe?"

"I told you. I believe in God. I think there's a higher power up there we all have to answer to."

"But you don't believe in what the *Bible* says. Isn't that the word of God? How can you believe in God and not in the *Bible*?"

"I don't know. Maybe they did exaggerate in the *Bible*. That was a long time ago. Why don't you tell me? You went to Catholic school all those years. What did they teach you about the *Bible*?"

"Only that I should believe every word and accept God's miracles as proof of his awesome power."

"Do you believe in miracles?"

"No, Jim, I don't. That's my point. If there were miracles Mom would still be alive, wouldn't she?"

"Come on, Cara, you can't put that on God. We're all free to make our own decisions. Me and your mom, we both made some bad choices. Hell, sometimes I think it's a miracle I'm still alive. I don't know if I believe in miracles, but it'd be nice to think your mom is up there smiling down on us. That's what I believe. You can believe it, if you choose to. It's all up to you what you believe in. Now, let's get some sleep. There's no use in talking about it. Either you believe it or you don't."

Chapter 15

Thank God I didn't have any dreams last night, none that I remember anyway. But I'm still all sweaty.

"Time to rise and shine," Jim announces as he pulls on the curtains to let the light in. "We've gotta pick up a load then we've got a long boring drive across Texas. Man, that's one flat stretch of land."

"Where are we going in Texas?"

"San Antonio."

"What's it like?"

"It's alright. The downtown area has a river running through it where all the good restaurants are, great Mexican food. I guess I should say Tex-Mex. We'll go when we get there."

"From Cajun to Tex-Mex, I can handle that."

A welcome surprise greets me as I lift myself up into the truck. It's my lizard, staring me straight in the face. "Hey, little buddy, where you been?" I wonder why he keeps hanging around. Maybe he's eating all the dead insects smattered across the front grill. That would keep him fat and happy. Then again, he has to kill his own food. He's a survivor.

There's a preacher on the radio talking about the importance of paying tithes to the church. According to him ten percent of your salary is a small amount to sacrifice for all the glory God brings into your life.

"Will you please turn that crap," Jim snaps at the radio.

"Alright, hold on, what are you getting so mad about?"

"I'm sorry. Guys like that just piss me off. I don't like to see people spending a lot of money on religion. That's one thing in life that should be free."

"I know, huh."

"Your grandmother, my mother, gave almost all her money to her church. The Church of Christ, I think it was. She used to spend all her time there and almost all her social security checks. No matter how hard I tried to talk her out of it she wouldn't listen. Like she was trying to buy her way into heaven. I don't know. Guess everybody kind of freaks out as they get closer to meeting their maker. I wish you could've met her."

"What was she like?"

"You would've liked her. She was really smart and stubborn as a mule. She worked as a legal secretary for some high brow lawyer, but she always wanted to go to college. She wanted me to go too, but you know how that turned out. I must've inherited my father's brain. Sometimes I think that's why I picked your mother. She reminded me of my mother."

"What was your father like? You never talk about him."

"I never knew him. He left my mother before I was born. I don't even know if she knew him that well. She never really talked about him."

"Why do you think he left?"

"I don't know, Cara. Maybe he was too young to handle the responsibility. Maybe he didn't know how to be a good father. Maybe he was afraid of screwing up. You know, it's easy to make mistakes when you're young. Mistakes you end up regretting the rest of your life."

"So, what do you regret?"

"I wish I'd a spent more time with you when you was growin' up. I wish I'd a gone to college. You know, really made something out of myself. I probably wouldn't have lost your mother. There's lot

134

of things I would've done different, but you can't turn back the hands of time."

"No, you can't."

"No use cryin' over spilt milk, right. Everything happens for a reason. Your mom did a great job raisin' you. Things would've been different if I was around more. All that arguing and fighting might've turned you into some kind of juvenile delinquent. She raised you right. You turned out great, a beautiful young lady and a good student, too. I couldn't be more proud."

"Thanks." It's nice to hear him talk about me like that. I wonder if he really means it or if it's just the guilt talking.

"You know, she wanted you to be a doctor. That's why she insisted on you goin' to that Catholic school. Nothing's more important than education. The sky's the limit for you, kiddo."

"Oh, great, so if I don't turn out to be some great doctor I'm a loser, right? What if I don't wanna be a doctor?"

"You don't have to be a doctor if you don't want to. I'm just saying you're smart enough to make it. There's not much advice I can give you when it comes to education and stuff, but I can tell you that if you wanna be happy in life, do something you really like. You know, something that you would do all day for free if you could. Don't worry about the money, it'll come. I don't know what I'd do if I couldn't drive the open road. Imagine me behind a desk or in a suit and tie."

"That's really not you. Mom liked being a nurse. She'd always tell me about how she assisted on these incredible surgeries. This one guy had a heart transplant. She said they actually cracked open his chest and pried his rib cage open with a saw and a vise to work on his heart. Could you imagine being part of something so important, saving someone's life?"

"Yeah, she was something." Jim smiles.

"I couldn't handle that, having someone's life in my hands."

"Me neither. Your mom was strong like that."

"Yeah, but she was weak, too."

"What do you mean?"

"She wasn't strong enough to stop drugs from killing her. I mean she was a nurse, it's not like she didn't know the risks. She even lectured me about it, telling me all these horror stories about people who overdosed or died from drugs. She even made me promise her I wouldn't do it. Ugh, what a hypocrite!"

"Hold on, Cara, it's not that simple. She was tryin' to warn you from her own experience."

"Did she even try to get help?"

"I don't know, Cara."

"So she just took drugs until they killed her. Why was she so sad? I mean I know she was lonely, you know, working so much and all, but I thought we were doing okay."

"I'm sure you were. You can't put it on yourself. Believe me. You had nothing to do with your mom doing drugs. Maybe it was the job. Maybe it was too much pressure. I don't know. Your mother used to talk to me about that kind of stuff, but that was a long time ago."

"I still don't understand it. I know you said she was caught up in her crowd, but that was just partying. How did she go from that to overdosing?"

"I think you understand a little bit more than you're letting on."

"What do you mean?"

"Why do you do drugs? And don't tell me you don't. I know what I know."

"That was only a little weed and I only did it 'cause I was curious. I don't do it all the time."

"That's what they all say at first. You're only fifteen. Don't you get it? If you're drinkin' and smokin' weed now, where do you think you'll be by the time you're twenty? This is where it starts, Cara. You get the taste for it, and before you know it, one high isn't good enough. You keep lookin' for something to take you higher and higher. Am I makin' any sense to you?"

"I don't know."

"I'm not just makin' this up. I never told you this, but I've been tryin' to stop drinking for years. It's hard being on the road all the

136

time. I try to catch AA meetings when I can, but it's hard. It's hard as hell to stop."

"Hey, I can stop anytime I want. I just tried it at a party, that's all."

"Yeah, I know," he smirks. "You say that now, but as easy as it was for you to break your promise to your mom not to do drugs is as easy as it was for her to keep going back to cocaine. It'll be the same way for you if you don't stop now."

"It's really not that serious. I mean you must've tried some things when you were young. Lots of kids try stuff, but they don't turn out to be addicts."

"That's kind of my point. We have a family history in this area, wouldn't you say? It might not be as easy for you to just say no as it is for other kids."

"I'm not like you. Just because you guys got hooked doesn't mean I will."

"I hope you don't. You don't want my grief. Just stop now, please."

"Okay, I get it already." We silently agree to drop the subject. "How much longer until we get there?"

"We've got about two hours to go."

"You were right. This drive sucks. There's nothing but flat road and dirt. What happened to the beautiful mountains?"

"Tell me about it. It's the worst part of the country to drive across. I've gotta take you to Colorado with me sometime."

"The Rocky Mountains, huh."

"Yep. If you liked the Appalachians you'd love the Rockies. All of Colorado is like one big post card. You can see the mountains in the background from anywhere you go in the state."

"And they're prettier than the ones in West Virginia?"

"Hell yeah. The Rockies are twice as big as the Appalachians. If you thought the view from 7,000 feet was cool, wait until you see it from 14,000 feet. You get a whole new view of the world."

"I bet it's absolutely gorgeous."

"Kiddo, it's like being on top of the world."

The next two hours go by fast. We keep the conversation pretty light. Jim tells me more about the Rockies and the Sierra Nevada ranges. I'd love to go to Yosemite. He says the giant redwoods are only a five hour drive from Grandma's. I've seen pictures, but a tree as tall as any building in Philly I just have to see for myself.

He stammers when trying to describe the Grand Canyon. He says there's no way he can do justice to its size and beauty. It's the most incredible thing he's ever seen. I make him promise me we'll stop there on the way to Grandma's.

We finally roll into San Antonio after what seems like forever. As usual, Jim drops me off at the hotel then goes to drop off his load. It's a nice hotel, like the one in Georgia, only smaller. It has an indoor, heated pool and a hot tub so I'll be fine. It's not like I'm gonna do laps or anything. I just like to lower my head below the surface of the water and turn on the bubbles so I don't see or hear anyone.

Everyone in the hotel stares at me walking by as if wearing black is some kind of crime. The lady at the counter literally gasps at my black nails when she hands over the room key. She's wearing one of those scarves that cover her head and part of her face. She must be from somewhere in the Middle East. She has the accent. I bet she's a Muslim. She's wearing a small pendant on the end of a thin gold chain that I recognize from the book, a crescent moon with a star, the symbol for Islam.

I go straight to the room and look up Islam in my book. I always thought Muslims and Christians were world's apart, but that's not true. Muslims believe in the same *Bible* as Christians do, from Adam and Eve to Noah to Moses to the birth of Jesus to a virgin mother. They just don't believe Jesus was the savior. They believe he was just one of a few special prophets God chose to be messengers of his word, like Abraham and Moses before him. For Muslims, Mohammed was the last great prophet, not a savior. They think we're still waiting for the savior.

Unbelievable, basically they both believe in the same God. All those wars and crusades over centuries and centuries over what, who the last prophet was?

We go downtown to the River Walk when Jim gets back. There's an inescapable calm that flows with the river. It reminds me of Lafayette minus the street performers and the sweet, sweet music.

I have a taco, an enchilada, and something called a chili relleno. I like the chili relleno best. It's filled with this spicy cheese and surrounded by this big, smoky flavored, green pepper. Everything's really, really good.

Jim laughs at all the hot sauce I toss on my food. I'm a little surprised at how much I like it, but there's something about the fire exploding in my mouth, the burning and the lingering sting that I like. I take a bite, endure the heat until I can't stand it, take a sip of coke, and repeat the process laughing with Jim and pointlessly fanning my mouth. I had actually forgotten I could laugh with Jim.

The next morning I see a younger version of the lady I saw the day before at the front desk. She's wearing the same robe looking dress that covers her whole body and head. She looks to be about my age.

"Hi." I'm drawn to introduce myself to her.

"Good Morning. Can I help you?" Her accent is not as pronounced as the other lady's, but she still sounds different. She has the same eyes and nose. This must be her daughter. She also has the same moon and star pendant.

"Yes, could you tell me where I can get a good breakfast around here?"

"Yes, there is a good diner around the corner." She points to the left. "And a very nice coffee shop straight down this street. I prefer the coffee shop. Some of the local artists display their paintings there."

"Thanks. The coffee shop sounds good."

She has an inviting, but business like smile. I want to know more about her. Why does she cover up so much? What's Islam really all about?

"That's a nice pendant you're wearing. What is it?" I ask.

"Thank you. It's a crescent star."

"Cool, what does it stand for?"

"Excuse me, stand for?"

"You know, I mean, is it a symbol for something?"

"It is for my religion," she answers timidly.

"Are you a Muslim?"

"Yes."

I can tell she's not comfortable with my questions. "I'm sorry. I don't mean to be nosy. It's just that I've been reading up on Islam and I thought it'd be nice to compare notes with a real person. I've never met a Muslim before. I was hoping you could help me out with my research. I mean, they make you all out to be terrorists on TV."

"I'm not a terrorist."

"I know. That's why I wanna talk to you. So I can find out for myself."

"The media is a jok," she replies with an angry tone. I can tell I've struck a nerve. "Are you writing a paper for school or something?"

"Something like that." Just as I answer I hear someone behind me clear their throat in an impatient tone. "I better let you get back to work. Can we talk later?"

"Sure, it was nice meeting you," she says then immediately acknowledges the impatient customer.

I wonder if she really is interested in talking later or if she's just trying to clear her line.

She was right. The coffee shop is one of those trendy spots designed to attract young, urban social climbers. Big, beautiful paintings cover every wall. Each local artist adds to the Southwestern theme. There's the rustic cowboy fervently chasing stampeding cattle, the lone prairie house with its tumbleweeds gliding across the front yard, and an absolutely beautiful painting of a huge sunflower using bright yellow, orange, red, and blue. My favorite is a painting of wild horses. Some are peacefully eating grass, others play, kicking up dust, happy, free and unburdened. How terrible it must be to be a horse today, wearing a saddle, pulled around by a bit in your mouth, giving kiddie rides at some local fair or pulling some carriage down Main Street.

I lay back on one of the big, red sofas with a caramel latte and a big piece of carrot cake, the breakfast of champions. I can't wait to learn more about Islam.

Just as I'm about to crack open my book a group of kids burst through the door and threaten my serenity. They spill into my space smiling and greeting me like they already know me. Oh well, so much for quiet reading time.

"Hey, Mike, over here." One of the boys sitting across from me shouts at a boy coming through the door.

He's absolutely gorgeous, tall, cute and full of muscles. I never really thought a lot of muscles mattered too much before, but they do now!

"Yo, what's up?" He makes the rounds slapping hands with his friends.

"Wanna coffee, Mike?" A pretty girl with a shy smile asks him.

"Thanks Alicia," he smiles back. "Okay guys; let's get this project organized. We have to be at the site by noon. Tony, you got the lumber from Home Depot last night, right?"

"It's covered."

"Tre, you're in charge of makin' sure the finished walls get painted today, okay? Don't worry, Denny, Monica and Tina are gonna be there to help you."

Who is this guy to command such respect and attention? I try not to stare at him, but I can't help it. He's in total control.

"You interested?"

Oh my God, he's talking to me.

"You wanna help out?"

He's looking right at me.

"Hey, my name's Mike. I couldn't help notice you were looking at one of our flyers."

He's standing in front of me with his hand extended. Say something. Say something.

"Cara," I shake his hand. "It looks like a good cause. What's Student Corps?"

Mark Miller

"We're a volunteer group. We do community projects. This Christmas we're working with Habitat for Humanities, building homes for the homeless. Last year we did a great Christmas dinner at the shelter. Nothing makes your day like watching a bunch of homeless dudes grub out on the first decent meal they've had in ages."

"That sounds cool. You guys do some great work."

"Thanks. What about you? What have you done to help somebody today?"

"Nothing."

"So why don't you come with us to the constructions site. We could use the extra hands."

"Okay," I agree without even thinking about it. He's so hot. And I can't remember the last time I did anything for anybody.

"Right on. So we're just hangin' out this morning planning who's gonna do what and bring what and whatever. Yo everybody, this is Cara. She's gonna be helpin' us out today. Cara, this is everybody."

"Hey...what's up...nice to meet you," they all wave and smile.

I introduce myself to them one by one. They seem pretty cool. I tell them I used to go to Temple, but now I'm between schools. They all think it's cool that I'm taking time out to "find myself". I don't like lying to them, but it feels good knowing students from the University of Texas can accept me as a peer. They don't need to know my age, especially Mike.

"What's that you're reading?" Mike asks.

"Just a book on religion."

"Yeah, I don't believe in that stuff."

"What do you mean?"

"Look, no offense, but I don't believe in God. I'm an atheist."

"For real, religion's for fakers." I never met any one before who just came right out and said it. It sounds so liberating hearing it out loud. Like his mind is free to think and do whatever he wants. He doesn't answer to anyone, not even God.

"So, what's up with the book?"

"I don't know. Guess I'm just curious. It's so crazy how so many different people believe in different things. Everybody thinks what they believe in is gonna bring them salvation, but nobody really knows. Do they?"

"Of course not. Look, religion is just a way for crooks to snatch more money out your pocket. Even if I believed in God, there's no way I would follow any religion that told me I had to cough up a bunch of cash to get into heaven."

"Oh no, you got him started again," one of the girls says.

"You've awakened the anti-Christ," one of the guys laughs.

"I'm no anti-Christ. I just don't choose to believe a bunch of stories man made up to help him cope with life. I don't believe in Santa Claus or the Easter Bunny either."

"Then how do you explain the creation of the universe?" the same guy asks.

"I don't. Hey, I'm man enough to admit I don't know how the universe was created. The big bang theory seems the most probable explanation, but I really don't know. But just 'cause I don't know doesn't mean I'm gonna make up some god to explain things away. That would mean I was no more advanced than our ancient ancestors who created gods to explain simple scientific phenomenon like rain, fire and the rising of the sun."

A girl with stringy red hair and freckles challenges him. "I don't care what you say. Science can't explain the perfection of our world. Everything just works too perfect. How do ants know how to build colonies, how do birds know how to fly back to their mating grounds year after year, how do we have the capacity to love and feel sorrow? And what about gravity? Science can't explain that."

"Sure it can. Evolution, adaptation, natural selection, it all makes perfect sense. Even the most basic life forms have the ability to do amazing things like change the structure of their bodies, organize into colonies, even reproduce without a partner. Anything they have to do to survive. And if you're not tough enough to survive, you don't make it, period. I don't think a higher power has anything to do with it, it's just the way nature works."

143

"That's my whole point," she persists. "Things don't just happen, they happen for a reason. It's not just nature, it's God. He created this world so that the animals could learn how to survive. How else can you explain the complexity involved in even a single cell. Each cell in every person or plant on earth runs like a well oiled machine. That has to be by design. Evolution is just too random."

"Oh right, intelligent design, the *Bible* says that God created the Earth to be perfect, right. So, if he did create all these creatures, why didn't he just make them perfect to begin with? Doesn't it make more sense that these creatures evolved over millions of years to learn how to survive in their environments?"

"He's right." I jump into the debate. "If God created Earth don't you have to ask where he came from. I mean did he have a mother and father? Is there a race of gods out there who go around creating universes?"

"Good point, Cara." Mike smiles, but everyone else just stares at me. "You know we could argue about this all day, but we need get back to work."

He starts commanding again, "John, you got the ladder? Tanya's in charge of clean up detail. B.J., you'll be coming to the carpet store with me later." He's obviously destined to be some great captain of industry or the president or something.

It's not the last time the subject of religion comes up. We debate many topics throughout the day from religion to global warming to our dependence on oil. Everyone gets to state their opinion. They argue passionately, even waving fingers and raising voices at times, but it's all in good fun. If this is what college is gonna be like I can't wait, sitting around debating the crucial issues of the world. I never had conversations like this with Crystal and Jennifer.

"Where you been all day?" Jim asks when I get back to the hotel.

"I met some kids at the coffee shop down the street. They do volunteer work in the community. I was helping them paint houses for Habitat for Humanities."

"Is that right?" He circles around me like a vulture, inspecting and sniffing. "Well, you ain't been smokin'. You don't look like you been drinkin'.""

"I told you where I was."

"I wanna believe you, Cara, but you know you have a track record."

"Whatever."

He keep looks me over like a TV detective investigating a crime scene. "You have paint on your jeans."

"Duh, I told you I've been painting all day. I'm going back again tomorrow. We have a lot of work to do on the houses." I'm not used to Jim sweating me about coming and going. Guess he's trying to do the right thing. "I'll be over there all day."

"Building houses, huh. That's a noble cause. Have you eaten?"

"We had pizza over there I'm stuffed. I'm going to the hot tub. My arms feel like spaghetti from painting so much."

"It's good to see you doin' something to help others."

Luckily, nobody's at the hot tub. I submerge completely, leaving only my mouth and nose above water and let my senses drown in the turbulent water. All I can think about is Mike. I did everything to catch his attention today, but all he wanted to do was talk about religion and stuff.

"Hi."

A small voice startles me and water splashes everywhere when I jerk my head out the water. It's the girl from the front desk. "Sorry, did I get you wet? I'm Cara. I would shake your hand, but I'm all wet." I'm careful to keep my arms and legs in the water so she can't see my scratches.

"It's okay. My name is Sarah."

"You coming in?"

"Oh no, I could never expose myself like that. Not in mixed company."

"What mixed company?"

"The men here. Father would never allow it, neither would Allah. That's one thing you should know about Islam. You do want to know about Islam, don't you?"

"Yes, I do."

"The *Qur'an*, that's our *Bible*, demands that we are modest in our appearance so we can avoid any temptations. We are not allowed to expose our head, legs, upper arms or the shape of our bodies. When I'm not in school, I'm not allowed to be around any men unless one of my family members is present."

"Really? How do you feel about that?"

"It's hard sometimes, but I understand. Men can be cruel when it comes to temptation and I don't want to risk losing respect. My family would be shamed if I were not a virgin on my wedding night."

"You mean you're gonna wait 'til you get married. Even if you met a boy you really love and he really loves you, would you still wait?"

"Yes, of course. No matter how much I want to. I could never shame my family." She pauses. "I want to ask you something, but I am embarrassed."

"Go ahead, you won't offend me."

"Have you done it with a boy?"

"Yes. I thought I was in love."

"And your family, do they know, have you been shamed?"

"Things don't exactly work like that in my family. I'm allowed to be around boys alone so it's easier to hide things. Anyway, my father wouldn't feel shame if he knew."

"What is it like, being with a boy?"

"It feels good when you're doing it, but when you're done," the words get stuck in my throat. "Just make sure you do it with someone you love and make sure they really love you, too. I mean for real, not just pretend."

"I won't have to worry about that. I'll be married. If it is as good as you say I can wait. Then I will have the rest of my life to enjoy that special time with my husband."

"So, no private time with boys, huh. What else don't you guys do?"

"We believe in living a clean and pure life as it says in the *Qur'an*. We don't eat impure meat like pork or drink alcohol, we believe in giving to those less fortunate than ourselves, we pray to Allah and respect that he controls all that happens. There is a saying in the *Qur'an*, "Whatever good happens to you is from Allah and whatever evil happens is from yourself."

"That doesn't seem fair."

"Sure it does when you think about it. If you steal from people or do drugs and alcohol bad things will happen to you. But if you follow the ways of Allah you will avoid the evils of the world and experience only the good. I have to go now. It's time for prayer."

"Thanks for talking to me. Have a good night."

"Thank you, you too."

What she said makes sense. If I wasn't out there drinking and smoking with Tommy I would've never been in the position for Jessie to do what he did to me. I am ultimately responsible for what happens to me. If I was living a clean and pure life I would've been okay.

Just when I almost convince myself to convert to Islam an image of Mike and his biceps pops into my head. I couldn't hang out tomorrow with my new friends if I was Muslim. I like the covering up part, a built in excuse to hide my scars. But no way I'm taking Jim with me everywhere I go. Plus, you have to pray five times a day every day of the week. That makes sense, too. It's hard to get in trouble when you focus so much time on God, but it's so much sacrifice. How are you ever gonna have any fun if you avoid everything that's not good for you? There's got to be a better way. Anyway, I'm not giving up my bacon.

I try to spend as much time with Mike as I can the next day at the project site. I don't know why I want him to like me so much, but I do. It doesn't even matter. He reminds me he has a girlfriend every time I try to flirt. One of the other girls sees how hard I'm trying and tells me it's no use. They've all tried before. He's totally committed. Isn't it ironic the atheist has more moral back bone than any boy I know? He spends his free time helping people and he's the only boy I ever met that showed any respect for women. If I had come on to any of the boys in Philly like I came on to Mike, I'd a been back at the hotel with a six pack of beer and my shirt over my head before I knew what hit me.

Shame is my blanket as I lie in bed trying to fall asleep. What the hell is wrong with me? Why couldn't I have been more like Sarah or Jennifer or Crystal? Maybe Jim's right. Why is it so easy for me to give into temptation? I wonder what Sarah would think of me if she knew what a drunk slut I've been. No wonder Mike didn't want me, he must've been able to smell the skank on me. No good boy wants a girl who's been used and worked over.

Chapter 16

We leave the hotel early in the morning. I wanna say goodbye to Sarah, but she's not around. It's probably for the best. I'm too unclean to be her friend.

We pick up another load of lumber and we're back on the road. Jim says we're going to some place called Hope, New Mexico. Hope, please, all I see is flat Texas highway.

We polish off our box of doughnuts in record time this morning, raspberry jelly with the white powder topping, but we mutually agree around eleven that we're ready for an early lunch. The first place we see is a no frills diner, dusty and rustic. I insist on a booth near the front window, so I can watch the wind twist the dust into tiny little tornados. Jim orders a standard scrambled eggs and bacon breakfast, but I go for the cheeseburger, fries and coke combo.

I don't know why I'm so hungry. You'd think I'd be worried about how huge my butt's getting, but I don't care. I don't even mind the flies bouncing off the window, desperately seeking the fresh air outside. It's just me and my burger.

"Damn Jews," I hear a grumbling voice over Jim's coffee slurping and the buzz of fly wings.

"Settle down, Nick," the man behind the counter warns. "We got customers in here."

"Right, sorry, I don't mean to get worked up. I'm just tired of havin' everything I read shaped by the media. Why can't they just tell it like it is? There used to be a time you could pick up the paper and get the truth, not just some Jew slant on things. You know the Jews control the media. They control everything."

"Yeah, I know, I know." The counter man rolls his eyes like he's heard it a thousand times before.

"You know they think they're the chosen people," the man continues to grumble.

He reminds me of a stereotypical, cruel, southern redneck, the kind that would've been comfortable as a slave master in a past life. Maybe he screamed at Rosa Parks to get off the bus.

"All high and mighty, like they run the world. They don't even believe in Jesus. Now that's just un-American."

"You gotta admit, Nick, most of 'em are angels next to you."

"Hey, Jesus already died for my sins. I figure that gives me a free ride to sin all I want."

"You goin' to hell for sure, Nick."

"What does he mean the Jews think they're the chosen people?" I ask Jim.

"What?" he grunts, too caught up in his eggs for conversation.

"He said the Jews think they're the chosen people. What did he mean?"

"I wouldn't pay too much attention to him if I were you. He sounds pretty ignorant."

"I know. It's just that I've heard people say that before. Why do they say that about the Jews?"

"I'm not exactly sure, but I think it has something to do with their belief that God picked them as his favorite people, the chosen ones who will receive eternal salvation."

"Really, what about everyone else?"

"I guess we're all just damned to burn in hell," Jim laughs.

"That's pretty ignorant. No wonder everybody hates them. But, you know, they're not the only ones who say if you don't believe in what we believe in, you're going to hell. Christians believe you can't get into heaven unless you accept Jesus as your savior."

"That's true."

"So, what's the difference?"

"I don't know. That's just how some people think. What does it matter? People believe all sorts of things. You know better than to blindly follow what other people say. I know you're smarter than that."

"I know. I used to do that a lot. I believed whatever they told me, at church or in school."

"A lot of things in this world don't make sense. You just have to do what you think is right. Come on, let's get outta here. We've got a lot of road to cover."

I like to lean my head out the window and stare at the sky as we cruise down the road. I love it when one of those huge birds goes gracefully gliding by. Jim reminds me that close up those beautiful, majestic looking birds are actually nasty, old buzzards waiting for an opportunity to suck the last remnants of life off some worn out carcass. They're still beautiful to me.

How great it must be to fly across the sky. Could anything in the world make me feel more free? Maybe I'll turn Hindu and be reincarnated as an eagle. That'd be better than a lizard. I'd be on top of the food chain. But eating mice and snakes, gross. Maybe a sea hawk. It'd be like eating sushi.

Jim can be funny when he lightens up. He has all these crazy stories about things he's seen on the road. Like the time he opened the door of the truck to find a naked, wrinkled, old woman sleeping in the front seat. He almost froze to death when he was stuck for hours in a blizzard with no heat. He's been robbed at gun point, stranded in the middle of a wild elk stampede, and he swears he's seen a U.F.O.

"I have a surprise for you," he says out of nowhere. "We've only got about an hour to go before we get to Hope, but we're gonna make a stop along the way."

I can't believe how quickly the time passed. We've been driving for hours. "Oh yeah. Where?"

"Ever hear of Carlsbad Caverns?"

"Carlsbad Caverns, yeah, I think I remember seeing something about that on TV. It's like this huge cave with all these stalactites and stalagmites, right?"

"Stalagmites?"

"You know, they're formations of rock that form over millions of years by condensation in the caves."

"If you say so."

"Anyway, they're beautiful."

"You wanna go?"

"Of course."

"Good. We're almost at the cavern entrance. We've been makin' good time."

The cavern is deep and dark with amazing rock sculptures reaching upward from the floor and dropping down from the roof. Some of them make thick white columns that glisten from moisture in the artificial light. Others look like icicles dripping into an upside down jagged mountain range of red, orange, brown, yellow and white.

They say bats live throughout the cave, but I know I won't see any. They pretty much sleep during the day. I feel sorry for them being blind and all, but I guess they make up for it with their sonar. That must be crazy, sensing everything around you without actually seeing it. But they fly around the caves at incredible speeds and never slam into the walls, evolved to navigate their surroundings perfectly. Since there's no light down here there's no reason for them to use their eyes. It makes perfect sense.

I used to believe God didn't give bats sight because they didn't need it. But if God created all creatures to fit in his perfect world, why didn't he make it so the bats could see even better in the dark? Like some kind of infra red vision or something. Bats needed to survive in a pitch dark environment, so they developed a sense of sonar. It's so much more logical. One step follows another and everything falls in line. God has nothing to do with it.

Jim has another surprise for me as we approach Hope. Instead of staying at a hotel, we're gonna stay on an Apache Indian reservation.

He has an old friend who lives there. I don't mind the hotels but this is gonna be sweet, something different. I have visions of weathered, old Indians wearing elaborate cow hide costumes, singing and dancing around huge bon fires. The reality is much different. They dress just like we do, but with a southwestern twist, lots of cowboy hats and boots. Everything else looks pretty much the same as any small town we've driven through. They even have a casino.

Jim explains all about the casinos on the way in. How the man stuck the Indians out on these reservations and forgot about them. When they found a way to make a decent living through the casinos, the government started bugging them about paying taxes. Why can't the man just leave them alone? I mean, didn't they put them on reservations because they didn't want anything to do with them? I'm happy the Indians have their casinos. They finally got to stick it to the man.

I was prepared to sleep in a tee pee or at least a tent under the open stars, but the hotel is nothing like that. It's not as nice as some of the others, but we're definitely not roughing it. Guess I should actually call it a lodge. That's what the sign out front says, a hint that you're staying in a hotel with just the bare essentials. It's cool, like I'm staying in an authentic log cabin, except for all the animal skins and heads mounted on the walls. They really give me the creeps.

"Jim, my old friend, welcome back." A tall Indian approaches us in the lobby with his hand stretched out.

"Jake, what's up, buddy?" They shake hands and give each other a quick man hug. "Jake, this is my daughter, Cara. Cara, Jake or you can call him Little Eagle. He's one of the tribal elders."

"Nice to meet you," I nervously stick out my hand. Elder? This guy looks like he could be my older brother. He's tall with beautiful reddish, brown skin and thick, flowing black hair. From his boots to his oversize belt buckle to his cowboy hat perfectly curved up on the sides, he's the Malboro Man come to life with an awesome tan.

"So what brings you back, Jim?"

"We're just passin' through on our way to Cara's grandparents in California. You know I couldn't roll through without looking you up."

"Good. We have a lot of catching up to do. You're just in time for dinner," Little Eagle says.

"Sounds good," Jim replies.

"Cara, nice to meet you. I hope you enjoy your stay here." Little Eagle smiles at me. I prefer to call him by his Indian name. It sounds more authentic. "You don't want to miss dinner tonight. We're having fresh venison."

"Venison, isn't that deer meat?" I ask Jim.

"Yep, and don't give me that face. It's good, you'll see."

I don't wanna think about eating Bambi so I drop the subject. We go to the room, drop off our bags, quickly wash up and we're ready for dinner. Fresh Bambi, ugh, maybe I'll just eat the veggies. I'm starving.

They serve everybody cafeteria style in a big dining hall filled with large wooden tables. The food is spread out like they're welcoming the pilgrims for the first Thanksgiving feast. There's a bowl with an assortment of beans, diced peppers and corn, a pan with some kind of brown rice with onions, carrots and peppers, big ears of corn grilled in the shucks, and in the center a huge bowl of stew filled with big chunks of meat. That must be Bambi.

I walk through the line, my eyes fixed on the center bowl. The timidly sweet smiling women plop a scoop of everything on my plate. I shake my head when I get to the center bowl, but they hit me with a scoop before I can refuse it. There he is, Bambi, sliced up in a sweet smelling brown sauce in the middle of my plate.

"What's the matter?" Jim catches me staring at my plate. "It's just meat, Cara. Just like any other meat. You don't have a problem chowin' down on all those dead cow burgers you love so much."

I hate to admit it, but he's right. Can't be a hypocrite. Dead animal is dead animal. I shouldn't discriminate just 'cause one is cuter than the other. It's not like they're killing the deer just for fun. They only kill what they need to feed their families. I slice a small piece off one of the big chunks. It smells good. The sauce is sweet and hot at the same time. The meat tastes like steak only wilder, like

154

I know I'm eating something that was once alive.

After dinner we all go down to a roaring bonfire they made in the center of camp. Jim sits next to me on a huge log and he teaches me how to roast marshmallows for our smores. It's harder than it looks, placing them close enough to feel the heat but not get burned. Watching the Apache kids play automatically relaxes me. How can I be stressed looking at some three year old twirl around and around until he falls down dizzy? I almost get up and join the kids dancing around the fire, bouncing up and down to the beat of an old man thumping on a crude drum. It's all so tribal. I am one with nature. I wanna howl at the moon.

Everyone gathers around the fire as one of the tribal elders tells stories of how his ancestors once roamed free across this land until the Spaniards and Europeans invaded their homes and stole everything. He talks about the buffalo that used to graze freely and the battles his ancestors had with the great beast. He speaks with great respect and admiration about the animal, like it's human, a worthy opponent defeated in honorable competition. He describes some of the tribal dances to celebrate the kill. Some of the kids give us a sample, but you can tell they're still learning.

The lodge guests are nice enough, but their chatter bores me to death. "Where are you from? How long are you staying?" Blah, blah, blah. I try to ignore them, but Jim has diarrhea of the mouth. He attracts them like flies. I move closer to the fire, let the heat close my eyes, and rock back and forth to the rhythm of the drum beat.

After a while the tourist crowd and most of the little kids fade away. Jim disappears somewhere with Little Eagle. I'm left in the circle with three of the men and an older woman. The old woman starts singing, but it's more like she's wailing a sad, slow beautiful cry. I can't understand a word she's saying, but one of the men tells me it's about a woman who lost her warrior husband in battle. The song brings back hard memories. She sings a few more songs, each one more melancholy than the last. One is a hunting song, another is about one of their great chiefs, and one they sing as a prayer to their gods for a good harvest. They all sound like they're about death and loneliness to me.

"Why do they call you Red Hawk?" I ask one of the tribesmen. I know real Indians take their names very seriously. They don't just pick some name out of the air like Bob or Jane. It has to mean something to them, something special in their lives.

"On the day of my birth my mother saw a red hawk in the sky. We honor the hawk as one of our brothers in nature. So, I was to be Red Hawk."

"It's a beautiful name, you know, strong. I love Indian names."

"Thank you, but I am not an Indian. That's the white man's word. I am Native American. Don't forget, my people were here long before Christopher Columbus or any of the others."

"I'm sorry. I didn't know. What's your Native American name?" I ask the man with the drum sitting next to him, quick to redeem my offense.

"It's okay, as long as you are willing to learn. I am Runs With Deer for my skill in hunting."

The last man anticipates my question. He has the deepest voice I've ever heard. "I am Screaming Bear because my father had a vision of me and a bear howling at the moon, as if we were brothers. The people say I carry the strength of the bear in my words."

"And what shall we call you?" the old woman says. "Lift your head. Let me see your face."

I tilt my head upward. The heat of the fire burns my face. She looks deep into my eyes. Like she's trying to see inside me.

"Cries Inside. You will be called Cries Inside." She looks at me with sympathetic eyes.

She can see right through me.

"What makes you so sad?" she asks.

"My mother died this past summer. I can't remember feeling right since then."

"You have suffered a great loss," she pauses. "You must never forget her, but you must learn to let her go. She belongs to the spirit world now. Her spirit can not rest easy knowing she is causing you such pain. You must let her go."

156

She must be some kind of psychic, Native American witch doctor lady to know me so well. Witch doctor or not, her advice makes sense. I don't know if Mom is part of a spirit world or looking down on me from heaven or whatever, but I'm not taking any chances. She has to rest in peace. But how can I let her go if I never forget her? Won't she be with me whenever I think about her?

"Do you believe in God?" I change the subject before I get too sad.

"We believe in a power that created the Earth and spirits who look over our crops and tribe."

"And what about the *Bible*, do you believe in that?"

"No, that is the white man's history. Our history has been passed down through our tribal traditions. Our bible is the wind."

"You mean it's all just passed down by word of mouth?"

"Is that so different from your beliefs? Are your traditions not the words of white men written in books? Our traditions are granted to us by our ancestors, passed down by generation after generation of loyal Apache."

"What about when you die? Do you go to heaven?"

"We are joined with our ancestors in the spirit world, just as you will be reunited with your mother when your spirit passes."

We talk in front of the fire until it's faded into a pile of glowing, orange embers. I learn about their warrior tradition and how the Apache were famous for their fierce bravery in battle. They were once a strong, powerful tribe, but they were simply outnumbered. I could listen to her talk until the sun comes up, but when the old woman decides to go to sleep we all follow her lead.

I spend a lot of time with the old woman the next day. We walk all around the reservation at a slow, steady pace. She's in great shape for her age or any other age. She doesn't even get winded when we climb steep hills like the one we take to the sacred burial grounds. She just walks and talks, telling me about the great chiefs and warriors that are buried here and the spirits who watch over and guide the tribe.

I learn about the binding spirit that runs through all of nature.

157

How we are all connected by the Great Spirit, alive in everything that walks the earth, swims in the sea or flies in the sky. Even the smallest insect deserves respect as a brother in nature. He shares a connection with the Great Spirit.

There are also spirits that control the weather, the oceans, the sun and stars, death and the underworld, and the animals. There's this big bear spirit that rules over all the bears on earth. They pretty much have a spirit for everything. It's kind of primitive like the ancient Greeks, but I guess it's really the same concept. I mean if you believe that there's a higher power that created the earth it's not too much of a stretch to believe there can be more than one god or spirit.

It's crazy. I could understand when people prayed to gods because they didn't understand how nature worked. The Romans thought the sun rose because it was carried across the sky on chariots driven by gods. If lightning struck, it was because they angered the gods. Entire cultures were based on appeasing the gods. But now with science and everything, how could anybody believe a prayer to some harvest spirit can bring in strong crops? If you're a farmer, you better learn something about weather patterns and the science of growing stuff.

It's a pretty cool idea, having respect for nature and all living things. Kind of like how Buddhism teaches respect for all living things. When I stand in the middle of a wide open space and stare up at the canopy of stars I know I'm just a little part of something so much greater. I think about the awesome forces of nature; hurricanes, tornados, earthquakes, floods, and fires that destroy millions of dollars of property and take thousands of lives while man stands by powerless. Nature is nature. Why are we so arrogant to believe we can understand or control it?

I don't see Jim again until dinner. I'm happy to see it's chicken tonight. I came to terms with the idea of eating Bambi, but I'd rather not.

"I heard you made a new friend today, kiddo."

"Yeah, she taught me a lot about the Apaches. They're an

incredible people. Thanks for bringing me here."

"No sweat. Glad to see you're havin' a good time."

"So where have you been all day?"

"Jake was showin' me around. They've got a pretty good set up here."

"Yeah, I can't wait for the fire tonight."

"It should be great. Some of the men are gonna do a traditional war dance."

I'm mesmerized by the dance, men twirling and stomping to the rhythm of pounding drums and wailing voices. The bonfire, twice as big as the one last night, glows off the spinning warriors' skin. They shimmer and shine like they're covered in gold. I love their elaborate head gear filled with a rainbow of colorful feathers, flowing down their backs almost to the ground. They hoot and yell strong, guttural exclamations of their manhood while thrusting their shields high in the air. Before they're done everybody's hollering. I can't help but get caught up in it. I never thought I'd find myself sitting next to Jim howling at the moon, but here we are underneath all the stars in the universe bonded together by nature.

After the dance most of the men retreat to their tribal meeting. I learn from eavesdropping on the women's conversations that the tribal meeting is actually less about discussing the well being of the tribe and more about seeing who can drink the most whiskey. No wonder Jim's so popular here. At least he hung out with me for a while.

Some of the older kids pick up the drums the men leave behind and one of the younger girls takes out a wooden flute. I'm not expecting much from such a young kid, but she starts to play a beautiful melody. The other kids join in perfect time with the drums. The young boys imitate the warrior dance and the girls dance in a circle off to the side. I feel one of the cute, little girls tug at my shirt. She wants me to dance with them. I can't resist her big, brown eyes.

The constant beat of the drums frees my body. It's better than any drug I ever tried. Nothing bad can penetrate this vibe; no heavy thoughts, no bad memories, no flashbacks of my past mistakes. It's just me, the beat, the fire, the stars and the children spinning and twirling, claiming all of nature as our own.

I'm reluctant to wake up the next morning 'cause I know it's time to go. We have breakfast in the dining hall before we take off. Little Eagle's there. He and Jim are obviously hung over from their "tribal meeting". They just smile and grunt at each other over especially large cups of coffee. The old woman comes in the side door and goes into the kitchen. I wouldn't feel right if I left without saying goodbye to her.

"Hi." I creek open the swivel doors leading to the kitchen.

"Good morning." She looks at me with a sweet smile.

"Good morning. We're leaving in a few minutes."

"Yes, I know. I wish you safe travels. May the spirits keep you away from harm."

"Thank you for teaching me about your ways."

"Thank you for listening."

"You never told me your given name?"

She stops picking at the assortment of beans she has neatly divided into piles in front of her and walks towards me. "I am Forever Weeping. I lost my only son at birth and I have been barren ever since. Now you understand. I see you carry the pain in your eyes. We must be strong for each other, Cries Inside. I will pray that your spirit remains strong."

I want to say I'll pray for her spirit too, but I can't form words. So I smile, look into her eyes and wonder if she'll always be so sad. As we drive away, waving to the children playing along the road side, my mind can't shake the depth of sadness in her eyes. Will the sadness remain in my eyes until I'm old and gray? Will I be forever weeping?

Chapter 17

Jim's way too hung over to talk much on our way to Las Vegas. I hate leaving the reservation, but I'll reconnect with Mother Nature when I get to Grandma's. Two days in Vegas, another concrete jungle, no doubt. I ask Jim if we can just skip it and head straight to Grandma's, but he insists we have to stay two days. At least I get to see the Grand Canyon on the way.

"Do we have to listen to that?" Some guy on talk radio is whining about gays in the military.

"You can turn it," he grunts.

Just as I'm about to hit seek the voice on the radio says, "Improve your life and achieve spiritual freedom. Our next guest is one of the world's most renowned authorities on Scientology."

"Scientology, what's that?" I ask Jim.

"I think it's some kind of religion. A bunch of movie stars are into it."

"Oh yeah, which ones?"

"I can't remember, some famous actor."

"Okay, let me hear what they're saying."

"Tell our audience. What is Scientology?" The processed radio voice asks.

"Scientology is a study of the truth," a strong voice replies in the tone of a salesman at a carnival game booth. "It explores man's capacity to unleash his unlimited capabilities. You see, Scientology believes in man's ability to solve his own problems, accomplish his goals, and gain lasting happiness by following scientifically proven auditing procedures to explore the source of your unwanted spiritual conditions and increase your awareness of existence."

"What the hell is this guy talkin' about?" Jim smirks.

"Shhh, this is interesting."

"You gotta be kiddin' me."

"Shhhhh."

"It explores your unconscious mind, those deep rooted thoughts that block your happiness," the salesman continues. "Scientology's dynamic philosophy will help you erase negative influences that depress your ability to enjoy your life to its fullest."

"That sounds deep," I think out loud.

"Yeah, knee deep in a load of crap," Jim adds.

"Shhhhh."

"First you must understand *Dianetics,* the only way to truly free yourself." He sounds like he's winding up to deliver an infomercial pitch. "*Dianetics*, it's a no nonsense guide to self awareness that will help you fight depression, achieve your goals and realize your most cherished dreams. You can get a copy at your local book store or you can simply call our 800 number and we'll send you the key to unlocking your inner spirit immediately."

"There's the money grab," Jim laughs.

"I don't know? It could be for real. I mean I think we should be more in touch with our inner selves instead of looking to God to solve all our problems."

"That's fine, Cara, but these guys are all about snatching the money out your pocket. Do you really need to give some organization a bunch of money to figure out why your life is screwed up? It's no secret you're gonna feel a little down if you lose your job or your wife leaves you or whatever. Explore the source of your unhappiness, give me a break. Don't you think most people already know why they're unhappy?"

"That's true."

"So why give some joker all your money just to tell you something you already know?"

"Maybe this guy is offering something more."

"Like what?"

"I don't know. Hope, maybe, something to believe in. The same thing any other religion is serving up I guess. At least this guy says they have a scientific method. You don't have to just blindly believe in something you have no proof of and you can't see."

"Hope shouldn't have to cost you an arm and a leg."

"That's true too. How much longer 'til we get to Vegas?"

"We've got a long haul, kiddo. We'll get to Vegas around nine or ten."

"At night?"

"Yeah."

"When are we going to the Grand Canyon?"

"Oh man, that's right. No big deal. We can spend the night at the canyon, take a good look in the morning and head out around noon. I'll lose a day, but that's okay."

We're lucky to get a hotel room in Grand Canyon Village. The lady at the desk says we would've had to book in advance if we came in the spring. We're both really tired so we crash pretty hard when we hit our beds.

I wake up the next morning well rested, bugging the hell out of Jim to take me to the canyon. It was too dark when we drove in to see a thing. The view is nice, wide open space spattered with patches of unthawed snow, but I don't see anything special from the hotel window. Nothing special on the drive from the hotel to the canyon site.

"You're about to see something amazing." Jim's smiling from ear to ear as we walk from the shuttle bus to the viewpoint.

"Yeah, I bet its all hype."

Unbelievable. I literally lose my breath when my eyes break the horizon of the parking lot and I get my first peek at the canyon. It's so, so big. I don't know how I'll ever be able to describe this place to anyone. I'm totally mesmerized. We spend hours walking around the

163

trail that circles the canyon's rim. I hold on to Jim's arm, maybe 'cause it's cold, maybe 'cause I feel closer to him than ever before. I barely even notice the other tourists meandering about in their own trances. Each few steps bring twists and turns leading to a new amazing view of the canyon.

"What you smilin' at," Jim says with a confused look on his face. He's not used to me smiling at him.

"Nothing. Thanks for bringing me here. It's the most amazing place on earth."

"It is pretty cool. Now you see why I couldn't describe it to you in words."

A park ranger explains how the canyon was formed by the slow carving Colorado River over millions of years. It's crazy to think about. They say God created the Earth and man in his image, but the Earth is millions and millions of years old and archeologists say man didn't show up on the scene until about 200,000 years ago. So, why the huge gap? Why would God create the Earth then wait millions of years before he made man? The dinosaurs roamed the Earth millions of years before man ever showed up. Did God create the Earth for the dinosaurs, then destroy them Sodom and Gomorra style and replace them with man.? Maybe the dinosaurs were God's first chosen creatures.

The idea of an asteroid taking out the dinosaurs and mammals rising up over millions of years, turning into cave men and eventually into us, makes a lot of sense. There's a complete fossil record of all those amazing, extinct creatures and the timelines match up. But it's just an idea based on historical records. Just like Christians and Muslims base their ideas on the *Bible* or the *Qur'an*, the historical records of their people. There's no way to know for sure who's right. Guess I'll just enjoy the view.

Jim practically has to pry me off the guard rail when it's time to go. I wanna stay for the sunset, but I know he has to deliver his load before dark. We get to this warehouse just outside of Vegas in time for Jim to handle his business. He's babbling on about all the great hotels and things to do in Vegas when he steps back into the truck.

Guess he caught a second wind. I just stare at the sun slipping behind a distant mountain range. I can't help thinking of Forever Weeping, her loss and all the spirits that live in the sky.

My stomach sours as the wide open space in my windshield is littered by strip malls, gas stations and convenient stores. Back to the concrete jungle. I miss the reservation already. It's like deja vu when we finally turn on to the famous Las Vegas strip. I recognize all the hotels from TV, but they're much more impressive up close. Everything's so big, it's crazy. There's the one with the huge Sphinx in front, the one with the Statue of Liberty and the one with the exploding volcano. Everybody's got a gimmick. No Holiday Inns here, for sure. We're staying at the one that looks like a castle.

There's a beautifully decorated tree in the front lobby and big, red bows everywhere, but it doesn't feel like Christmas. From the time we step through the door, to the wait in the check in line, until we get in the elevator, the persistent ringing of slot machines invades my ears. Maybe I can pretend they're jingle bells. I want to explore, but Jim reminds me I'm too young to gamble.

As he drags me through the cosmopolitan crowd, I realize people from all over the world come to Vegas. A group of kids with piercings and dyed hair passes by and I know I'll have no problem disappearing into this world. Everyone is welcome here.

Jim insists we hit what he says is the greatest buffet on the strip before we even go to our room. We wait in this long winding line for half an hour before we're finally seated. It better be good. We could've had McDonalds by now.

The buffet is so big I can't tell where it begins or ends. They have everything; prime rib, pizza, pasta, fried fish and chicken, pork chops, turkey and dressing, macaroni and cheese, all kinds of veggies, a huge salad bar, crab legs and shrimp, and a whole section with Chinese food and sushi. I pile my plate with as much as I can fit. Jim keeps reminding me I can go back, but I can't hear him. I'm on a feeding frenzy. Oh my God, I didn't even notice the dessert bar. A whole section of the room devoted to cakes, pies, candies and ice cream. They even have two fountains with white and dark chocolate

165

continuously flowing from the beaks of two golden swans.

I can barely hear Jim's voice over the symphony of clanging plates, scattered voices and munching, grazing herds. We're a swarm of gluttonous beasts and I'm the leader. I fall back into my chair and discretely unsnap the top button of my jeans. I don't want another bite, but chocolate truffles have the ultimate power.

We rub our bellies and smile at each other, proud of our pile of empty plates. I'm looking forward to stretching out in the room, maybe playing some cards, then checking out the hotels together later. But Jim has to go meet up with an old friend. He says I should be in bed by eleven and threatens to check in on me. Yeah, right, same old Jim. I shouldn't be surprised. This is sin city. People don't really change.

The hotel has four floors of amazing shops and entertainment. I could imagine I'm walking down an authentic medieval village road, except for the blatant commercialism. I'm pretty sure Gucci didn't sell handbags on the street corners back then. They even have an authentic jousting dinner show. I peek inside a huge arena and see two men in full knight's armor sitting on colorfully decorated horses charge at each other across a big dirt floor. The hostess and all the servers are dressed in medieval gear. This is more like the days of Robin Hood. The hostess asks me if I want to be seated so I decide to leave, but I've gotta talk Jim into going tomorrow night since we're gonna be here two days. There's a magic show, too, in the main lounge. One of those famous illusionist guys I've seen on TV. So much to see and so little time.

It's almost eleven, but so what. Time to explore the famous Las Vegas strip. Everything looks totally different against the dark of night. Each casino boasts a dazzling light display that reaches high into the sky. Looking down the street, an electric light parade overwhelms my senses. I've never seen a concrete jungle look so alive.

I walk up and down the streets for hours staring at the lights, watching the erupting volcano and dancing water show and popping in and out of hotels. I get lost in the maze of multi-colored carpet and endless slot machines in every casino. They're all the same, but each has its own thing, transporting me into a fantasy in a different part of the world at a different place in time. The Mirage has these incredible albino tigers in the lobby and a full size aquarium with sharks. The New York hotel has a rollercoaster on top right next to the Statue of Liberty. It really feels like I'm walking down a city street inside that one. Cesar's Palace has these huge sculptures that look like they're right out of my history book. I wish Jim was here.

This is truly the city that never sleeps. I wander among the herds of people in the casinos and on the streets, but nobody says a thing or even notices I'm alive. I'm just here. I close my eyes and pretend the bustle of passing people is really the twirling and hollering of Apache kids. I'm dancing, hand to hand in their circle. I feel a part of something again until the bump of a passing tourist brings me back to reality.

It's two in the morning when I get back to the room, according to the digital alarm clock on the night table. My feet throb from all the walking. Jim's not here, but I can fall asleep thinking of my stay with the Apaches and all the cool things I've seen tonight.

I only remember bits and pieces of the nightmare. It was Jessie again and Tommy. Each one had one of my wrists and I was hanging off a cliff, naked. They must've dropped me because I felt like I was falling when I wake up sweating. Jim's tossing in his sleep. I want to tell him, but he's no help to me now. He has too many of his own demons to fight. I feel like scratching, so I do.

I don't dare go back to sleep, so I spend most of the morning at the pool. It's almost five and the sun's just starting to rise. There's not many people around. Guess the party animals are just getting into bed. I enjoy the time away from the crowds, reading my book on a reclining pool chair near an artificial waterfall, relaxed by the sound of falling water.

Chapter eight outlines how religion helps fulfill man's four basic needs. First, man needs to believe in some kind of life after death. From our earliest ancestors mankind has held beliefs that there is more to being human than just our flesh and bones. We have an innate desire to feel like our soul, the real essence of who we are, will live forever. The book says belief in an afterlife also helps us deal with grief. It's an internal mechanism that allows a mother to bury her child and live on with some solace that they'll be reunited in the afterlife.

Second, people need religion to turn to when they're in desperate times or facing circumstances that are out of their control. When natural disasters occur, the only way mankind can cope with such a loss of control is to turn to a higher power that controls the elements man fears so much. According to the book, man believes that if he can appease the higher power then he has some control over the elements or any other aspect of life he feels is out of his control.

Third, the book claims religion serves as the ultimate companion to people who are truly lonely. When people need a shoulder to lean on and they have no where else to turn, they can always find a place with God. Neighborhood churches provide a sanctuary for millions who feel they have nowhere else to turn. It allows man to feel like he is never truly alone.

Fourth, religion provides a strong sense of community. Churches have brought like minded people together for centuries. They form social bonds and create an environment that offers a safe haven from a sin filled world, especially for families.

The book makes sense. Man made up religion to help cope with life. Religion offers hope and companionship. When all else is lost you can always turn to God. Guess nobody wants to be alone.

Jim's scrambling around the room when I get back.

"You eat yet, kiddo."

"Yeah, like hours ago."

"You got up early this morning, huh? Well it's only one o'clock. That's early in Vegas time."

"Yeah, right."

"You should've seen me last night. I was on fire. I thought the dealer was gonna cry."

"Black jack?"

"Yep. I'm on a roll. Can't wait to get back out there. I'm gonna triple my money by the time we leave. I'm hotter than a river of fire flowing through hell."

"So, you're gonna spend all your time in the casino? What about me?"

"Come on, kiddo. We're only gonna be here one more day. You have any idea how long I've been waiting to get on a roll like this? As long as I'm winning I've got to keep playing. That's how a streak works."

Silly rabbit. Doesn't he know the longer you play, the higher your chances of giving it all back?

"Yeah, I know exactly the table," he rambles on like a junkie planning his next fix. "You seen my watch? Never mind. You'll be okay here won't you? They've got a great pool and I know you haven't seen all the hotels yet."

"Yeah, whatever. Can I at least have some money to go see a show or something?"

He must be feeling guilty or maybe he really did win a boat load 'cause he gives me two hundred bucks. Then he quickly snatches his keys and cigarettes off the night stand and bolts out the door. "Wish me luck kiddo."

I hope he loses it all in an hour. What the hell am I supposed to do all day? Guess there's still some casinos I haven't seen yet, The Belagio, Circus Circus, a few more.

Lost again in the maze of shops, restaurants, slot machines and exhibits. Time moves so fast in the casinos I don't even notice its passing. The sun is already gone when I emerge from The Mirage. The lights of Vegas explode with the color of a fireworks show on the Fourth of July. I'm definitely gonna see a show, but which one? Maybe one of those great magicians that can levitate and make airplanes disappear. I know it's all mirrors and stuff, but I think I could figure out how they did it if I saw it live. There's a few concerts going on, but most of the bands are way before my time. Anyway, I can see a concert anytime. A larger than life billboard of Cirque De Soliel fills my eyes as I walk down the street. They're playing here at the Mirage. They look so amazing the times I've seen

169

them on TV with all the crazy costumes, acrobats and dancers. Cirque De Soliel it is.

No wonder Jim gave me so much money. These shows cost big time, but I have enough for the show, dinner, and a taxi there and back. I could go back to the buffet for dinner, but it'd be weird sitting alone, surrounded by all those people. The Hard Rock Café is less crowded. It's easy for me to find a seat in a corner away from everybody. Cirque De Soliel doesn't start for a couple of hours, so I have time to read my book.

I realize that every culture over the history of mankind needed religion to believe in a higher power and an afterlife. It must've been so hard back then, when you were either a king or a slave, when you had to work the land and fight the elements just to feed your family. Maybe life was so hard the afterlife was all they had to look forward to. But just because people need something doesn't mean it's really real. I still don't see any proof that God exists.

My pleasantly overweight waitress keeps coming around with her plastered on smile asking me if I need anything else. She's rushing me off her table, but I don't see why. The restaurant's still pretty empty. I leave after the fifth time she asks if I want more coffee.

For the next two hours I am transported into a fantasy world of twirling, flying, leaping, contorting, dancing Cirque De Soliel performers. It's absolutely amazing the things they can do with their bodies. I'm so disappointed when the show's over I just sit there staring at the empty stage as if by sheer will I could bring them back for an encore.

Time for another walk around sin city. It's still kinda early. This really is a place to quench all your hedonistic thirsts. If you're hungry for greed, gamble all day and night. If you're hungry for food, gorge yourself at a buffet. I heard some guys talking about how you get free drinks in the casinos, so I guess you can drink yourself silly. No wonder Jim loves the casinos. Bet he's on a streak alright, a free drink streak. I stop at a newsstand that carries magazines filled with women advertising their services right next to copies of the

U.S.A. Today. Guess if you're hungry for sex you can get that, too.

I wonder what Sarah would think about this place with enough vices to make a good Muslim girl lose her mind. Her father probably wouldn't even let her out the room. It must be weird being her, having your father control every aspect of your life. There's so many things she's missing out on. But then again, I went out, dated boys, drank and smoked and look what happened. I can't help but envy her. It looks like she's trapped, but it's more like she's protected. Like her father has her all wrapped up in a safe little cocoon where she'll grow free from harm until she's ready to emerge as a beautiful butterfly, untainted and unspoiled.

All of a sudden, I feel the need to be by myself. I watch TV for a while when I get back to the room hoping The Jeffersons or Taxi will help me laugh a little. It doesn't work so I cruise through the music channels. Only country music fits my bluesy mood. They sing about losing the love of a good wife to the grim reaper, losing the love of a good husband to another lover and losing your dignity when the love you offer is not returned. My life is a country song. The more I listen the more I think about everything I lost and everything that was taken from me.

"I hurt myself today. To see if I still feel. I focus on the pain. The only thing that's real," a sad, scruffy voice struggles over a lonely guitar. It's like he's whispering straight into my ear. I'm not alone after all. Somebody out there feels the pain. I run my nails against my legs, but I need to get deeper. Jim left one of those pocket knives on the night table. It stings a little as it cuts into my skin, but it feels so good to see the blood run down my leg. It's such a release.

Chapter 18

We don't end up leaving Vegas 'til about one in the afternoon. Jim's so hung over he can barely speak. It's better that way. I think I would puke if I had to hear another word about his streak. I'm so ready to get to Grandma and Grandpa's. We've been on the road for over two weeks and today is Christmas Eve. I imagine a real traditional Christmas with a big tree, lots of presents and lights everywhere. Nothing says Christmas like a house lined with red and white lights. Some people like the blue and green ones, but when it comes to Christmas lights, I'm a traditionalist. I bet Grandma's gonna cook an awesome meal. She can really burn. She taught Mom how to cook and Mom could really burn, too. I wonder if she'll teach me.

Harmony is just like I remembered, beautiful rolling hills, cool cypress trees and wide open spaces. Nobody's around and there's only a few buildings scattered here and there, but nothing over two stories high. It's pretty much a ghost town. We drive through what looks like the only stop light in the whole town. I can't help but smile when we drive past a field full of cows. It's like the reservation here, peaceful and quiet. Grandma's house is up on a hill with a few homes nearby, but far enough away to feel like you don't have any neighbors.

The house is smaller than I remember. Of course everything

looks bigger to you when you're a little kid. Jim says there's three bedrooms and two bathrooms just like our townhouse in Philly. I hope I get a bathroom to myself.

"Oh, thank God, they're here, Calvin, they're here, they're here." Grandma shouts and bounces down the driveway like an excited puppy dog as we pull in front of the house.

"Well, it's about time you got here," Grandpa waddles up behind her as fast as his aged legs can carry.

"Jim, what took you so long? We thought you'd be here yesterday," Grandma barks at him.

"I told you we were gonna see the sights along the way," Jim snaps back.

"You should've called," Grandma grabs me in her arms and gives me a big hug as I step off the truck. She has the unique ability to smile at me and scowl at Jim at the same time.

"Hey, let's not worry about that," Grandpa soothes the tension. "Come here, sweetheart. I'm so happy to see you," another great, big hug. "How do you like the lights?"

"They're great." He has just the red and white ones sprinkled across two short palm trees on either side of the walkway to the front door. I like the ones running across the front of the house dangling from the roof like icicles. He put a lighted three foot tall Santa in the center of the yard with three cardboard reindeer silhouettes outlined with white lights. It's just enough, but not too much.

"They'll look better when the sun goes all the way down," he grins.

"We saved decorating the tree for you to get here," Grandma says. They're both holding a hand, leading me into the house.

"Wait 'til you see it, its huge," Grandpa says.

The tree is huge with a stack of presents piled underneath. The whole house is full of Christmas. There's a ceramic two foot tall Mrs. Claus holding a candle accompanied by smaller elf and reindeer statues, a small nativity scene on the coffee table, and stockings for everybody over the fireplace.

"Wow, the whole house looks amazing. You guys really go all

173

out for this Christmas thing, don't you?" I walk around the room checking out all the cool little decorations.

"We want you to feel at home sweetie," Grandma says. "Let me show you your room."

She leads me to the end of a short hallway. It looks okay, except for it's all pink. Like my room used to look before everything happened.

"What do you think? Do you like it?"

"It's all pink."

"I know, honey. That's the way your room has always been.

"It wasn't that color the last time you saw it."

"No, it was that dreadful black."

"Black's my favorite color. I hate pink."

"Since when?"

"For a while. Can I paint it black?"

"What? Get serious, honey."

"If it's supposed to be my room, why can't I paint it like I want it?"

She glances awkwardly toward Grandpa. I think I've turned her.

"Well, maybe we can paint it a different color, but not black, honey. That's a little too extreme for me."

"Why don't we talk about it later? You just got here. You should be eating, not fighting," Grandpa butts in.

"I heard that." Jim comes through the door with some of my things. "What's for dinner?"

"Well, I thought we'd have kind of a light dinner tonight. You know we're going to be eating all day tomorrow. We've got tacos. The meat's in the pot on the stove and the shells are here on the counter. You have your tomatoes, onions, lettuce and cheese over here so help yourselves. Grandpa and I have already eaten. When you've finished, we'll decorate the tree. And everybody make sure you wash your hands before you touch the food."

"Can I open a present?" I ask rummaging through a pile of beautifully wrapped boxes to see which ones are mine.

"No, sweetie," Grandma says.

174

"But Mom always let me open one present on Christmas Eve."

"I'm sorry, but we never open any presents until we get back from church Christmas morning. We have to give thanks before we enjoy our blessings. That's the tradition in this house. Now come on and get your dinner."

We spend the rest of the night eating tacos and brownies, decorating the tree and cooking. Grandma's a magician in the kitchen. I help her slice, mix and stir, trying hard to listen to all her recipes, but she's moving way too fast. She's got like five different things going on at one time, a cake, a pie, two kinds of cookies, and some kind of soup slowly simmering in a big pot. I don't know how she does it all. Of course I get to sample all the goodies as they come out the oven. For the first time in a long time, I go to bed full and happy.

Grandma wakes me up at eight o'clock to get ready for church at nine thirty. I don't have the heart to tell her my views on God and religion. It'd just hurt her feelings and she doesn't deserve that.

"Good morning, sweetheart," Grandma says, too busy stirring her coffee to raise her head to look at me. "We have orange juice, coffee and muffins for a quick breakfast, then we're off to church and when we get back we'll open our presents and have a great big brunch." She lifts her head and looks at me with disappointed eyes. "Oh, sweetie, please don't tell me you're going to church dressed like that. She can't go like that, can she Grandpa?"

"No, Cara. You know this is a special day. It's Christmas. Can't you find something better to wear than jeans and a sweat shirt?"

I think about rebelling for a moment, but when I see Jim come out of his room in a button down shirt and a tie, I know I can compromise for one day, too. I dig through my clothes and find a pair of black slacks and a nice dark grey, silk blouse. That's a fair compromise. Christmas or no Christmas, there's no way I'm wearing a dress. I don't even have one that'll cover my legs and arms.

"That looks much better," Grandma says and everyone smiles at me in good clothes.

"That's the little princess I remember," Grandpa adds.

"Can I open my presents now?" I ask.

"No, sweetie, remember I told you last night. No presents until we come back from church," Grandma explains.

"Well what are we waiting for? Let's go." The sooner we leave, the sooner we'll get back.

I almost forgot what a snore Catholic services can be. All the kneeling and standing is the only thing that keeps my eyes open. Why couldn't we be Baptists and go to one of those cool churches where they really know how to celebrate religion, dancing, singing, and shouting in the name of the Lord? Like those TV preachers working the congregations into a fury with their sermons. They don't just stand there delivering a monotone sermon like this guy. I could really get into a rockin' band with one of those hand clapping, foot stomping choirs. But I'm stuck here, forced to listen to the most boring man on Earth.

I'm the first one through the door when we finally make it back to Grandma's. I guess you never really outgrow Christmas. The first box I see with my name on it is kinda small so I put it to the side looking for the bigger boxes. There's one, so big I have to use two hands to pick it up. I carelessly rip the beautiful wrapping paper, tossing it to the side to reveal a plain brown box. Grandma, Grandpa and Jim are all smiling those Kodak moment smiles as I shake the box trying to figure out what's inside. It's a really nice leather back pack with suede accents on the pockets. This is definitely not the kind you get at Wal-Mart.

"Thanks a lot. This is really nice." I smile at them. "Who's it from? I ripped the wrapping off so fast I didn't even notice the tag."

"It's from us, sweetheart," Grandma says. "We figured you should have something nice to carry your books back and forth to school."

"Thank you, it's really great."

The little box has a pink sweater in it. I try to smile as wide as I did with the back pack, but my disappointment is hard to hide. One day they'll realize I can never be their little pink sweater girl again.

"Open mine kiddo," Jim wants to join in the fun.

I have to admit he did pretty good. I got a long sleeve t-shirt with a beautiful picture of the Grand Canyon and a souvenir poker set from Las Vegas. Grandma snaps at Jim for giving me such a sinful gift, but I like it. I didn't bother to collect any souvenirs for myself on our trip so, now I have two. "Thanks Jim, it's perfect."

I got Jim a pretty cool snake skin belt from the gift shop at the Grand Canyon. I think he really likes it 'cause he stares at it for a while, grinning from ear to ear. I didn't know what to get Grandma and Grandpa so I just bought them a gift pack with an assortment of gourmet coffees. I know they drink coffee every morning so I'm pretty sure it's a safe bet.

It's a perfect day. It turns out the soup Grandma was working on last night is some kind of seafood chowder she was saving for our brunch. It has scallops and shrimp in a creamy mushroom soup and it's absolutely amazing. I thought that was going to be it, but she brings out a sausage, mushroom and cheese quiche that's simply the most wonderful thing I've ever tasted. And that's still not it. She made this incredible banana bread and a fruit salad with watermelon, cantaloupe and honey dew melon. It's like I'm staying at a five star bed and breakfast with Martha Stewart as my hostess.

She starts right in on Christmas dinner after brunch. She's a one woman cooking factory, seasoning and basting the turkey, baking rolls, boiling greens, spreading marshmallows on yams, and mixing the dressing, cranberries, and mashed potatoes. Every burner on top and rack inside the stove is occupied. Grandpa and Jim lay sprawled out on the sofa watching some football game. I watch Grandma with pure admiration.

"Is there anything I can do to help?" I ask.

"Not really, honey. Everything's pretty much done. It just has to cook now, but you can keep me company while I watch over it. You know you can't just leave it alone. You have to watch over it every step of the way to make sure it turns out right."

"That makes sense."

"You know, Cara, things are going to be different for you here. Your Grandpa and I know that you were probably used to doing your own thing while you were living with Jim. You're going to have to go to school and if you skip even one day, I'll know. Is that going to be a problem?"

"No, Grandma, it won't. I've always wanted to go to public school. I've been looking forward to it."

"Good. You know we go to church every Sunday."

"I know, but I don't think I can make it to church." Going to church on Christmas Sunday was one thing, but there's no way I'm going every week. I've got to nip this in the bud.

"Why not?"

"Well, Grandma, I just don't feel like I used to about God anymore, you know, since Mom died."

"Don't say that, Cara," she drops her head and stops wiping off the counter. "You know as hard as it was for you to lose your mother, it was just as hard for me to lose my only daughter, my only child. No mother should ever have to bury her child. But through it all, I never questioned God's plan. Never."

"I'm sorry. Don't get mad. It's just that I've been doing a lot of thinking and I just don't have faith in things like I used to anymore."

"I think if you start coming to church again you'll feel differently. The Lord is still with you, sweetheart. He always has been. You're feeling lost right now, but you're in good hands now. You don't have to feel alone anymore."

"It's not about feeling alone, Grandma, not really. I just don't think there's anybody up there listening to our problems and helping us through our days. I mean, sure I could go to church with you and pretend to believe, but wouldn't God know I was just faking it? Anyway, how do you make yourself believe in something you really don't believe in anymore?"

"You mean to tell me you really don't believe in God, not at all?"

"No."

"So, what do you believe in, all that evolution stuff?"

"You have to admit it makes sense when you think about it."

"I don't think so, Cara. I know, with everything I am, that I'm

178

not related to some damn ape. And I don't care what all those scientists say. They can twist their theories around to make you think whatever they want. I believe in what the *Bible* says."

I'm tempted to question Grandma about her beliefs. It would be so easy for me to ridicule all those fantastic stories in the *Bible* and engage her in the ultimate debate, the creation of mankind. But I know it's really no use. She's not a curious college kid trying to unravel the mysteries of the universe. She's set in her ways, too old to change. I have enough respect for her not to try.

"Your faith in the *Bible* used to be so strong." She looks as if all the air has been taken out of her.

I want to tell her the truth, the whole truth. I want to tell her about how her God took my mother, and left me to be raped. I want to, but why ruin Christmas? It's not like she could do anything about it anyway. It happened, that's all. "I'm sorry Grandma. I don't know what I'm talking about. It's just something I was thinking about, that's all."

"So, you'll go to church with us?"

"I really don't think I can right now, Grandma. I hope you understand. It just wouldn't feel right."

"I understand. You need more time. You've been through a lot, but I know God lives inside you. One day you will come back to him."

I just smile at her leaving her thinking she has reached me. That way she can enjoy her Christmas without having to worry about her only grand daughter's soul burning in hell.

For some reason I think about my lizard. It occurs to me that I haven't seen him in days. I excuse myself and go to check out Jim's truck. I don't see him anywhere. I'd like to think he made it and he jumped off the truck to find a nice new home somewhere in Grandma's yard.

We have a huge traditional Christmas dinner and spend the next couple days lazily lounging around, eating everything in sight. Grandma teaches me how to play gin rummy. She says it's a more dignified card game than playing poker. She's pretty good, but I

179

manage to win a couple of hands.

"Well, guys, I'm gonna turn in. I've gotta roll out tomorrow," Jim interrupts our game.

"Where you headed?" Grandpa asks.

"I'm pickin' up a load in Oakland and droppin' it in Seattle. Then I'm back on the road headed back east again."

"It's been good seeing you again, Jim. You make sure you get plenty of rest tonight and take your time on the road. There's a lot of crazy drivers out there during the holidays," Grandma warns.

"That's for sure. Thanks a lot for your hospitality. June, you're the greatest cook on the planet. You know that, don't you?"

"Thanks Jim." It's the first time I've seen her smile at Jim since we got here.

"Cara, why don't you help me pack? I'd like to talk to you for a minute?"

I follow him to his room, hoping he's not expecting some tear jerking goodbye scene, not after the way he dumped me in Vegas.

"Cara, I wanted to thank you for spending the last couple of weeks with me. I wish things could've been different between us, but I hope you know you can call me if you ever need anything. I'll always be your father and you'll always be my daughter. I won't forget that."

He walks towards me like he's gonna give me a hug or something. I guess I don't mind, but it is kinda weird. We nervously hug each other for no more than a second or two. Neither of us is comfortable with the ritual. I walk out the door wondering if we'll ever really be close.

Chapter 19

The first day back to school is finally here. I'm scared, excited, nervous, and a little queasy. All new kids in an all new school. I'll probably be Morticia all over again. Oh well, making friends isn't exactly on the top of my list. I'm really gonna have to be more careful this time. Can't end up anybody's sofa meat again.

A bus is coming to pick me up around seven. Coastal Beach High is about six miles away in a bigger town called Cambria. I can't wait to get my license and check out the town and beach. Of course I'm gonna have to find something to drive. Maybe I can talk Grandma and Grandpa into a new car. Maybe I'll meet a hot surfer boy with a convertible, perfect for the California sunshine. On second thought, maybe not.

I hate the way I left things with Crystal and Jennifer. How could I be so mean to my best friends? So absorbed with that rapist pimp I couldn't see they were trying to help. Anyway, that doesn't matter now. They're not here and I've got to find a way to fit in all by myself.

The school looks normal enough from the outside. There's a really cool sculpture of seals lying around a rock formation next to the flag pole out front. The soft, steady breeze, cool but not too cold, tingles my face and reminds me how close we are to the ocean. Of course, it's not the outside I'm worried about. It's all about the cliques. I know for sure I won't be a cheerleader. It's not always good to be a part of the popular crowd. How would I know who to trust? They're all so fake and phony. Maybe I should just hit books and become super geek. Everybody would leave me alone. I wouldn't have to deal with boys or dating or anything. I could just stay to myself like an old maid and do my own thing, whatever that is. Anyway, it really doesn't matter. They're gonna think what they wanna think about me no matter what.

I pretty much mastered the ninja like art of being around people without really being seen. Stay close to the lockers when walking among the crowd in the hallway and always sit in the back row in class. The cafeteria's the worst. There's no place to hide and hardly ever a completely empty table. I look for a quiet table away from the chatty, popular kids. Most of the kids at these tables are trying to hide, too. We just sit there sheepishly looking down at our lunches, avoiding conversation, trying to make it through the day unnoticed.

One day I see a table of kids that looks kinda like me. I don't know why I didn't see them before. They're all wearing black, each with their own unique hair style. It's like they're saying I'm different, so what, deal with it. I wanna walk up and sit down at their table, but I'm too shy.

Everyday at school's the same. I am the invisible girl. Nobody even talks to me except to ask me to pass a note in class or give them an answer on a test. One day in class a kid in a black Led Zeppelin t-shirt, black jeans and bright orange hair cut really short on the sides keeps bugging me for answers. She's sitting right next to me so I can't really avoid her pleas, but I don't really mind too much. She's got style.

"You're really smart, you know. Where you from?" she asks.

"Who, me?"

"Yeah, you. You don't see nobody else back here do you?"

"I'm Cara. I moved here from Philadelphia."

"Yeah, how you like it so far?"

"It's okay, you know, warmer."

"No doubt. Thanks for lettin' me copy."

"I don't care. Math's lame anyway. You never use anything you learn past the eighth grade again in life anyway."

"True that."

The bell rings and she smiles at me as we both go to different classes. I see her again at lunch waving at me to come to her table. She's at that table where the kids wear all black. Never thought I'd meet a whole group of kids that look just like me. *Be cool, Cara, Be cool,* I tell myself as I approach the table.

"Everybody, this is Cara. She's from Philadelphia," the orange haired girl introduces. "Cara, this is Kevin, that's Wendy, Billy at the end, and I'm Trina."

They all wave or nod, acknowledging my presence.

"Pop a squat," Kevin says. He has the most jet black hair I've ever seen. "You like Green Day?" he asks with his nose turned up at my t-shirt.

"What's wrong with that?" I respond.

"Well, they're okay, but don't you think they're a little over commercialized?"

"I don't know. I just like their music, especially the lyrics."

"Don't mind him," Wendy says. "He hates any band everyone else likes. No matter how good they are."

"They're okay, I guess. They're just so popular," Kevin says.

"I don't care how many people like them. They're good," Trina adds. "Your problem, Kevin, is you're always too worried about what other people think. You don't want no one to know you could possibly go along with the crowd, so you deny liking them, even though you really do. Man, don't you see? You're denying yourself what you really like just to appease the mob."

"The ultimate irony," Billy says. "Cara, what do you think?"

"I think you should do what you wanna do and screw what everyone else thinks." The answer flies out of my mouth.

"That's what I'm talkin' about," Billy shouts slamming his hand on the table. "I knew I liked this girl for some reason."

"You guys always go back and forth like this?" I ask, surprised by their passion.

183

"Kevin knows we love him even if he has no mind of his own." Trina giggles and Kevin playfully nudges her pretending to push her off her seat.

Could I be so lucky to find a group of cool people so quickly? They invite me everywhere they go, the mall, the coffee shop, and the beach on days when the wind isn't blowing so much. The beach is my favorite. Staring at the sun fall behind the horizon, I never though I'd see anything as vast and beautiful as the Grand Canyon. No wonder nobody's ever found when they get lost at sea.

We debate every topic in the world from terrorism to abortion. Everyone thinks they hold the answers to creating world peace, solving the energy crisis, and tackling any other problem that gets in the way of creating a utopia.

The best thing about my new friends is their talent. Each one has an incredible skill. Kevin's an awesome artist, always sketching pictures of over muscled ancient warriors and princesses. Billy draws too, mostly super heroes he gets from his comic books. Wendy and Trina write really cool songs and poetry about being in love or wanting to be in love or losing love. I wish I could write like that, but I don't think I could ever write anything so beautiful. Trina has some really crazy songs about death and torture. Wendy says her parents are real losers and they left her kinda twisted. She seems okay to me, but they do say still waters run deep. I think I found my clique.

We usually hang out after school at Kevin's or Trina's. Their parents are never home so we have the house to ourselves. Kevin usually talks his older brother into buying us some beer and sometimes he can bum a joint. Wendy and Billy don't ever smoke weed. They say it just makes them feel weird and tired. I don't do it as much as I used to, just take a couple of puffs to relax. Then I leave it alone. I don't want to smell like it or look to hazy eyed when I get home.

I can't get away with stuff like I used to with Jim. Grandma and Grandpa are always at home and they always wanna know where I am and who I've been with, every minute of every day. I told

Grandma about my new friends so she lets me hang out after school, but I have to be home by 6 p.m. for dinner. She thinks it's good that I'm making new friends and she's always bugging me to meet them. I wouldn't mind except I don't think Grandma and Grandpa could deal with my new friends. Kevin, Billy, Wendy and Trina all look so different with their nose rings, tongue rings and different color hair. They're still having a hard time with my black clothes and fingernails. I guess that's just the way for people who choose to be different. Everybody's too busy looking at the outside to appreciate the real person inside. Never mind the great drawings and poetry they create and all the great ideas they have on solving the world's problems. I truly believe Billy could be some kind of politician, maybe even the president. He always seems to have the right answer no matter what the problem.

January 20th, my 16th birthday. I'm what they call on the cusp between Capricorn and Aquarius. They say Capricorns are supposed to be organized and logical thinkers and Aquarians are supposed to be very creative. You'd think being in the middle of both signs at least some of it would've rubbed off, but I don't see any of those good qualities in me. It's Sunday, so I get to sleep in undisturbed. I know Grandma and Grandpa want me to go to church with them, but they've been really good about not bugging me to go. They left a card for me neatly placed between a tall glass of orange juice and a stack of pancakes and some bacon they left for breakfast. I didn't even think they would remember. They come back from church all smiles and hugs. I almost cry when they hand me a gift in a shiny small box and start singing happy birthday. I figure it to be some kind of jewelry by the size and shape of the box. I really don't even like wearing jewelry, but I have to pretend to like it no matter what it is. It's a Saint Christopher pendant hanging from a brilliant gold necklace.

"That's fourteen carat gold, I hope you know," Grandpa boasts. He always makes some kind of announcement whenever he spends more than twenty bucks on anything.

"Do you like it?" Grandma asks. "It's Saint Christopher. As long as you wear that you will be protected from evil."

"Thank you, I love it. It's so pretty and expensive looking. I'll have to save it for special occasions." It is pretty, but I really don't plan on wearing it. That would just be too hypocritical for me. I can only imagine the hell Trina and the crew would give me for wearing something no reputable self professed atheist would be caught dead with.

I hang out most of the day with Grandma watching her make my birthday cake and what she calls my special birthday dinner. We're having jumbo shrimp sautéed in butter, olive oil and garlic, cheesy mashed potatoes, corn on the cob, and for dessert my very own special strawberry short cake and vanilla ice cream with, caramel, and nuts. One good thing about wearing black, it hides all the extra pounds. I was gonna hang out with the gang today, but I think I'd rather let Grandma and Grandpa spoil me. It's been so long since anyone did so much for me.

"Grandma."

"Yes Dear."

"Can we talk about changing my room color to anything but pink?"

"Sure, what color do you want it? Anything except black."

"What about grey?"

"Yes, a nice light grey to catch the sunlight."

"No Grandma, dark grey. I like it dark. It helps me sleep."

"All that darkness isn't good for your spirit. It's depressing, Cara. Your Grandpa and I are worried about you. You never smile and all that black. Why all the black?"

"You know there are worse things than wearing black. It's just how I feel. I don't know. I guess I still really miss Mom."

"We'll always miss her, honey, but we have to learn how to live on. Do you think she would be happy seeing you mope around all day with those black fingernails?"

"I don't mope. And just because I dress different doesn't mean I'm some kind of freak or something."

"Don't get upset, dear. I know it's been hard for you."

"Mom grew up here. I mean pretty much all her life, right?" I have to interrupt her before she starts in on the pity party.

"We moved here after your Grandpa came back from the war and we've been here ever since. You're staying in your mother's old room, but it's you're room now."

"What was Mom like when she was my age?"

"Too much like you, I'm afraid. She always had to be different, always wanted more out of life. You know your Grandpa and I have always been pretty simple people. I don't know where she got all that ambition from, but she couldn't wait to get out of Harmony. She always had bigger plans than this little town could offer."

"Did you know she had a problem with drugs?"

"I knew. I think I always knew. I should've done something about it when she was your age, always staying out late with her friends. She said they were just hanging out, but I knew better. I just didn't want to admit she might be drinking or doing drugs. It was a different time then. Grandpa always said kids need something to do to blow off steam. We figured there was only so much trouble she could get into in our small town. I guess hindsight really is twenty-twenty. Now you see why I worry about you and your new friends."

"What about my friends?"

"I hear you've been hanging out with those kids with all the weird hair and tattoos. You know those kinds of people do a lot of drugs."

"Really? You don't know them. For your information, they don't do drugs. Everybody wants to stereotype us as druggies, but it's not true. You're just as bad as the rest of them. Just 'cause you look different from everyone else doesn't mean you're a bad person. How can you pass judgment on people you don't even know?"

"Okay, Cara, you're right. I shouldn't judge people until I get to know them. But how can I get to know them if I never get to meet them? Why don't you bring your friends home some time? You're not ashamed of them are you?"

"No."

"Good, then it's settled. I want to meet them all. Invite them to dinner tomorrow."

"Tomorrow, no way."

"Why not?"

"No way I'm gonna let them see that powder puff pink room you guys have me living in."

"You really hate it that much?"

"Yeah, Grandma, I do."

"Okay, we'll paint the room this weekend."

"Dark grey?"

"Yes, if that's what you want."

It's been a perfect day. It doesn't even occur to me until I go to bed that Jim hasn't called or anything. Out of sight out of mind, I guess. I got a lame card from him a few days later. Whatever, he'll always be clueless.

Chapter 20

I woke up this morning with a queasy feeling in my stomach, like I'm gonna throw up. Too much cake and ice cream, I guess. The guys almost flip when I tell them about dinner. They agree, but I can tell they really don't want to. I'm not too crazy about the idea either, but a deal is a deal and my room is how I like it now. Maybe it's for the best. Once they see how creative and smart all my friends are they're bound to like them. Then I'll be able to hang out with more freedom.

"So, I hope your grandparents aren't expecting us to dress up or nothing," Wendy says with nervous disdain in her voice.

"I ain't got no good clothes." Trina looks just as concerned.

"You don't have to dress up for them. Just be who you are." I reassure them.

"Yeah, since when do you care about what anyone thinks about you?" Kevin jumps in.

"I know what I'm wearing, jeans and a t-shirt, just like always," Billy affirms.

"Look guys, this really is no big deal. They just wanna know who my friends are, that's all. Just be yourselves. It's really not gonna be that bad. My Grandma's an awesome cook."

"My mom can't cook a thing," Kevin says. "This might not be so bad after all."

I'm not half as nervous about the dinner as they are. I just hope Grandma and Grandpa don't ask them a bunch of stupid questions or make fun of the way they look.

Kevin and Wendy are old enough to drive on their own. Kevin and Billy get here first in Kevin's Honda. It's a pretty nice car, cool enough to cruise around in. Kevin has a job at the record store in the mall so he can afford to buy a good car. Wendy and Trina pull up right behind them in Wendy's BMW. Her father's some kind of hot shot attorney, but she sees him about as often as I see Jim. They got a really great house in the nicest part of Cambria. The BMW's a hand me down from her mom who just had to buy a new Mercedes to keep up with her country club crowd. You'd think Wendy would be all stuck up with all the money and stuff she has, but she's really cool, you know, down to earth. I'm the only one who doesn't have my license yet. I've really gotta do something about that

I meet them all in the front yard and we stand around the cars talking for a few minutes, reluctant to go inside. I guess there's no use delaying the inevitable, besides I can see Grandma peeking through the window.

Grandma pretends to be busy in the kitchen when we walk through the door.

"Hey Grandma, everything smells great."

"Hi everybody, hope you're hungry," Grandma turns toward us with her warming smile.

"Grandma, this is Kevin, Billy, Trina and Wendy."

"It's so nice to meet all of you. Cara never tells us anything about you. I hope you like lasagna."

"Oh, hi everybody," Grandpa walks through the back door.

"Grandpa, this is Kevin, Billy, Trina and Wendy," I reintroduce them all.

"Welcome, make yourselves at home. Our house is your house. Come on in and have a seat." Grandpa smiles.

We sit down on the couches in the family room. They're both being really nice making the usual small talk, but I can tell by the look on their faces that they're surprised at my friends' appearance.

It's kinda awkward in a subtle way. Everybody's smiling and saying the right things, but there's a thin film of tension hovering above us all. I can almost hear their thoughts. *Why would someone walk around looking like that? Why do they want to be so different? Don't they have anyone to guide them? Poor, little lost children.*

"Well, it's going to be a few minutes until dinner's ready. Does anybody want something to drink?" Grandma asks, "I have Coke, Seven-Up, and apple juice."

"No thanks," everybody says collectively.

"I'll take a beer," Kevin says under his breath, loud enough for us to enjoy a good laugh, but too low for Grandma and Grandpa to hear.

"You guys wanna see my room?" I suggest a diversion to relieve the uneasiness.

"Man, your grandparents are about as straight as they come." Trina busts out laughing as soon as we're all in my room with the door closed.

"Yeah, they're definitely super, duper old school," I agree.

"I think it's cute," Wendy says. "I bet they've been married, like, forever, huh?"

"I guess."

"That must be nice," she says with a slight, sad smile.

"Yeah, whatever," Trina interrupts. "I like the grey on these walls. It's so dark and mysterious."

"You have some cool old school posters," Billy comments standing in front of my picture of Kurt Kobane.

"Now that guy really knew how to feel," Wendy says.

"It's a shame he took his own life. I'll never understand how people can do that. I could see if you were locked away in some prison for the rest of your life or something. I mean, if you got nothing to look forward to you might as well go ahead and end it. But this guy was on the top of the world. Fame, fortune, groupies, everything. I don't get it." Billy looks sincerely disappointed.

"For real, man, he could have any girl he wanted. He was a certified rock star and he threw it all away," Kevin says.

191

"I don't know. A lot of people commit suicide. People do it every day. You don't know what was really goin' on in his life," Trina says.

"He must've been very depressed," Wendy says.

"Depressed, over what? He had it all. Whatever his problems you know he had the money to fix it, you know, go to rehab, get a therapist, whatever. Get over it, man, damn."

"I'm sure you don't see it that way when you're depressed," Wendy explains.

"You hear all the time about stars who feel all alone, like they don't know who to trust. I bet it is hard. I mean you never know who's hangin' out with you for who you are and who's just in it 'cause you're a celebrity or whatever," I add.

"When I become a famous poet you guys better not get all weird on me," Trina giggles.

"Yeah, no matter how many groupies I get from being a famous illustrator, I'm never gonna let it get me down," Kevin boasts.

"Yeah, right. Comic book geeks don't have groupies." Trina's still laughing.

"Man, you need to see the girls at the comic book conventions. I'm talkin' smokin' hot. Right Billy?" Kevin defends himself.

"Right, whatever." Trina has us all giggling now.

"Dinner's ready." Grandma's voice echoes down the hallway.

"Come on, guys, let's go. And remember to be on your best behavior," I wave my finger, a playful warning.

"Man, that smells good," Kevin says pushing his way to the front of the line. They all look anxious to eat, especially Kevin. I bet he smoked a joint before he left home.

"You kids should know Grandma's lasagna is legendary," Grandpa says.

"Oh, Calvin, stop telling lies."

"Don't be modest Grandma. You know you're a great cook."

"Thank you, Cara."

Once the food hits the table the only sounds heard are the clang of fork against plate and lip smacking jaws working overtime.

"You out did yourself this time June," Grandpa comes up for air.

"This is really, really good," Wendy adds and everybody grunts in approval. I think it would take an earthquake to get Kevin, Billy or Trina to interrupt their grazing.

"Don't forget your salads and the garlic bread goes really good with the lasagna," Grandma says.

There's no response, just constant munching.

"Man, that was great," Billy blurts out when he's cleared his plate.

"There's plenty seconds for anyone who wants," Grandma says.

"Sounds good to me," Grandpa says. "Just pass the tray around. It looks like everybody's ready for another round. So, how are you kids doing in school? Are your grades okay?"

Grandpa's got enough food on his stomach to start in on the embarrassing questions.

"They do okay." I try to deflect the question. "Billy's a genius."

"Oh yeah, Mr. Straight A all the way," Trina says snapping a flat hand against her brow in a mock military salute.

"Well, I think it's wonderful that you take your studies seriously young man," Grandma smiles at Billy.

"He doesn't take anything seriously. He's just smart like that," Kevin says in a bitter tone.

"That's not true," Billy looks embarrassed.

"Oh come on, sure it is. You know you never even study. Man, I've seen you read the chapter the night before a history test and get an A without blinking." Trina mimics Kevin's disdain.

"It's not his fault he's smart. I wish I was so lucky," Wendy says.

"Does that hurt?" Grandpa says staring at Wendy's mouth.

"Excuse me?" she's startled by the interruption.

"The thing in your tongue? Does it hurt?" Grandpa persists.

"What thing? Calvin, what are you talking about?" Grandma asks.

"That thing, it's like a ball or something. Don't you see it?" Grandpa won't let it go.

"Oh, my goodness, how can you eat with that thing in there?" Grandma looks closely at Wendy who is more than happy to show off her tongue ring. She definitely gets off on the shock value.

Everybody drops their forks to join in on the laughter. The look on the old folk's faces is priceless.

"You like my nose ring?" Trina turns toward Grandma hoping to get the same reaction.

"It's interesting, I suppose." Again the concerned look on her face reveals her shock. "That must have hurt. Why would you do that to your face?"

"I always wanted one." Trina shrugs her shoulders.

"And you?" Grandma looks at Wendy.

"I think it's cool. It shocked the hell outta my mom. I thought she was gonna have a heart attack," Wendy giggles. "And yes, it did hurt like hell when I got it, but it's cool now."

The tension eases into curiosity. "How long did it take to heal? Did it get infected? What did you eat until it healed? Do you have anything else pieced?" Grandma and Grandpa are relentless. They see everything from the belly rings to the tattoos. I can't believe how much they want to know about my friends. But not in that weird, nosy way most adults butt into your business. We're all just having fun. Grandpa has a way of doing that, putting everyone at ease. His jokes are the corniest ever, but it's good to be around someone who never takes things too seriously.

We spend more time hanging out in my backyard after that dinner, drawing, writing and eating. The patio has really comfortable chairs and a great view of the rolling hills. Grandpa builds great fires to keep us warm and Grandma always has something for us to eat, fried chicken, home made soup, chili, sandwiches. I don't think Kevin's parents feed him at home. The solitude and serenity makes it a perfect place to be creative. I even start writing some poetry. They all tell me it's good, but I know it sucks, especially compared to Trina's and Wendy's. I really don't care, it's mine.

Chapter 21

I wake up wanting to throw up again, but there's nothing on my stomach to let go. I'm sure I didn't eat anything bad last night. Must be some kinda crazy stomach flu 'cause I don't feel like eating anything for breakfast. I'm queasy, tired and funky all day. Still not much of an appetite when we meet for lunch, so I let Billy and Kevin fight over my ham and cheese sandwich.

Chemistry's my least favorite class. It's usually tolerable 'cause I just came from having lunch with the crew, but today's gonna be unbearable. My teacher's monotone rambling about the periodic table is boring my stomach into a churning caldron. All of a sudden my head starts spinning. I try to excuse myself and make a dash for the restrooms, but my legs give way. The last thing I remember is the feel of the cold floor on my face and some idiot's comment. "That goth freak's probably wacked out on drugs."

"What happened?" I wake up in the nurse's office lying flat on my back.

"You fainted, but you're okay, I think." The nurse is a short, sturdy Asian woman who looks at me with the sympathetic concern of a mother.

"What do you mean, you think?"

She stands firmly in front of me. "I saw your arm when I took your pulse. You're hurting yourself, aren't you? I've seen this before, with other girls. It's not the answer. Do you have anyone you can talk to about this?"

"No. No, I mean, I don't need to talk to anybody. I just got scratched by a cat, that's all." I never really thought of it as hurting myself until I heard her say the words. It always makes me feel better.

"Those aren't cat scratches. It's okay. I know. Whatever it is, you don't have to face it alone. There are people you can talk to, even if you can't talk to your parents. There are people who will listen to you and help you."

I want to tell her. I want to free myself of all the humiliation, guilt and shame. I want to shout out I've Been Raped, but I can't say a word.

"I have to tell a counselor about this. I hope you don't think I'm invading your privacy, but it's the law."

She waits for me to respond, but I can't even lift my head. It's like my terrible secret is about to be exposed. Everyone will know I'm a freak.

"You need to talk to someone about this. You can talk to me. I want to help."

It's hard not to believe her trusting smile and sincere eyes, but how can she help? Can she bring back Mom? Can she give back what they stole from me?

Grandma and Grandpa look at me like I'm a mental patient or something after that. They've never looked so worried. They keep telling me how much they love me and asking me if I'm okay. I tell them I am, but I'm really not sure. They say I have to see a therapist to help deal with my issues. Whatever. I was just starting to feel right again. I've got cool friends and school is actually tolerable. Now I'm gonna have to dig everything up just to explain to some stranger why I'm so sad. Like I need some therapist telling me why I'm depressed. Mom died, I got raped, I got sad. Just let me deal with it.

I haven't had a dream for a couple of weeks, but now they're back and stranger than ever. Sarah and Jason are at a party drinking, obviously flirting with each other. I'm like a fly on the wall, there but not really there. I see him lure her up the stairs, just like he did me. I see them having sex. She's moaning like one of those girls in the porno movies we used to watch when we skipped school to hang out at Tommy's. Then, all of a sudden, Sarah and I are in a ditch dressed in burkas. An angry mob is throwing stones at us yelling, "Whores, sluts, kill them."

Sarah turns to me and says, "Why did you make me do it?" She gets hit in the head with a rock and falls with her arms stretched out on both sides of her body. Her legs remain straight one lying on top of the other. Blood drips from her slumping, tilted head. I wake up before I feel the fatal blow from the charging stones. My heart is racing and my sheets are damp with sweat. How did Sarah get mixed up in all this? She's the sweetest, most pure person I've ever met. How did she become part of my sick, twisted world?

I rub my hands across my arms feeling the scars that bought me so much relief from my pain. I want to do it again, but I have to see that stupid therapist tomorrow. Who cares? They already know I'm doing it. The little pocket knife I use is perfect to press hard into my skin until it's the only pain I can feel. I let it slice deep enough to see blood, instant relief. Now I can sleep.

Chapter 22

The therapist's office looks nice enough from the outside, lots of pretty flowers all round and even some big palm trees in the waiting room. Here I sit, waiting for the diagnosis, unbalanced, disturbed, crazy. At least it's not crowded. There's only a couple of other kids here with their cheerleading parents pushing the, "Everything is gonna be ok," speech. Their kids have that, *I'd rather be anywhere but here*, look on their faces. Just like me. The walls are covered with posters that say crap like, "The first step of getting out of a hole is to stop digging." "Be yourself, an original is always better than a copy." "Attitude is a little thing that makes a big difference." "Self control is knowing you can, but deciding you won't." Give me a break.

"Hi, you must be Cara. I'm Susan." A pretty, thin woman with bright red hair and freckles comes out to greet us. "And you must be Mrs. Hartfield. Nice to meet both of you. Did you have any problem finding us here?"

"Oh no, your directions were perfect." Grandma replies.

"Cara and I are just going to go back to my office and talk for about an hour or so. Can I get you anything while you're waiting, coffee, water?"

"No, thank you. I'm fine," Grandma politely smiles.

"We have some vending machines right down this hall if you

change your mind. You ready, Cara?"

"I guess."

My feet drag down the hall, but my mind tells me to make a break for the front door. She has one of those posters on her office door. It says, "Only positive attitudes allowed past this point". What is it with these people? Do they really believe they can fix people's problems with slogans?

"I'm glad you came to see me, Cara. Make yourself comfortable. The first thing I have to do is ask you a few questions to get to know you better. Now I want you to be honest with your answers. It's all confidential. Everything we talk about in here, every word you tell me, is confidential. I want you to feel completely free to talk about whatever you want."

"You won't tell anyone, not even my grandparents?"

"No one, not even your grandparents."

"Okay."

"You're here because you've been cutting yourself?"

"Yes."

"How long have you been doing it?"

"I don't know, a while." She seems to be listening, but she's also scribbling away on a clipboard. She's probably not even paying attention.

"And you live with your grandparents?"

"Yes."

She goes on to ask me question after question starting with my family history. She wants to know if I ever had any major illnesses or any mental health issues before. She asks what kind of student I am and if I ever had a behavior problem in school. When she asks about my drug history I'm honest about what I've tried, but I lie about how much I did it. I do the same when she asks about my sexual activity. She even asks about my religion. I just tell her I was raised Catholic.

"How old are you?" I figure it's my turn to ask a few questions.

"Twenty nine. Why do you ask?"

"I don't know. My mother was thirty nine."

"You grandmother told me she passed last summer. That must have been hard on you."

I don't respond.

"Were you and your mother close?"

"Yes."

"And your father?"

"Jim? He is who he is, I guess."

"You call him by his first name?"

"Yeah, he's always been more like an older brother who went off to the military or a distant uncle than a father. He wasn't around much when I was growing up."

"Where was he?"

"On the road. He's a truck driver."

"It must've been hard not having a father around."

"Not really. I mean, I always had Mom."

"Can you tell me your fondest memory of your mother? What do you miss about her the most?"

"I miss our breakfasts. She worked a lot, but we always had breakfast together in the morning."

"What was it about the breakfasts you liked so much?"

"Just being with her, I guess. She always listened to me and tried to help me when I needed it. I don't ever remember talking about her own problems. It was our time."

"Sounds like she was a wonderful mother."

"She was." It felt good talking about Mom like this. Everyone else was telling me how to forget about her. "She always helped me with my homework. She was really smart, smarter than some of my teachers. She was the smartest person I've ever known."

"You said she worked a lot. What kind of work did she do?"

"She was a nurse. She loved to help people."

"You must've been very proud of her."

"I am. She got to help a lot of people before she died."

"What would she think about the marks on your arm?"

I pull down my sleeves below my wrists, but I know she already knows they're there. "She wouldn't understand. I don't even know why I do it except it makes me feel better for some reason."

"Some of the other girls I've worked with have told me they do it because it helps them deal with their emotional pain. Losing a mother is a hard thing to deal with at any age, but especially when you're young?"

"When I do it, it's like it takes my mind off everything. I can just release all the bad memories through the knife."

"You have bad memories about your mother?"

"No, not about Mom, other things. I don't know."

"It's okay. We don't have to talk about it if you don't want to. What happened the other day at school? You fainted? Has that ever happened to you before?"

"No. It was the weirdest thing. I got so dizzy all of a sudden. I've been throwing up a lot, too. And I'm like tired all the time."

"Did you tell your grandparents about this?"

"No, they're already worried enough as it is. Anyway, I figure it's just the flu or something. It'll go away."

"Have you ever had the flu before?"

"Yes."

"The way you feel now, does it feel like the flu when you had it before?"

"No."

"Cara, I think I know why you've been getting sick."

"Why?"

"Have you been sexually active?"

"Yeah, but what does that have to do with the flu?"

"When was the last time you had your period?"

"I don't know. It's been a while. I guess I didn't have it last month. Between the move and everything I didn't even notice."

"So, you skipped a month?"

"Yeah, I guess I did."

"I've worked with a lot of girls your age and your symptoms sound very familiar. I think you might be pregnant."

"What?"

"I'm sure you knew this could happen if you were having

unprotected sex. I'm sorry I shocked you. I didn't mean to just throw it out there like that. I have a bad habit of saying exactly what's on my mind. I have to work on that."

"Did you say what I thought you said?"

"Yes, Cara, I think you might be pregnant. I'm sure you've heard of morning sickness and you say you're tired all the time. Fainting isn't as common, but it can happen, especially if you've been throwing up a lot and not eating right. I know this is a lot to take in, but if you are pregnant you're going to have to start taking care of yourself."

"Oh my God. What am I gonna do? I can't have a baby. I don't want a baby. I can't do it. Look at me. I'm a basket case. I can't raise a kid. This can't be happening."

"Whoa, Cara, relax, calm down. Just breathe in slow and breathe out. We don't even know if you're pregnant or not yet. I'm going to refer you to a doctor so they can give you a pregnancy test. I know it seems overwhelming, but you're not going to have to go through any of this alone. You have options and you have your grandparents, don't you?"

"Yeah, but a baby. I'm not ready for a baby.

"Let's not get ahead of ourselves. We'll see what the doctor has to say first."

"Do you have to tell my grandparents?"

"Don't you think they should be involved in this whole thing? I assume you don't have the resources to raise a child on your own. I don't see how you can't tell them, do you?"

"They're gonna flip."

Susan agrees to wait until I see the doctor and get an official positive test result before I mention anything to Grandma and Grandpa. I didn't know what to expect, but Susan turned out to be pretty cool. She doesn't talk down to me like most adults do, lecturing and commanding.

It seems like the hour passed way too fast and before I know it I'm in the car trying to figure out how I'm gonna break the news to Grandma. Just wait until after the doctor appointment like Susan said. I know I'm pregnant. I am different inside. I can feel it.

The doctor confirmed everything, no surprise. Susan suggests Grandma and Grandpa come to my next session so I can tell them as soon as possible. She's good at twisting the conversation so that I feel like it was my idea, but that's okay. I wanna tell them anyway and it'll be so much easier with Susan there.

"Come on in and have a seat," Susan says in her calming voice. "I'm glad you both could make it."

"We'd do anything to help Cara. What can we do?" Grandpa says desperately, like if he just said or did the right thing all my problems would magically disappear.

"Cara has something she wants to share with you."

I sit there staring at the floor. I wanna say something, but there's a lump in my throat the size of a grapefruit. How can I look Grandpa in the eye and tell him I'm pregnant. He still thinks I'm a virgin. The guilt and shame rolls over me like an avalanche. I want to be his innocent, little, pink sweater girl again, but my innocence is gone and it'll never come back. Everybody's staring, waiting for me to say something. Susan's office isn't that big, but the room seems so much smaller now. The walls are closing in on me.

"Its okay, Cara, take your time." Susan's voice calms me, a little.

"That's right, honey. We love you, whatever you want to tell us. We love you and we'll do whatever we can to support you." Grandma reaches out and holds my hand.

They will support me. I know that. She gives me the courage to speak. "I made mistakes. I've done bad things, wrong things." Tears start to drip from my eyes. I still can't raise my head. It takes every ounce of energy I have to get the words out. "I'm gonna have a baby."

"It's okay honey, it's okay. We'll get through this together. Everything is going to be fine. I promise." Grandma moves closer and puts her arms around me. She rocks me back and forth like a baby in a craddle. Most parents would've freaked out. I know everything is gonna be okay, but I still can't stop crying.

Grandma makes a great dinner when we get home, fried chicken, cheesy mashed potatoes, green beans, and her famous home made biscuits. They both encourage me to eat up, reminding me that now I'm eating for two. After dinner we put on a DVD and get cozy with a big bowl of popcorn. It's a comedy about an old baseball player who gets a second chance. It's pretty funny and it leaves us with a good moral at the end. The team is always more important than the individual. Just like a family, I guess. We do a lot of smiling at each other and hugging throughout the night. Trina calls me, but I let Grandma take a message. I'll see her tomorrow at school.

I go to bed thinking everything's gonna be alright, but I still can't sleep. There's too many thoughts running through my head. I rub my hand over my stomach, but I can't feel anything yet. There's a real human life growing inside me. I'm eight weeks along, but the doctor said I won't start to show until about twenty to twenty four weeks, that's six months. It's a relief to know I have a while before I get big as a house. Oh God, I'm gonna get big as a house. That's gonna suck.

I'd be lost without Grandma and Grandpa. No way I could raise a baby on my own. No way I'd get an abortion either. It's not the baby's fault I was a drunk slut and got pregnant. Just 'cause I can't feel it doesn't mean it's not there. And if I don't destroy it, it'll grow into a baby. I could never live with the guilt, taking a human life. I don't know about adoption either. I'm not going through the pain of squeezing out that huge baby head just to give it up. But I guess I'd have to if I was on my own.

Should I tell the father? Jason, Tommy, neither would care. God, I hope it's not Jessie's. Please, not the demon seed. My baby's gonna look like some kinda creepy troll. If it's Tommy's or Jason's at least he'd be good looking, but he'd have the moral back bone of a jackass. It doesn't matter. None of those fools are getting anywhere near my baby. For what? Like they'd ever be there for me.

My baby's gonna be born into a secure family, smothered with love. Maybe one day I'll find a good father to help me raise him or her. Right, nobody wants a girl with a wide butt and a baby. I don't care. I have my baby now. I'll take care of him or her and it'll love me back no matter what. My baby safe will be safe and I'll be there for whatever he or she needs.

I have to force myself out of bed to go to school in the morning. I don't feel like eating, but I have to keep something on my stomach, so I carry around a bag of saltines and a big piece of French bread to munch on. I still end up running to the bathroom all the time. Why do they call it morning sickness when it happens all day?

"Man, you look like hell," Trina says as I approach our lunch table. "How come you didn't return my call last night?"

"I know I must look terrible. I went to bed early last night. Look guys, I have something to tell you."

"What is it," Billy says looking concerned.

I can't think of any other way than to just say it. "I'm gonna have a baby."

"What!" They all gasp at the same time.

"I'm pregnant. I'm gonna have a baby."

"Oh my God, when did you find out," Trina asks.

"A couple of days ago."

"What does it feel like?" Wendy asks.

"I feel like hell. I'm tired all the time and I've been puking up a storm."

"When are you due?" Wendy keeps on.

"The doctor said the last week of August."

"Man, you're gonna have a baby. That's so trippy," Trina laughs.

Kevin and Billy just sit there staring at me. Just the thought of a baby automatically paralyzes any guy. It stops them dead in their tracks like a deer in headlights looking for a way to dart away from the danger.

"So, you're really gonna have it?" Kevin asks.

"What do you think she's gonna do, pinhead?" Trina snaps at him.

"I hear what he's sayin'. That's a lot to take on all at once," Billy says.

"It'll be okay. My grandparents are gonna help me out. They've

205

really been great about it. I couldn't do it without them. Besides, I could never do what you're talking about. I just couldn't do it."

"Hey, I think congratulations are in order," Trina exclaims. "An addition to our little family."

"Yeah and we get to be Aunt Wendy and Aunt Trina." Wendy gives Trina a high five.

"I can teach him how to draw," Kevin says.

"Things are gonna get kinda weird for you," Billy says looking across the cafeteria like he's staring down the enemy.

"Yeah, there was a pregnant girl in my sister's class. She said they called her all sorts of names," Wendy says.

"Anybody says a word and they're gonna have to answer to all of us," Kevin boasts.

It feels good knowing I have so much support. My body's already going through some crazy changes. I'm always running to the bathroom either to throw up or pee. I can't keep anything down. Any strong smell really sets me off, like the cheese on the nachos of the kid who passes by me in the cafeteria. The worst was the time I made the mistake of taking the short cut through the gym during wrestling practice. The pungent odor of sweaty boys, smelling like stinky feet and old gym socks, sent me straight to the nearest trash can.

My boobs are bigger now too, much bigger. I was never really small or anything, but this is ridiculous. They must be full of milk already and the baby's not gonna be here for another seven months. They're really tender too and it hurts to carry them around. Grandma told me they were gonna hurt for a while. No wonder I haven't been able to sleep on my stomach for the past month. I was actually looking forward to my boobs getting bigger, but this really sucks.

I'm sweaty, bloated, and on edge all day at school. The least little thing sets me off. I screamed at this kid in class just for tapping his pencil on the desk. He looked at me like I was certifiable.

I knew my body was going to rebel on me eventually, but I didn't think it was gonna be so soon. The funny thing is no one can tell anything is going on from the outside. I've been wearing big sweatshirts to hide my boobs. If they only knew on the inside my body is raging volcano of hormones erupting in ways that would blow your mind. Between the churning stomach, sore boobs, hot flashes, headaches and super nasty attitude, I'm too tired to go anywhere after school so the crew comes by to hang out with me at home. That makes it bearable. They say my poetry is getting pretty good. I wrote one about being pregnant.

> What's happening to me
> I don't know, I can't tell
> But I think my whole body is starting to swell
> I think I'm about to get bigger and bigger
> Like a beach ball with no form and no figure
> But I have a secret that nobody knows
> Deep inside something wonderful grows
> It zaps my strength from my head to my toes
> But that's okay, 'cause I'm all that it knows
> It relies on me for everything
> So I try to be careful and do the right thing
> I have no choice, that's my baby inside
> And I'll be there to wipe every tear that it cries

Trina and Wendy tear up a little when I read it. Trina always says you know you've written something good when you get an emotional reaction out of someone. A laugh, a cry, it doesn't matter as long as they express some kinda raw emotion. The crying is a good thing.

I have my weekly session with Susan tomorrow after school. It's something I've looked forward to over the past couple of weeks.

"Hi Cara, you look great." Susan meets me in the lobby as usual. She's about my height, but what I wouldn't give to have her figure. She's the cute, little, sweet petite I always wanted to be. I bet she can date any guy she wants.

"Yeah, right. I know I look terrible."

"How have you been feeling?" She asks as she closes the door to her office.

"I wouldn't say I was glowing yet, but I'm alright. Just sick and tired of being sick and tired all the time."

"Have you been taking your vitamins?"

"Oh yeah, all of them, every day."

"Well, I'm sure it'll get easier as you go along. They say the first trimester's the worst. Your body has to get used to carrying another life inside."

"I guess. Have you ever had a baby?"

"No. I'm still looking for the right guy."

"Yeah, you wouldn't want to end up like me."

"I didn't mean it like that."

"I know."

"It's just that I try to be very careful with life decisions. You know those really big decisions that can affect the rest of your life. I'm especially careful about who I sleep with. You have to be with all the STDs floating around out there."

"I was never careful. I was so stupid. I fell for the first guy who paid me any attention and he turned out to be a total asshole."

"How old was he?"

"He was seventeen and I was fifteen. He was my first. I thought I was in love with him. I was so stupid. It was all my fault."

"What was your fault?"

"Something happened to me. Something I never told anybody about."

"You may find it helps if you tell someone about it. You can tell me, Cara, that's what I'm here for."

"I got all drunk one night at a party and my boyfriend gave me this stuff called ecstasy. I ended up passed out on a couch." I pause for a moment.

"Take your time, Cara."

"He let one of his friends rape me while I was asleep. He knew about it. He was there. He told him to do it."

"I'm sorry that happened to you, Cara, but it wasn't your fault. It wasn't right for you to drink and do drugs. That's true. But no one has the right to touch your body without your permission. Nobody. There's no way that's your fault. I know you feel like it is, but it's not."

"Yeah, but if I wasn't such a drunk slut they never would've been able to take advantage of me like that. I know that now."

"There's no excuse for what they did to you. I don't care how many drinks you had. Unless you gave them permission to have sex with you, it was wrong."

"I don't know. There must've been something I could've done about it."

"Well, there wasn't. What do you want to do, live in the past? That's just like banging your head up against the same old brick wall over and over again. There's nothing you can do about the past, but there is something you can do about the present and the future.

Cara, everybody gets crapped on at some time in their lives. Unfortunately, you've had to deal with a lot of it at a very young age. Most of us don't have to deal with the death of a parent until we're in our fifties or sixties. And the rape, no one should ever have to go through that. But you lived through it all and you're still here, working to get better. I admire you for that. The bottom line is, in life, shit happens. How you deal with it is who you become. The good news is you don't have to face it alone. I hope you'll let me help you deal with it."

"I have to deal with it. I have to be strong for my baby."

"Yes, Cara, you do. Well, you know what they say. If it doesn't kill you, it can only make you stronger. You're a very brave young woman. You're a survivor. I think you were given this child for a reason."

"For a reason?

"Sure, just think how much stronger you're gonna be at the end of this experience. You'll experience things and learn more than anyone your age. And everyday you'll grow right along with your child in ways that you can't even imagine. In the end, you'll come out a much better person."

"You make it sound like I'm joining the Marines or something, you know, 'be all that you can be', but I guess you're right. I wish I was as confident as you. Susan, do you believe in God?"

"Yes."

"How do you know he really exists?"

"I don't, not really. I just know my faith brings me peace and that's good enough for me. And you?"

"I used to before Mom died, now I don't really know. I don't think so. I mean it's gotta be a miracle for me to have another life growing inside of me, right? But then again every animal on earth reproduces in one way or another. Is it really all that special? I don't know. I don't know if I believe in God."

"Well, that's something you have to figure out for yourself. No one can tell you what to believe in. You have to feel it. When you can be true to your feelings, you will have strength in your faith."

I always have a lot to think about after my sessions with Susan. It feels great to finally let my secret go. At first, I thought all her clichés were just a load of bull. "If it doesn't kill you, it'll make you stronger", yeah right. But when you really think about it, it's true. I know it's gonna be hard, but if I can raise this baby and get my college degree. Look out world. There's nothing holding me back.

I guess clichés become clichés for a reason. A bird in the hand is worth two in the bush. You do reap what you sow. And the grass is always greener, until you get to the other side.

Chapter 23

Grandpa finally came through on his promise to teach me how to drive. He's more relaxed than I thought he'd be. Maybe the fact that we're in an empty parking lot has something to do with it. It definitely makes me feel better knowing there's nothing around I can hit. I thought I could handle his mid-size Chevy truck after driving around in Jim's monster rig for so long, but it's harder than I thought, especially when we get to the streets. I'm a nervous wreck. Grandpa almost had to grab the wheel to keep me from freaking out one day when this big truck passed us on a curvy road.

After two months of practicing, I get the nerve to take my test and pass on the first time. I should be celebrating, planning a freedom drive across country or something, but I don't want to go anywhere. I'm home. There's no place I'd rather be.

Sixteen weeks, the time has been flying by. My stomach is growing, but no one can tell through my oversize sweat shirts. I actually feel better than ever. I haven't been throwing up, I got more energy and my appetite has definitely come back. I've heard women talk about cravings, but it's like I crave everything, especially if I see a good food commercial. All it takes is the image of a double cheeseburger filling the TV screen to make me rush out the door. Grandma is always ready to take off at a moments notice when I feel the need for McDonalds, Wendy's or Taco Bell. She always tries to talk me into a salad or one of those chicken sandwiches, but when I want a cheeseburger I just have gotta it. She's always trying to make me eat something healthy like fruit and veggies. She says whatever I eat goes straight to the baby and all that fast food just isn't good for either of us. I see where she's coming from, but I just don't want that healthy crap. And french fries *are* a vegetable. Grandpa's been helping me cheat a little by hiding snickers bars and cookies around the house.

Grandma's cooking tastes better than ever. She piles it on at every meal. That's the one good thing about being pregnant. You can totally pig out and no one cares. They just smile at you, say you're eating for two, and offer you more food. I'll eat almost anything, but for some reason I now hate onions. Even the smell of them makes me ill.

I still freak out when I think about how much responsibility a baby is gonna be, but talking with Susan really helps. Just having someone to talk to about everything makes all the difference. She's helped me deal with what Jessie and Tommy did to me and all my crazy dreams. I still have them. But now instead of cutting to relieve the pain, I write about the dreams and my feelings and I share them with Susan. I wrote a poem about the rape I shared with Susan at our last session.

"You thought that you could take from me
Something you can't even see
Something I hold dear inside
And guard with my shame and pride
You thought that I was just a toy
Something to share with all your boys
Something easy, something cheap
You never saw what lies beneath
You thought I would just shrivel up
But I decide I can be tough
And you were just a bad mistake
What you stole I can remake

212

What I am deep in my soul
Is something only I control
And what I am and what I'll be
Is more than you can take from me"

Susan looks at me with a sweet smile and tells me it's the most beautiful poem she's ever heard. She has the same smile looking at my ultrasound pictures. I realize to other people the pictures are merely a little white shadow against a black background, but to me it's the most beautiful thing on earth. She asks if I'm having a boy or a girl. Just like everybody else, she's surprised when I tell her I don't know yet. The doctor keeps asking me if I want to know, but I always say no. I totally want it to be a surprise. It'd be like unwrapping the ultimate Christmas present if I knew ahead of time.

Week twenty, no matter how big the sweat shirt, my belly shows. Everybody stares and whispers behind my back at school, Coastal Beach High's starring attraction. I have to trade in my black jeans for looser fitting pants thanks to the bloating and my incredible stretching stomach. I let Grandma talk me into some colors other than black. I honestly don't feel like wearing black anymore. I don't want my child to be born into darkness. I want his or her life to be filled with brightness, color and happiness. I don't ever want my child to see me dressed in all black, sad and depressed. Even when I'm down, I'll have to put on a brave face and show my baby nothing but a smile.

I can actually feel the baby moving now, tossing and turning, rolling around my stomach. It's so weird that a real live human being is actually growing inside of me. Maybe it is a miracle. Everybody says it is.

One day, while I'm sitting out on the deck, Crystal and Jennifer pass through my thoughts. I haven't thought about them in months. I left things so bad with them I don't know if they'd even want to talk to me. We were best friends for years. I have to let them know.

"Hi, is Crystal there." My voice is shaky.

"This is Crystal."

"Crystal, it's me, Cara. What's up?"

"Oh my God. I don't believe it. Where are you? Where have you been? You just left without saying a word."

"I know. I'm so sorry, but I have something I have to tell you, something important."

"Wait, Jennifer's here. Jennifer, Jennifer, pick up the other phone. She's gonna freak when she hears your voice."

"Hello?"

"Hey, Jen, it's Cara."

"Cara. Oh my God, Cara. Where have you been? Are you ok? Why didn't you call us before?"

"I'm sorry, I really am. But my grandparents came and before I knew it I was driving across country with Jim."

"Jim, no way," Crystal shrieks.

"What do you mean?" Jennifer asks.

"My grandparents wanted me to move to California to live with them, you know, because of my grades and everything. But instead of flying, Jim made me drive out there in his big, old truck."

"No way. Did you wanna die?" Crystal shrieks again.

"I thought I would at first, but the whole thing turned out to be pretty cool when I think about it. I mean, I got to see the Appalachian Mountains, I ate Creole and Tex-Mex food, I stayed on an Indian, I mean Native American reservation, I saw the Grand Canyon and Carlsbad Caverns, I stayed at a really cool hotel in Las Vegas, and I met some really amazing people. All in all, I'd have to say the whole thing was pretty great. Even Jim was bearable."

"Wow, sounds like you had a great time. What was the reservation like?" Jennifer asks.

"It was incredible, but that's not really why I called." I hesitate.

"What's up?" Crystal barks and I'm quickly reminded how impatient she gets when the gossip is good.

"I...I...I'm gonna have a baby."

Silence.

"Did you hear me? I'm gonna have a baby."

"Oh my God, Cara, oh my God," Crystal breaks the silence in

dramatic form.

"How far are you? I mean how pregnant are you? I mean, when are you due?" Jennifer rambles.

"August."

"Are you still with that guy, what's his name, Tommy?" Jennifer asks.

"No, not for a while."

"Is he the father?" Crystal asks.

"I don't know. I mean he could be."

"How many others could there be?" Jennifer asks in a snotty tone.

"Look, I didn't call to get ragged on. I just wanted you to know, that's all."

"Cut it out, Jennifer," Crystal scolds.

"I'm sorry, you're right," Jennifer apologizes. "So how are you doing? Is the baby healthy?"

"Yeah, everything's going according to schedule. I'm starting to look like a little piglet, but the doctor says the baby is healthy, so it's all good."

"Are you okay with it? I mean, you are gonna be a mother. That's so much responsibility. Do you need anything? Are you gonna be okay?" Jennifer's tone changes from judgmental to concerned.

"Yeah, everything's cool. My Grandparents are the best. They're so excited about helping me raise the baby. My new school's nice too and, yes, I'm definitely still going to college. They have some pretty good schools near by. I think I'm gonna like it out here. It's really nice and quiet and the beaches are beautiful. There's these really cute seals, like everywhere. It's the perfect place to raise a baby."

We stay on the phone for over two hours and talking about my trip and all the crazy things my body is doing. They want to come out and visit after the baby is born. We decide the best time would be next summer, after they graduate. That way the baby will be one year old and more active and alert. I promise to send them pictures

215

as soon as the baby is born and we promise to keep in touch. It was great talking to them again.

Another month passes and I'm getting bigger and bigger everyday. My stomach is going through these crazy contortions. I've been taking birthing classes at the hospital and it definitely feels like what they said contractions would be like. This can't be happening. I'm only six months. I don't think too much about it the first few times I get the tiny little contractions, but when I keep getting them I run to Grandma.

"Grandma, something's happening. It feels like I'm having contractions."

"What? How does it feel?"

"Like they said it would in class. My lower stomach cramps up tight for a while, then it stops."

"Have you timed them? Are they coming in regular intervals?"

"No, they just come and go whenever."

"Does it get more intense as you go along?"

"No."

"Well, I don't think you have much to worry about. I had these things called Hicks contractions. Most women do. It's like a false labor, but it's just your uterus getting ready for child birth. We'll call the doctor just in case, but I'm sure that's all it is."

The doctor confirmed Grandma's diagnosis. I'm amazed how much she remembers. It must've been forty years since she was pregnant. I bet when you go through something so painful you never forget. I try not to think about the pain. I'd rather believe in the magic of the epidural and its power to ease the pain of a grapefruit sized baby head squeezing through my secret spot. Anyway, my spot's not that much of a secret anymore.

Thank god, school's out for the summer. The last thing I want is to go to school everyday, waddling around like a side show freak. I get to just lounge around the house in my t-shirts and draw string warm up pants, trying to stay comfortable. Grandma and Grandpa spoil me to the point I'm almost tired of being babied.

We've all been working on getting my room together for the

baby. We mutually agree dark gray is not a good color for a baby so Grandpa bought two kinds of paint, light blue for a boy and serene peach for a girl. I just can't go back to any kind of pink. The peach will work. It's light and subtle, but it's not pink. We already have the crib, a stroller and all the baby clothes we need, most of it donated from Grandma's church friends. Grandma wants to throw me a baby shower, but I just don't want all that attention. People are pretty much giving us everything we need anyway. I guess that's one good thing about being a member of the church. There's a real sense of community there. Like everybody has everybody's back.

Today is the first day of my seventh month and I feel like I'm hitting the home stretch. My back really hurts a lot. We've been using hot water bottles and cold ice packs, but nothing seems to work. The pain just keeps coming back. My head aches too, much worse than before. I don't like to take anything for the pain 'cause of the baby so I just put up with it. Those little false contractions are getting worse too. Guess my body is just preparing me for the pain of child birth, but if this is just the warm up, I don't know if I'll be able to handle the main event.

I try not to complain too much. Grandma and Grandpa are trying so hard to make me comfortable. Grandma makes great dinners. Tonight it's a big oven roaster chicken stuffed with dressing, mashed potatoes, collard greens and macaroni and cheese. As soon as I get a whiff of the macaroni and cheese my stomach revolts on me with a fury I've never felt before. A stream of vomit spews from my mouth and covers the table, food and all.

"Oh my God, Cara, are you okay?" Grandma shouts.

"Are you okay, Cara?" Grandpa echoes.

"I'm sorry," I try to apologize for ruining dinner, but the flood gates rush open again. Guess my stomach wants to make sure no spot on the table is left uncovered. Grandpa brings me a trash can from the kitchen. My head is pounding, my back is in knots and my stomach tells me the barforama isn't over yet.

"June, she don't look so good," Grandpa says nervously.

"Get the keys, we're going to the hospital," Grandma answers.

217

The look on her face says it all. Something is wrong.

I hold my stomach in my hands and plead all the way to the hospital, "Please, please, please let my baby be okay, please".

The pressure in my stomach grows so bad I need Grandpa's help to get through the hospital parking lot. I don't know if it's 'cause I'm such a mess or Grandma's desperate ranting at the front desk, but the nurses take me right back to a room.

"How do you feel, darling," a nurse comes into the room.

"Like hell. What's going on?"

"We're not sure yet. We're going to run a few tests and keep you here for a little while just to make sure. You'll be fine. I called your doctor." She turns to one of the other nurses, "Let's get some urine and blood and get a monitor on the baby."

"Is my baby okay," I ask frantically. Everybody's moving so fast, going here and there. I need to know what's going on.

"Your baby's going to be fine, darling. Now just relax your arm." The nurse puts one of those blood pressure things over my arm. She's a large Black woman, not fat, just big. When she talks all the other nurses listen. She seems to know what she's doing and that puts me at ease, a little. Grandma is by my side, too. Grandpa sits in the corner offering a brave smile. The look on the nurse's face turns when she sees my blood pressure results. "Just relax now, the doctor should be here soon," she says and quickly leaves the room.

Grandma squeezes my hand, "Don't worry, honey. This kind of thing happens all the time. The doctor will come in and give you something to settle those contractions and we'll be home before you know it."

"Yeah, home in time to clean up dinner." I laugh, but the crippling pressure on my stomach turns my laughter into moaning.

It's not long before the doctor arrives. He checks me over and asks about the contractions. "How does it feel? Is it pain or pressure?"

"Both," I tell him. "I don't know, it just feels weird and it hurts."

He tries to hide it, but his face changes when the nurse tells him my blood pressure. "Put her on an IV." He looks at Grandma, "Her

218

blood pressure is high and it's escalating. If it gets too much higher, she and the baby could be at risk." He turns to me, "The pressure you're feeling is from the baby. It wants to come, but your cervix isn't ready yet. We're going to have to perform a cesarean section to deliver the baby safely. It's a fairly common surgery. You'll have a scar, but it gives the baby the best chance at a less traumatic delivery."

"Will it save my baby?"

"It definitely gives us the best chance at a safe delivery for you and your baby."

"Okay, whatever you have to do. Just save my baby. Please save my baby."

They rush me off to the delivery room and put me under. The next thing I know I'm lying in a recovery bed with Grandma and Grandpa on either side. Grandpa is watching some game on TV, but I can hear Grandma faintly praying.

"Where's my baby?" I try to shout, but my voice comes out weak and coarse.

"Cara, you're awake." Grandma leans over me and smiles. "You have a beautiful baby boy."

"He's a tiger alright," Grandpa perks up.

"Where is he? I wanna see him. I wanna hold him."

"You can see him, honey, but you can't hold him." She rubs her hand over my forehead. "He's in an incubator. His lungs aren't fully developed and his blood pressure is high."

"I don't care. I wanna see him. Please, where's my baby?"

"Okay, Calvin, will you get a nurse. We're going right now, honey, try to stay calm."

"Is he gonna be alright Grandma? Don't lie to me. Is he gonna be okay?"

"I don't know, honey. The doctor says his organs are all developed pretty good except for his lungs, but his body fat is low. He's especially concerned about the baby's blood pressure. He said there's nothing they can do but monitor it and hope it comes down. You have to relax, honey, your blood pressure is up, too. The doctor says a lot of bad things can happen if your blood pressure gets too high. Honey, you could have a stroke."

"And my baby, he could have a stroke, too?"

"Oh, honey, don't even say it. The doctor says he looks strong. He's a fighter."

I can only see him from behind a large glass barrier. The nurse won't let us any closer. I'm embarrassed when she has to point my child out from the other fragile, thin babies. I should be able to pick out my own baby by some maternal instinct, but they all look the same. Like the offspring of some frail, shriveled skinned alien. He looks so tiny in that incubator. He's all alone in there, fighting for every breath. Fighting to grow and live.

"He's going to be fine, Cara." Grandma puts her hand on my shoulder.

I can hear her praying under her breath. I'm praying, too. I don't know if anyone up there can hear me. I just know that my beautiful baby boy is lying there, helpless, barely alive. There's nothing I can do about it. The doctors have done everything they can. There's no where else to turn for help. "Please God, please let him live. I'm sorry for everything I said about you. Please don't let him die." I want to believe he is there. I want to believe he can help so I keep praying.

"Let him live. Please. Let him live. Let him live." That night I repeat the words over a million times as I fall in and out of sleep. The more I say them, the more I believe there is hope. Someone, something must be up there. There has to be a God. "Please, hear my voice."

Grandma is sitting over my hospital bed when I wake up. "What time is it?"

"It's early, honey, go back to sleep."

"How long have you been here?"

"Since before the sun came up, I guess. I couldn't sleep at home knowing you were up here alone."

"How's my baby. I wanna see him."

"I just saw him. He's sleeping. It looks like he's breathing fine."

"So, let's go."

"Slow down. You're going to tear your stitches."

I do have to move slowly, but pain or no pain, I'm going down that hallway. He looks so sci-fi with all those tubes hanging from his body. But he's a fighter, seven months old, weighing in at three pounds, four ounces. He's my little warrior. Grandma tells a nurse to get me a wheel chair so I can sit in front of the glass.

"Honey, I brought you something from your room I thought you might want."

It's my St. Christopher pendant. She puts it around my neck and we fall into silent prayer.

"Grandma," a thought finds its way into my head and I have to interrupt our praying. "Do you realize that my son was born on the same day Mom died?"

"Yesterday was the anniversary day, wasn't it?"

"Yes, it was."

"Isn't God amazing." Grandma smiles.

"What do you mean?"

"On the day we are meant to mourn the loss of your mother, God blessed us with a gift. Now we can always remember this day as a day of birth and life, not death. Your son is truly a gift from God."

"He is a gift. I only hope God lets us keep him."

"Have you picked out a name for him yet?"

"No, not really. I've been too worried to really think about it."

"Michael means gift from God. What about Michael."

"Michael Hurst, I like the sound of that, my little gift from God. Michael Hurst, Michael Hurst." As I say the name out loud I realize it doesn't sound right. Hurst is Jim's last name. It's my last name too, but I got it from Jim. "Grandma, does he have to have my last name?"

"What do you mean?"

"I was just thinking Michael Hartfield sounds a lot better than Michael Hurst. I mean he was born on Mom's anniversary date. Mom changed her name back to Hartfield after she divorced Jim and he is gonna be raised in the Hartfield home. I think that's the way

221

Mom would've wanted it."

"That's a wonderful thought, Cara. Your grandfather is going to be so proud."

"Maybe I can change my name to Hartfield, too. Is it possible? People do that, right?"

"I'm sure you can if that's what you want."

"That's what I want. So the whole family can be Hartfields. Grandpa's name is Calvin, right?"

"Yes."

"Michael Calvin Hartfield, it's perfect." I smile and Grandma smiles back.

They keep me in the hospital for five more days until my blood pressure stabilizes. The crew comes by to see me a couple of times. They really lift my spirits. Billy has a new theory linking President Bush to global warming. I don't know if I agree with it, but it helps me forget the pain Michael must be going through. They're pumping oxygen in his incubator, but he's still struggling for every breath. I wonder what it must feel like for him. One moment you're floating safe in a cocoon of amniotic fluid and the next you're lying on a sheet, tubes hanging out your face, fighting for every breath. What a messed up way to meet the world.

I don't want to leave the hospital without my baby, but they won't let me stay another night. The first night at home without Michael is crazy hard. I can't sleep and there's only so many prayers I can say. I hope my prayers are heard, but I feel the need to offer more, so I write a poem to God.

> Listen God, please hear my plea
> For what I ask is not for me
> It's for my baby pure and sweet
> Who asks for nothing, but to be
> What has he done, where has he been
> He hasn't had the chance to sin
> Or cheat or steal or heal or love
> It's not his time to live above

Please let him stay and live with me
I'll give him all a child could need
We'll give thanks and pray each day
And try to understand your way

I'm at the hospital as much as they'll let me. Grandma is here with me most of the time. Grandpa has taken the role of chauffer and all around errand guy. Sometimes I think I'd just be better off if I pitched a tent in the hall outside the NICU. The other mothers and families are here praying for their babies. I want to reach out to them, but I'm afraid I won't be able to handle anyone else's grief right now. Going home each night sucks. I can't shake the image of Michael lying there, alone, his only line to life a bunch of tubes. Every night I'm tempted to snatch him up, hold him in my arms and nurse him to health. I would press his face close to my breast so he could hear my heart beat and know he is alive. That's something all those tubes could never do for him.

Chapter 24

After two long months, the doctor says Michael is strong enough to come home. Grandpa boasts that he knew Michael would pull through the whole time. After all, "The boy is a Hartfield." We paint my room light blue with serene peach around the borders. It looks really nice. Michael's crib is already set up for him in the corner right next to a fully equipped changing station. I'm not as nervous as I thought I'd be. Probably 'cause I know if I have any problems Grandma's right down the hall. It's like having the ultimate nanny at my disposal. After what we've been through there's nothing I can't handle. I'm just glad Michael made it home alive.

"Dear Lord, let us give thanks and praise for the miracle of life you have bestowed upon us," Grandma says grace before we eat.

I used to just roll my eyes and wait until this part was over, but now I pay attention.

"We are eternally grateful for the blessing of Michael upon our home. You have tested the strength of our family, but we know everything happens for a reason. You have made us grow stronger as a family. We will not question your ways, only ask for the strength to be worthy of such a precious gift. Bless us, oh Lord, for these thy gifts which we are about to receive through Christ our Lord. Amen."

Grandma speaks so passionately I think she could be a TV evangelist. The meal is great, of course, but we're all fixated on

Michael. We watch him intently focusing on every little move he makes as if it were Neil Armstrong's first step on the moon. Michael is the bond that ties our family together. Doing what's best for him will always come first. There's an easiness floating around the room. Like everyone is where they are supposed to be. This is our safe little haven, our family. I don't know why or how, but it feels like God lives here.

Grandma teaches me everything I need to know when it comes time to put Michael to bed. I used to listen to music as I fell asleep, but now I like complete silence so I can hear Michael breathing. He's only a few feet away, but it feels like he's in the other room. I wish I could have him right next to me in the bed, but I know he's still way too fragile. The doctor said he was definitely lucky. With his blood pressure so high he was sure there'd be some kind of major complications, but there weren't. Michael's as healthy as any other baby. He just needs time to grow into himself.

The silence has a way of freeing your mind and letting you think. I remember what Grandma said at dinner about God having a reason for putting Michael through such an ordeal. Do things really happen for a reason? Was it really part of God's master plan for Michael to be born on the day Mom died? I don't know, but it seems too real to be just a coincidence.

Maybe there is no great big plan. People make mistakes, then, they turn to God to make it easier to live with those mistakes. I mean if you just say God is responsible for everything, you don't really have to be responsible for anything. I got drunk. I took drugs. I got raped. I got pregnant. Now I have to raise my son. I guess it's like Susan says, "Shit happens; how you deal with it is who you become."

Grandma tells me Jim called and he's on his way to see his new grandson. I've already decided that Michael should know who his grandfather is. It's not like Jim will be there for him anyway. His great grandfather will be his real grandfather and father really. Anyway, it couldn't hurt to let him know Jim.

In a way I'm looking forward to seeing him again. Susan has

225

taught me to remember the good times more than the bad. I think of the time we spent on the reservation. Jim can be pretty cool when he wants to be. One night, after dinner, we hear a knock on the door.

"I bet that's Jim." Grandma gets up to answer the door. "He should be coming tonight."

"Where's my boy?" Jim comes through the door loud and happy.

"Hi Jim, keep it down, the baby's sleeping," Grandma tells him.

"I'm sorry. How are you June? I just can't wait to see little Michael Hurst." Jim grins with pride.

"You mean Michael Hartfield." I was happy to see him until he came in claiming my son. "Michael Calvin Hartfield, to be exact."

"Cara, come over here and give me a hug. I hear you went through hell bringin' that baby into this world. I'm so proud of you." He snatches me up and gives me a big hug. "How you doin', kiddo. You look great."

"Thank you. I'm still sore, but I'm okay."

"What's all this about his name?" Jim asks.

"He's gonna have Mom's family name. Hartfield's gonna be my last name, too. I don't want him to be confused about anything growing up."

"What do you mean? You're changing your name?"

"Yeah, Jim. My son's gonna have the name of the family that raises him. Does that make sense to you?"

"I understand," he lowers his head. "That's the way you want it?"

"That's the way I want it."

Michael is sleeping soundly, so we have to endure Jim babbling on about how much he can't wait to see his grandson. It's cute, but annoying. I wish he would've taken that much interest in me as a kid, but I guess everyone learns at their own pace.

I wake up the next morning to the sound of Jim quietly knocking on my door.

"Cara, are you awake yet?" Jim waits patiently at my door.

"I am now. What do you want?"

"I just wanted to know if I could sneak a peak at Michael."

"What time is it?"

"Eight o'clock, everyone else is already up."

"Alright, come on in, but be quiet. He's still sleeping. He's usually awake by now, but he woke up in the middle of the night hungry as a bear."

Jim quietly enters the room and hovers over the crib. His eyes grow large and his smile brightens the room.

"Michael, that's your Grandpa," I whisper and Jim's face fills with joy.

"Cara, I know I'm not gonna be around a lot to help you with the baby, but you know you can call me if you ever need anything, anything at all. I'm gonna be sending you money for the baby just in case he needs braces or something."

"It's gonna be a while before he needs braces, Jim."

"I know, I know. I just want you to know that Michael will never want for anything. Whatever he needs, he's gonna get. You can count on that. Put the money away in a college fund or something."

Jim stays for a couple more days then he's on the road again. I think he's sincere about the help. He's always been good at sending checks. When I think about it, Jim is gonna make the perfect grandfather. All he has to do is make an appearance on holidays and spoil his grandson with gifts and money. Anyway, I'm gonna need the money and all the help I can get raising Michael.

I haven't seen Kevin or Billy much this summer. They came by the house to see Michael when I brought him home, but I think they'd rather be hanging out than babysitting. Wendy and Trina come by the house more often. They really love Michael. Every now and then they try to get me to go hang out with them, but I just don't want to leave Michael. School's going to be starting soon and I want to spend all the time with him I can.

I've been going to church again. The first time was weird because they made me stand up with Michael and introduced us as new members of the church. After service everyone always wants to make funny faces at my baby. They're all so welcoming and friendly. Grandpa reminds me that we are part of a community now.

227

We are among friends and we will never be alone.

Should I raise Michael Catholic? I really like the sense of community, but I still can't figure out how to believe in organized religion. Can I be a Catholic if I really don't believe Christians are the only ones who will receive eternal salvation? I came up with a theory that helps tie everything together in my mind. I think all mankind is connected through evolution and there is only one God who exists for all of us. Maybe God put the first cell on the earth and just sat back and watched it evolve over millions of years. Maybe we are just some kinda grand experiment. Or maybe God did create the earth in six days and mankind in his own image. I don't know. I do know that I believe in God. This world is just too magically perfect for it to all have happened by chance. From the plants that suck up our carbon dioxide to the insects that eat our waste, we all fit together, depend on and need each other. It doesn't matter if you call him God or Vishnu or Allah. If you live a good life and don't hurt others, if you have faith in a high power, your soul should be saved and you should get to survive in the afterlife. God is God for everyone. Religion is just something man made up.

I'm not sure if I'm ready for school or not, but ready or not, today is the first day back. I pick out a nice pair of jeans and a cute top to show off my post baby body. I only gained ten pounds. Since Michael was premature I didn't gain as much weight as I should've. I guess I'm gonna be popular again. Everybody'll know me as the girl with the baby. That's okay. At least I won't look like a bloated freak anymore when they stare at me.

Even though I know he's in great hands, it's so hard leaving Michael behind. After I drive off to school with Wendy, I won't see him again for another eight hours. What if he does something amazing like say momma or stand on his own two feet? I know he's still too young for all that, but it could happen. It's gonna happen one day, probably while I'm at school. It's gonna be so hard to concentrate at school when I'm thinking about my baby at home.

I hear Wendy blow her car horn and reluctantly I ease out the door, blowing one last kiss to Michael while he sleeps. I can't believe what I see staring up at me from a rock as I'm walking down the driveway. It's my lizard. At least I think it is. It looks like him. It has to be him. He made it. I hope he lives here in the yard with us forever.

On the way to school Wendy fills me in on everything the crew has been up to the past few weeks. "Like it or not, you're gonna be popular now," she says as we drive into the parking lot.

"Yeah, I know."

"I think you're the only girl in school with a baby. That makes you almost famous."

"Don't you mean infamous."

"You ready to go in?"

Trina, Billy and Kevin are waiting for us in front of the school. We hug each other and spend a few minutes ragging on all the cliques we will be excluded from. The more we rag on them, the more I realize how little I really care about all that. I'm a mother now. All that will I fit in crap just doesn't matter anymore. I have something much more important to focus on.

On the way up the steps I pass by a girl in a tight t-shirt that says, "Meet me after school". God, I hope she knows what she's getting herself into.

Mark Miller

Also by Mark Miller:

Baby Club

Every girl wants love. But for Tynise, Lauryn, Ruby and Marisol, finding love in one of the roughest projects in Chicago's inner city is no easy task. The four fifteen year old best friends believe having a baby will fill a void in their lives. They decide to place a bet on which one can have a baby first and *Baby Club* is born. How far will four teenage girls go for unconditional love?

The Inner Light

Out of every dark corner a light will shine. Trouble is born into a life of drugs and gangs, a world of darkness. When his mother is arrested, he discovers a unique gift. He sees an inner light that emanates from the faces of people who treat him well. Follow Trouble as the light guides him through the foster care and juvenile justice systems, the void of an absent mother, and a quest to find his inner light.

For additional information regarding *Chasing Faith, Baby Club* or *The Inner Light*, visit:

www.markmilleronline.net